Under Witch Aura

MARIA E. SCHNEIDER

Bear Mountain Books

A Bear Mountain Books Production
www.BearMountainBooks.com

Under Witch Aura
Maria E. Schneider

Printing History: POD printing December 2011
E-format 2011

Cover Art: Valentino Sani

ISBN-13: 978-0615533926 (Bear Mountain Books)
ISBN-10: 0615533922

Acknowledgments

Many of the usual suspects are guilty of helping: Mom thanks to your respect for spiders, you either scarred me for life or inspired me. To Dad, who always comes to the rescue in real life. Grandmas, avid gardeners both. Grandma C, I still miss your tortillas.

Nancy Fulda because you share your wonderful skills as a reader and a writer. A special thanks to Kindle-aholic for her "White Feather" suggestion for the cover, and to my wonderful cover artist, Valentino Sani, who made the cover what it is. To LeAnn because you let me get away with nothing. With your help, my writing might rise to the next level. To April for your friendship. To Dee and Joan for last minute advice. To Cinderspark for suggesting Aura was a better title for book two than book three.

A special thanks to awesome author John Levitt for reading and insisting it could still be better. And to anyone and everyone who ever rescued a feral cat or homeless dog—bless you.

Most of all to my husband, who is the wind beneath my wings.

Under Witch Aura

Chapter 1

Ghosts don't usually cause much trouble; they knock things over or rattle the eaves enough to be annoying. I didn't know Sarah all that well in life, and I had no desire to know her better after death. It took a pretty angry ghost to appear in full form and do damage on the plane of the living.

Sarah wouldn't have been able to reach me at all had I been inside my house. I'm no dummy; after my first home burned down due to an evil spirit trapped in Aztec gold, I built the new one with the best protection a witch could spell. No witch, not even a dead one, could get through.

Of course, the problem was that I wasn't safe inside my little house. I was unloading groceries from my rattletrap Civic, trying to grab all three bags because I was too lazy to make an extra trip.

The howl split through the air, an angry, fighting growl that rose to a feral scream. In one motion, I dropped my groceries and spun around. Instinctively, I snapped my silver-decorated wrists in front of me. I didn't carry a silver dagger to the store, although these days, just to get a parking spot, I probably needed a gun.

Sarah was within inches of touching me, but she stopped as though she hit a wall when I raised silver. She didn't look much different than the last time we'd met, except for the fact that I could see right through her to the front porch.

There should have been nothing in my yard between the car and my porch besides moonlight, but not only was there a ghost, there was a cat. The feline had let loose the feral scream, not Sarah.

I didn't own a cat. I hadn't the faintest idea where it came from, but it had saved me. Its warning screech had turned me around in time to keep Sarah from touching me. If she was trying for possession or for violence from the grave, thanks to the cat, she had missed.

Unfortunately, my raised silver did not cause her to disappear. Her groping arms faded into barely visible stubby fingers even as they reached for me.

I retreated carefully, keeping my silver exposed.

In life Sarah hadn't been my rival, but neither had she been a close friend. Sure, she was a witch, but her witchery involved the spiritual; inner healing and the like. I didn't mess with that stuff, and we rarely crossed paths—or clients.

Like me, her appearance didn't shout "witch" unless you considered her gray frizzy hair. She was my age, twenty-seven, but her hair had been gray since high school. Mine was still black and thankfully pulled into a ponytail, out of the way.

Sarah wore jeans, tighter than mine, with a flowery, ruffled shirt. There was a huge dark stain below her left collarbone. Rather than sad like I'd expect from a ghost, her eyes were as wild as her hair.

"Sar..ah?" Collecting my breath, I realized then that her shirt wasn't ruffled, it was in tatters, flapping away from her body as though floating from some unseen force. When had I seen her last? A month ago?

How long had she been dead?

"Sarah?" I repeated pointlessly. With another few sideways and backwards steps, I'd have a clear path to the porch. There wasn't a lot of protection there, but she'd be less real in the porch light, and the small amount of silver lining the deck might keep her at bay.

Sarah wailed, an eerie, sub-audible sound, leaving me witless and cold with fear.

I edged away, but she followed, her mouth moving mournfully. Stealing a glance towards the steps, I noticed the cat again. It hunched on the railing, illuminated by a pool of porch light. Mottled browns rippled across its body.

It was far too small to be my shape-shifter friend and sometime-employee, Lynx. Not that I had ever heard such a hair-raising feral scream from Lynx, either in his human or cat form.

The cat leaped from the railing, darted off into the shadows, and howled again. I swung around to find Sarah close enough to breathe on me had she still had breath.

"Stop." I pushed out with one hand as though I could strong-arm her. Backing up, I flashed silver behind me with my other arm. Watching every direction was impossible.

She flinched, wailing. Her angst was strong enough that the noise vibrated through me, grating painfully through my bones. The sound was far more ominous than the cat's live screech.

How long would the silver protect me? So far as I knew, ghosts didn't have a lot of limitations or power. But then again, I had never met one this audible or visible.

Sarah's mouth moved again, petulantly this time, and she rubbed at her chest. I couldn't read lips, and her hollow groaning wasn't discernible as words. With the porch light behind me now, her arms showed almost as much damage as her chest. The wounds were either disease from the grave or she'd been peppered with shrapnel.

I scooted away and jumped over two steps straight onto the porch landing. "What do you want from me?"

"Adriel. Heeeelp. Meeee." The three words were forced across planes of existence that weren't meant to be traveled in reverse. The sound was as clear as daylight, something in short supply at ten in the evening.

I stood directly under the light now, but made the mistake of blinking. That fast, she vanished.

I spun around, ducking, but there was nothing behind me. There was no one on either side of me. I clung to the side of my house like a new layer of paint. My eyes searched the shifting shadows. The Civic was a giant monster at the edge of the darkness. Shadows...

"Eeep!" My heart missed a beat, but the movement across the yard was just a tree, rustling in the breeze. Although it was early September in Santa Fe, my shivers arose from fear rather than the cool evening breeze.

Ghosts could easily brush through a person. Sometimes they wanted back on the side of the living badly enough to attempt possession. Sarah had to have some amount of power just to appear at all. From the damage and pain she exhibited, letting Sarah touch me wouldn't be a pleasant experience.

My fingers gripped the rough adobe. The darkness shifted, but it was only the juniper tree continuing its swish back and forth. The potted cactus on my porch didn't bend, nor was it large enough to hide anything in its shadow.

I edged carefully to the front door. "Sarah?"

I thought I heard a "meow," but it could have been the breeze flapping the plastic grocery bag that lay in the dirt next to the Civic. The night whispered; crickets chirping, the ticking of the car engine, sand shifting. A faint hint of gasoline fumes from the Civic wafted through the air.

I unlocked the front door and dodged inside. As fast as my feet would move, I ran to my workroom and grabbed my silver dagger even though I hadn't the slightest intention of going back out there tonight. Maybe not even tomorrow.

No, I was calling for backup. From the looks of the sizable hole over her heart, Sarah had met a brutal end, and I didn't want to run into her again tonight, or worse—encounter whatever she might have led to my front door.

Chapter 2

Witchery is far more mundane than you might expect. Mostly I mix and measure chemicals from Mother Earth and add important "firing" mechanisms. Occasionally, casting a spell involves mysterious words, but it's far easier and safer to set off a spell by crushing a membrane containing a chemical catalyst.

While I generally had a spell or two on my person, they were usually protections that had been concocted in advance. None of my spells worked against ghosts, at least not that I was aware of. I hadn't even known silver would ward off a ghost because silver was certainly no threat to a living witch.

There would be time for research and spells later. Sarah had obviously not died a peaceful, easy death, and right now I wanted the comfort and protection of the living more than anything else.

I snatched up the phone to call White Feather. Although he still called me at least once a day, I had barely seen him the last two weeks. Our relationship had been on the cusp of "getting warm and wonderful" when he retreated, got busy or got cold feet.

I wasn't sure why we hadn't been spending more time together. When we first met, he had posed as an undercover cop investigating problems in the paranormal community. He thought I was an old decrepit witch; one of his best informants.

It turned out his brother was the cop. White Feather was really a wind energy consultant by trade and a wind warlock covertly helping his brother investigate supernatural crimes now and then.

Whatever he was working on could wait. Sarah was dead, and the stain on her front hadn't been from a few sips of spilled coffee. White Feather could involve his cop brother Gordon when…The thought of finding Sarah's actual remains spooked me more than the thought of her ghostly form. At least the wraith had been animated. A dead body had a different and very definite finality.

"Hello?" White Feather's warm, mellow voice dispersed the worry, replacing it with a shock of longing. It had been too long since I'd seen him.

"White Feather, it's me."

"I know." He sounded exactly as he had the last few times we'd spoken, his deep baritone happy to hear from me.

I was breathless, something he could do to me without any help from a ghost. Usually, I covered the worst of my reaction so that it wasn't too obvious that he could have me wrapped around his finger, or his body--just about any time he asked.

My voice stuttered when I said, "I've got an issue. A possible issue really. It's small, I think, but I'm pretty sure it's going to be an issue."

"Are you in danger?" Keys jangled and what sounded like a door closing came from the background.

"No, no, I'm fine." Sarah couldn't cross into my home without an invitation, and she wasn't likely to hover out in the yard waiting for me to come out. Or was she?

She had faded completely after a scant minute of trying to communicate. But what had summoned her in the first place? She had no reason to seek me out before death, much less after.

"Adriel?"

My pause had been too long. "Your brother needs to search for a body," I squeaked, "to go with the ghost that showed up on my doorstep."

He may have dropped his keys. "Call me on my cell if it shows up again. I'm on my way."

I hung up, checked the window and paced. There wasn't time to research ghosts, but there had to be some basic precautions that would help.

I hurried back to my lab and surveyed the shelves full of bottles, beakers, special stones and piles of notes. The potent cayenne of a rista worked the same way garlic did against vampires. Since creatures that crept about in the dark were the problem, it might come in handy.

A gun would do me absolutely no good at all, silver bullets notwithstanding. I added another crucifix to my neck, put a spare in my pocket and kept my silver dagger handy.

On the way back to the living room, I caught sight of myself in the mirror. My golden-hued skin was abnormally pale. The funny green hazel streak in my left eye stood out against the otherwise ordinary brown.

I smoothed the wrinkles from my t-shirt with my hands, but it was hopeless. With White Feather on his way, I should be wearing something more attractive. My iron hadn't been used on clothing since...probably ever. It was in the lab for heating spell packets.

If I had bigger boobs maybe the wrinkles would stay stretched out. My figure was average, and like most Hispanics, on the short side, stretching to hit five six. At least I wasn't fat. Witches got a lot of exercise chasing clients and practicing spells. At least I did.

Thinking of spells refocused my attention on the problem at hand. If Sarah threw a ghostly spell at me, it wasn't likely to be an act of kindness. "Arrowheads!" They were an effective tool against evil spirits. Since they tended to interfere with my own spells, they weren't in the lab.

Scurrying into the living room, I counted three stones up from the fireplace mantle and one over, muttering a release spell. The silver box hiding behind the stones wasn't heavy.

The arrowheads inside were almost like Mother Earth, calling my essence, but unlike the steady drumbeat of her song, it was a gentle siren, tugging without offering anything back. It was a calming feeling, but at the same time, a smothering one.

I selected the obsidian arrowhead because obsidian had natural protections against illness. Who knew what diseases Sarah might have picked up from her new, dead friends? Maybe those spots on her arm weren't from anything that occurred while she was alive.

With the arrowhead in my pocket, I positioned myself next to the window. If any ghosts attacked White Feather, they'd better have an open portal to return to their home base because I'd hit them with enough spells to re-kill them three times over.

It wasn't long before the headlights of his Prius sedan cut across the yard and merged with the light from the porch. The only things out of place were my unlucky groceries, scattered on the ground, forgotten.

The car, like the man, was stealthy, coasting to a silent stop. White Feather took his time, shutting the lights off and allowing his eyes to adjust to the dark before easing out of the car.

Not taking chances, I raced to the front door and yanked it open, ready to go out fighting or usher him in if he had to make a run for it.

He retrieved the grocery bags without breaking stride. Only the turn of his head and the tautness of his shoulders indicated his wariness.

I couldn't sense his magic, even though I knew its caress; the heady perfume of a nighttime breeze, the elements of heat carried on the wind, and the scents of life in the air. While my magic was of the earth, White Feather's talent was of the wind. He compelled it and controlled it. The way I spoke to Mother Earth, he spoke to Father Sky.

Tonight, he kept his wind close. His magic barely brushed against me as he reached the porch. It was only the lightest of touches before it was gone.

He stepped inside. I slammed the door.

He held out one of the grocery bags. "I didn't see anyone." He smiled at me then, but he didn't touch me.

My heart stopped anyway. His eyes were the color of trees; a deep green with black lashes that matched his thick, wavy hair.

"Anything," I corrected. "You didn't see any*thing*."

I finally accepted the grocery bags. Sadly, I heard a sickening crunch. It only took a minute to confirm my suspicions. "Rats. Only two of the eggs survived." Gourmet cook I was not. Since dating White Feather, I had been wined and dined--until he had suddenly become preoccupied. For the last two weeks, I had been forced back to my previous diet of omelets and pasta.

"What happened?" White Feather asked. His eyes flicked around the living room and kitchen. A counter divided the two rooms. An ancient round oak table and chairs sat in the combined dining and living space. My parents' old, brown leather couch hugged one wall and a newer, beige easy chair sat next to it. Unless you counted the fireplace, the only other piece of furniture was a square table where I had kept my television until it stopped working.

My lab was the largest room in the house and the most frequently used. It contained my computer, which, with the television broken, filled in as a purveyor of news. Apparently it wasn't sufficient because when I finished telling White Feather about the ghost, he seemed to know more than I did.

"Was this Sarah person one of those nuts claiming homestead rights on forest land and living in a shack?" he asked.

She had no address, because it was pretty much as he described. "Yes, she lived near the free range land, but in the hills, toward the ski resort. Her place was an old ranch or mining property she claimed belonged to her grandfather before the forest became forest land."

"That's the one. No one could prove she wasn't the grandkid because no one could prove who lived there. She's been squatting out there for five years while the government argues with her. There was a fire at her cabin three days ago. My brother mentioned it because of the explosion, and the fact that he didn't find anyone. He figured she'd moved on."

I gulped. "Not in time."

"Apparently not." He stuffed his hands in his pockets and paced away from the kitchen counter. "You checked the rest of the house?"

"I went in the lab. I don't think she can cross the threshold into my house. I'm not sure what attracts a ghost in the first place, but she is still a witch, right?"

"Technically, yes." His face was pensive, tired. He combed his hair back with one hand, but he hadn't cut it lately so the ends curled against his neck.

"My various protections against other witches and evil spirits *should* keep her out. Of course, I'm not certain she's an evil spirit. All I know is that she didn't like me raising silver against her."

"Would that have bothered her in life?"

"Not that I know of. She wasn't a shifter."

"Hmph."

While I fumbled with putting the groceries away, he checked the place over. I felt the flash of his wind and a stir in the air as he sent his magic out ahead of him. Neat trick and one I wanted to learn. I had been meaning to ask him how he did it because I intended to devise a similar spell using earth magic, but lately, I wasn't all that sure where I stood with him. He hadn't shut me out, but he'd been too busy—or something.

Just looking at him made my heart ache. Or tingle. Well, both.

When he returned to the living room, I wiped my hands on a towel and asked, "So, uh, what else is new?"

He laughed either at my nervousness or the lameness of the question. "Hell if I know." He stepped toward me and then stopped at the counter, bracing his body against it with his hands in a half leaning position. "I've had to spend a lot of time at home lately."

"Oh?" My heart beat faster, hoping the reason would somehow be good news.

"There's something in the wind." White Feather didn't use that statement as an expression. The wind for him was a link to a whole different level of information. It could mean that the wind carried a message from the past or future. It could be a warning or, on the more mundane side, just portend a bad storm on the way.

"I've got wards at the house, and every time I leave it feels like they've triggered, but when I get home, everything seems fine. I can't figure out what's wrong. All the way over here, there was pressure from the wards, and this incident of yours has me thinking. Maybe it's a ghost. At my place."

"You think so? Sarah didn't set off any of my protections. But the silver definitely bothered her. Did you know Sarah?"

"No, but it wouldn't have to be her. I guarantee you that something is messing with my wards. Now that I'm inside your house, the warning isn't as intense, but if I hadn't already had dozens of false alarms in the last couple of weeks, I'd be positive that someone was at my house breaking in."

The protective spells around my house were set to keep out all forms of evil, spells and other mischief. His were likely similar only in a wind form rather than earth. "My spells might be blocking whatever is in the wind. Or even the wards from your place."

"Possibly. After adding more wards, I was certain I was closing in on the problem, but now I'm not so sure." He tapped one finger on the counter. "One problem at a time. First thing we should do is take a look at Sarah's house in the morning. We might spot something Gordon missed. The police crew wouldn't have expended more than the basics on the case because with her gone it was actually a problem solved."

"Okay." I turned and hung the towel across a cabinet door to hide the confusion in my eyes. Why hadn't he told me something was in the wind two weeks ago? He hadn't asked for my help either, and that stung a bit. More than a bit.

"Was Sarah a wind witch?" he asked.

"Not that I know of. She was into aromatherapy, but her main talent was healing auras—grounding oneself, finding spiritual peace and stuff like that. Matilda would know more about what she might have been into lately." White Feather had only met my best friend in passing, but everyone knew Mat.

She ran the most popular witch shop in Santa Fe, flaunting her abilities in front of the world. Since most witches didn't want a public face or reputation, Mat was also a rare witch who sold other witches' spells on consignment. "Before we go out to Sarah's house I'll talk to Mat. She might have some of Sarah's spells for resale that will help us trace her."

"You don't have anything of hers?"

"Not a thing. It doesn't make sense that she came here. We weren't close at all, even though I've known her since high school. She admitted openly that she was a witch, but she didn't like competition."

"She must have been keeping track of you."

"She had no reason to. I see her..." The truth still hadn't settled in my brain. "I used to see her around Santa Fe a few times a year in the grocery store, but that was it."

He said, "Well, if she's dead," I snorted rudely, but he continued, "I'm guessing there's a body out there somewhere. We may as well find it."

Someone had to look for her, and it appeared that we had been nominated. "I'll stop by Mat's shop as soon as she opens at ten and see if she has something of Sarah's. We could head up the mountain by eleven or after lunch." Matilda was not a morning person. If she hadn't had four cups of coffee, I'd get a dose of attitude with muddled answers to my questions.

It would also be nice if we could go to lunch together before hiking up the mountain, but I didn't want to push it. Feeling vulnerable, I avoided his eyes.

As my gaze shifted nervously, I noticed his knuckles. He held onto the edge of the counter hard enough to bruise his hands. The muscles across his wide shoulders were bunched and tight, but his voice didn't betray any tension.

"Sounds good. I'll pick you up at eleven." He turned toward the door. "You'll be okay tonight?"

"Sure," I said, not having any idea if it was a lie or the truth.

"I'll take one more look around before I go."

I stayed in the kitchen, pretending there were still groceries to put away while he prowled through the two bedrooms and my attached workroom.

"Nothing and no one," he announced as he came back into the living room.

"I'm pretty sure she can't come into the house. I'll do some research on ghosts and see if there are protections I can add."

"Good idea. I don't want you in any danger. Maybe she found you through me somehow."

"That doesn't make any sense."

"Neither does whatever is in the wind. Call my cell phone if she shows up again."

I nodded.

He started to leave, but changed his mind and pulled me in fast. As kisses went, it was almost sterile; quick and hard, but I wasn't about to complain. He let me go and grabbed the doorknob. "Do you have any salt? It's a weak protection, but it will keep most ghosts at bay."

Salt was a good blocker against evil spirits, and the adobe already had some baked in, but an extra sprinkle wouldn't hurt.

My kitchen cupboard yielded a large container of Morton's best.

He took it from me and said, "Lock up."

From past experience, I knew he would listen for the locks. From the window, I watched him disappear around the side of the house, sprinkling the salt over his shoulder. The porch light showed the salt landing in a precise line, pushed there by a helpful air drift from White Feather.

When he finished, he didn't bring the salt back inside. He stood still for several seconds, his head tilted as he listened to the secrets that the wind shared only with him.

He was in his car and driving away before I accepted he was leaving. He'd never made me any promises unless you counted him saving my life. My heart counted that, even if my mind was willing to let it go. Him leaving wasn't precisely a rejection, but my heart didn't seem to know that either.

My brain barely overpowered the part of me that wanted to burst into frustrated tears. He hadn't stopped calling. He had been worried enough to come over here...he was obviously tense. Very tense.

I tapped my foot. Something was amiss. While he'd said he felt better inside my house, he hadn't exactly been relaxed. He hadn't even seen the ghost, but he had been plenty on edge.

Hard as it was to put my ego aside, maybe this wasn't about me. White Feather was obviously holding something back, and if he thought something in the wind was dangerous, he wasn't likely to invite me to investigate.

Well, lack of details had never stopped me from tackling problems before. He might not be willing to ask for help, but as far as I was concerned, an invitation was an unnecessary formality.

Chapter 3

If I had only wanted Matilda to check her inventory of spells, I could have called earlier than ten. She would have grumbled, but even half-zombie, she could check her inventory. More important than Sarah's spells, I was curious about whether Mat had seen Sarah as a ghost. That wasn't the type of conversation to have over the phone with Mat half asleep.

Matilda knew almost every witch in New Mexico and probably a great many more elsewhere. While most of us were either too competitive or too secretive to openly discuss witchery, Matilda ran her business openly just off the Santa Fe plaza. She sold to tourists, groupies, regular clients, and artists. If there was ever a group of people likely to hire a witch, it was the artists. Whether they needed to get in touch with their inner self or touch someone else, sooner or later, nearly every artist in the area made their way into Mat's shop.

My friend played to the needs of her clients well. She embodied mystical; cultivating the persona like an ever-changing work of art. When I walked in, she was fluttering about the shop in full regalia. Her swirl of tie-dyed robes, multiple rings and bright colored makeup were fit for a crystal ball queen. Strangely, she was missing her usual headpiece, which varied between a tiara and a veil. Today her hair was in an elegant French twist rather than a teased mass of red curls that shouted, "Goddess."

Instead of greeting me with her usual happy squeal, she was a quiet mouse fretting over a customer. Said male customer was intently perusing the shelves as though they contained great tomes of knowledge rather than pretty bottled potions that promised to grant wishes.

Matilda offered me a subdued wave. Her eyes flicked quickly from me to the customer. I had no idea what she wanted me to do.

"I can come back—"

She shook her head sharply. Bad guess. I tried again. "I'll just browse—"

Her hand fluttered in panic. Well, if I couldn't leave and couldn't stay, what was I supposed to do?

The guy swiveled my way. Matilda immediately pasted an innocent expression on her face, while I stood there sputtering like a fish out of water. He smiled at Matilda and then at me. "I'm Jim."

Jim reminded me vaguely of White Feather, with dark good looks. He was shorter than White Feather, but probably close to the same age, thirty or so. His shoulders were wide, like a wrestler. Dark eyes smiled and his skin was pure Hispanic gold, a lovely shade of tinted sunshine and Mother Earth.

"Uh, hi." Matilda didn't introduce her customers to one another because anonymity was part of the creed in her shop. I certainly couldn't start asking my questions in front of him.

Jim and I both looked at Matilda for cues, but she had become as still as a store mannequin.

"I'm Adriel," I ventured cautiously.

Mat's eyes lit up and her shoulders relaxed. Ah. She wanted to introduce us, but with the unspoken rules, didn't want to overstep. She rushed to fill in the gap. "Adriel, I'm so glad you stopped by. Jim, this is Adriel, my friend." She batted her eyelashes at him, but in a subtle flirt rather than her usual flamboyant show.

He offered his hand over the clothing rack that marked the middle of the store. "Nice to meet you."

"You too." Since the cat was out of the bag as far as us being friends, I added, "I'll wait in the back. I stopped in to ask Mat about getting together for dinner later this week."

Jim smiled and returned his attention to Mat. "Oddly enough, so did I."

It was hard to keep from giggling at the pleased expression on my friend's face. Since I hadn't come about dinner, and we could eat together any old time, Mat's happiness certainly wasn't on account of my suggestion. I ducked through the scarves that separated Mat's living quarters from the store. It was impossible not to eavesdrop, especially since her couch faced the shop.

There was no point in pretending disinterest. Giggles overtook me the second the shop door closed behind him.

Mat appeared in the doorway. We both waited until the bell at the front door stopped jingling. Mat even checked over her shoulder to make sure he was gone before saying anything. Then, we both talked at once.

Mat said, "I met him at the Small Business Association meeting. He didn't know I was a witch, but after we went out twice, I mentioned it in passing, and he didn't bat an eye!"

"Niiiice," was my comment.

"This was his first visit to the shop. He was in the middle of checking everything out when you came in. I wasn't expecting him or anything!" She wrung her hands for a half second and then said, "Hang on, I'm gonna close the shop for fifteen so we can talk!" She raced to the outer door, glanced outside, put her sign up and threw the locks.

I asked from the doorway, "What if he returns, and you just closed for a break?"

She skidded to a halt, but then she gave me a chiding glance. "Oh, stop it. He won't come back right now." But she did double-check the walk outside, which prompted a stifled laugh from me.

"I'd ask what you think," she said, "but it isn't like it *matters.*"

"Of course not." I shook my hand and blew on my fingers. "Hot."

"He is all of that, isn't he?" It was her turn to giggle. "We've only been out a couple of times. I figured once he got a bead on my business, he'd drift off, but he doesn't seem to care."

"Awesome! It's hard to find a good man, and it's almost impossible to keep one after you come clean." Normals came in three types: They either didn't believe in witches, they believed, but were drooling groupies, or they thought all witches were loons. "What does he do?"

She shrugged. "He's an engineer."

"At Los Alamos?" My heart gave a nervous flutter. The engineer status wasn't the problem. When White Feather wasn't helping Gordon, he consulted on wind projects, but unlike the majority of engineers in Santa Fe, White Feather wasn't employed at Los Alamos. My limited experience with scientists there hadn't been all that positive.

"No, Jim works with computers." She smiled reassuringly, because she knew about my recent experience.

"Ah. That sounds safe."

We chitchatted for a couple of minutes, but once her nervous energy dissipated, I said, "I wanted to ask you about Sarah Damico."

"Sarah? Up on the hill?" She waved in the direction of the eastern mountains.

I nodded. "What was she into? Did she mess with wind?"

Mat shook her head, but then clarified, "Well, aromatherapy and spiritual healing could be considered air arts."

"Did she sell much here?"

"Oh, yes. She's exceptional with aromatherapy potions. You bought some of her stuff for that big party you went to, remember?"

"I did?"

"I know, I know, I don't identify who sells what, but that's the kind of thing she does. She makes potions for atmospheric effects with a lot of herbs to create the right vibes for healing and stuff. I don't know if you used it because you had several potions from different witches."

Even without a more obvious hint, I was almost certain which spell had been Sarah's. I also had an inkling of how and why Sarah might have chosen to visit me. "Have you seen her—I mean—"

Mat answered before I could explain. "It's been, oh, a couple of weeks at least. She comes in about once a month to collect her profits and ask if I need more inventory."

"I meant--" I gulped and started again. "I've got some bad news." Haltingly, I shared my encounter with Sarah's ghost.

Mat stared at me, her mouth working. "Oh. My. But...Well."

"I must still have one of her spells."

Mat frowned. "You probably do. But if she came to you because you have some of her spells, why didn't she appear in front of me?"

"Maybe you were in bed where normal people belong at ten at night?"

She shook her head. "Lately, I've been out past ten a lot." She blushed. With her milk-white complexion there was no hiding it either. "Oh my gosh, can you imagine how embarrassing it would be if Jim dropped me off and she appeared?" Her eyes bulged, and the becoming flush deepened to a crimson of worry.

"Maybe the concrete around here interferes with her ghost abilities. It tends to block me from Mother Earth to some degree."

Mat nodded, but then shook her head. "My magic works fine." She chewed on her lipstick. "She might still show up here. Wouldn't that be interesting?" She obviously couldn't decide whether seeing the ghost was more important than the consequences if she did.

"You might want to try to avoid her until we figure out what is going on. In the meantime, can I buy one of her spells? I want one that is definitely hers."

"Hmm. Let me see what I have left. I keep records of what everyone buys also. If she is attracted to something you still have, I can tell you which spell it is." Mat moved to her desk.

Sorting the records on her computer only took her a few seconds. "Oh darn. I only have one of hers left. I'll have to charge a premium since it can't be made again." She cross-checked her shelves and quickly located a coarse pottery jar. Her thumb rubbed along the edge as though soaking up the vibes.

"You might not want to sell it to the general public until we determine whether or not Sarah plans to follow her spells around and make appearances."

Mat tilted her head. "You're right. That might make it even more valuable."

That hadn't been what I was getting at. "Mat--"

"Let's check which spells I sold you." With great care, she set the jar on the computer table. Her fingers danced over the keyboard again. "You bought two of hers. Serenity—it's a gorgeous blue smoke that sets a soothing mood spell, and one other that does essentially the same thing in a green jar labeled, 'Forest.'"

It wasn't hard to remember which spells I had employed during the party because the special effects had saved the life of my client and quite possibly my own skin. "I must still have Forest."

Mat touched the jar. "So I can keep this? I'll sell it to you if you need it."

I smiled, completely understanding. The spell was valuable and likely to grow more potent over time. Depending on the witch and how each spell was ultimately used, in the hands of the right witch, the remaining spell held a lot of potential.

"I'm certain I still have the forest one. If I can't find it, I'll let you know." I hated to think what Mat would charge me. We were friends, so she would be reasonable, but that in itself was a charge—on our friendship.

Mat grinned happily and followed me to the front where we exchanged hugs. She stood in the doorway while I retreated across the broken sidewalks of Santa Fe. No doubt she was daydreaming over whether she could make more money by waiting to sell the spell or by selling it now because it might come with a ghostly visit.

I rubbed at sudden goosebumps. No one deserved to run into Sarah's miserable ghost.

I drove home, eagerly anticipating the next couple of hours with White Feather, even if it meant investigating Sarah's musty old cabin.

My mood took an instant nosedive when I pulled in my driveway. The scrawny brown cat from the night before waited on the porch railing. Its tail twitched as it watched me watch it from the car. There was no howl this time, and it was broad daylight, but I surveyed the area very carefully before edging out of the car.

The cat was even smaller without nighttime shadows dancing across it. Hunched down, it was barely bigger than a kitten.

My heart beat faster. I listened so intently it was impossible to actually hear anything.

We stood, facing off, for at least thirty seconds. When the blood stopped rushing around my head and nothing suspicious appeared, I finally asked, "Well? What are you here for?"

It regarded me unblinking and soundless.

My yard wasn't overgrown, but it was outside the city limits with no close neighbors so it was in its natural desert state. It could hide a careful live person and certainly a determined ghost.

I approached the house sideways to prevent anything from sneaking up behind me.

The cat tired of the game and sauntered off the left side of the porch. A delicate pattern of ribs warred with the stripes of brown and rust. "Do you want food?" The cat, most certainly a small female now that her tail end was clearly visible, did not deem me important enough to answer. She seemed uninterested, but I knew better.

Whoever had abandoned her hadn't given her much of a chance. If the coyotes didn't make a meal of her, an owl or hawk would. If she managed to escape those fates, the desert would claim her by refusing to provide enough water.

Once inside, I filled a bowl with water and emptied a can of tuna in another. I left both bowls on the porch. The cat had saved me, whether it meant to or not.

White Feather drove up just as I finished my self-appointed task. Unless he wanted to wait, we'd have to hunt for Sarah without a witching fork. Setting the willow to Sarah's essence would be more complicated than usual because I needed a way to extract bits of her remaining spell without using it up entirely.

Ah well. How hard could it be to find a dead body if one really looked?

Chapter 4

White Feather brought lunch. It was almost a date since we ate the takeout burritos in the car on the way up the base of the Sangre de Cristo mountains. Neither of us said much because our mouths were full.

I was not a slow eater during the best of times, and since I wasn't driving, my fingers were licked clean before we reached Hyde Park, not even halfway to the Upper Tesuque Trail. I rolled the window down and inhaled pine-scented fall air.

Mountains had so much magic, how could anyone, mundane or witch, not feel the sheer weight of their power? As we climbed Artist Road toward Hyde Park, Mother Earth drummed a steady beat all around us. The wind carried her scent, brushing magic along my skin. The auras were so intermingled, it was impossible to separate one bit of magic from the other.

"I should have brought my herb basket as long as we were coming up here."

White Feather's green eyes lingered on me for a few seconds. The winding curves of the road couldn't be ignored for longer than that. "Let's hope it stays peaceful."

It was an opening, at least of sorts. "Something in the wind still bothering you?"

He flexed his shoulders and then his fingers. "Doesn't get worse, doesn't get better."

We reached the turnoff. White Feather parked in the small space afforded for hikers. "The cabin isn't that far."

It was probably no more than a fifteen minute hike, but I retrieved my backpack from the back seat. It housed my water bottle, and more importantly, it contained a few basic spells.

White Feather grabbed his own backpack and locked the car. The start of the trail was a clearly marked forest road.

"According to Gordon, Sarah used to park at this turnout. Since her vehicle wasn't here after the fire, he hoped she wasn't home when it happened."

"Her car was a real clunker. I'm not sure how it made the climb up the mountain."

"Gordon has a bulletin out for it—rusted, brown Chevy with a blue door."

"Did you tell Gordon about her ghost?" I waited nervously for his answer.

"Of course."

He trusted my judgment, enough to tell the story to his brother. I was immensely relieved.

The trail we were on was part of the upper Tesuque. After less than a mile, a string of yellow tape marked where we needed to head down.

Sarah's place was tucked along a ridge, far enough from the trail that most hikers wouldn't come across it. She must not have come in and out the same way all the time because there was no defined trail. The few broken branches and slide marks were probably from Gordon's team.

"Did you come out here with your brother?" I worked to keep my balance on the loose incline.

"No. The report stated the incident as a fire accident, likely cooking over an indoor fireplace. Gordon only sent me the electronic file after I told him about the ghost."

I had been to Sarah's shack once, uninvited. A couple of summers back while harvesting wild herbs, the odd scent of magic had drawn me there. I had expected the remnant of an old ranch site where someone had practiced magic. Instead, Sarah was toiling away in a small garden patch next to a rustic cabin.

We drank cold tea while we pretended to catch up, but we had little to talk about.

When White Feather stopped, I had to step to the side or slide right into his back. The view through the aspen stand brought me to my own dead halt. "Moon...light madness."

Sarah's cabin was charred down to almost nothing. The old tin roof was halfway down the hill, pieces of it propped up by trees. Of the shack, only one section of a side wall was left standing.

"*Cooking accident?* Are you kidding me?" Where her fireplace had been, there was now a giant hole.

He acknowledged my disbelief. "If we find her body, they'll be interested in the real cause of the fire, collecting DNA, the works. Until then, it's just an accident."

In the world of cops, DNA was the rough equivalent of auras. Gordon believed in witchcraft; his brother was a full warlock so it would be hard for him to ignore. Nevertheless, the police didn't look for auras. Most of them didn't believe in witchcraft, werewolves or any other magicals. That was White Feather's unofficial role. He filtered information from the underground to Gordon so that justice could be meted out even when the subculture of magicals was involved.

We paced forward at the same time, drawn to the ashes that marked where the front door had been.

The place still smoked in spots, a stray puff here and there when the wind shifted the ashes. "Will our auras mess up the investigation?"

"The property isn't insured and belongs to no one officially. It's been left unsecured for several days now."

I shook my head and stepped carefully inside what would have been a wall. No one had combed through the mess. There were piles of melted plastic, a pipe sticking straight up out of the ground, and some shattered bricks from the fireplace. "One heckava a pot of soup gone wrong."

White Feather stayed at my side as we took the three steps necessary to reach the hole near the fireplace. A small line of bricks was the only indication that the fireplace had been there.

I knelt down and fingered a piece of blackened, gritty clay tile. It was all that was left of an Indian sand painting, a depiction of one of the sacred ceremonies to call the spirits to ask for intercession. Too bad it hadn't protected Sarah.

Dropping the piece, I stood. On the south side of the house where the garden had been there were no plants, just a rippled line of sand as if the explosion had happened in a wave, depositing a sandy border all the way across that side of the property. The front door had been on the north end. Black ashes there formed another, almost straight line.

White Feather muttered, "If we manage to find her somewhere in this mess, we stand almost zero chance of proving how she died. This fire was too intense."

"If her body burned, her ghost wouldn't be able to come back, would it?" I hadn't had time to do much research, but incinerated vampires couldn't come back. Surely the same held true for any burned body.

"With proper preparations done before she died, it's possible. A lot depends on how strong a witch she was."

Goosebumps danced across my arms. "This is crazy. The only way this could have been a cooking accident is if she had been baking dynamite over the fireplace."

"The investigation report said something about finding parts to a grill in the area. There was speculation she had been using propane inside the fireplace and that it sparked the explosion."

At least White Feather said "the report" which implied he wasn't a big believer in the theory. "There was certainly an explosion in the fireplace," I agreed, peering down into the hole. The bits under my foot crumbled and landed some six feet down.

White Feather stepped back and pulled me with him. "Careful."

"Good idea. Thanks."

There was no real delineation of rooms because the place had been too small. A very short stub of adobe jutted into the center and might have enclosed a kitchen or maybe a small bedroom. A lone metal pipe in the rubble was twisted and broken. Pipes made no sense because there wasn't any running water.

White Feather pointed to the garden. Another pipe lay there, less twisted, but also unattached to anything. "She must have had collection barrels up higher and let water run down through pipes."

"Should we take a look? Or maybe we should wait until I spell a witching fork to see if we can track her."

"You can do a tracking spell in this mess?"

"I doubt it. Matilda had a spell in her shop that belonged to Sarah, and it turns out I have one in my lab. The problem is that if Sarah was blown up in this mess, the spells won't be effective. She'd be everywhere." I kicked the ashes at my feet. To my surprise, the ashes didn't settle; they kept moving.

I knelt down to take a closer look.

"Be careful," White Feather warned.

He must have had a premonition or maybe there were better ways to explore blackened dust. The ashes rose and moved at me, a black missile with legs and a raised, stinging tail.

"Eeep!" I fell backwards, landing across the charred doorway. Without standing, I scrambled away as fast as my awkward feet and arms allowed.

White Feather's wind brushed around me, targeting the scorpion. In his hurry, fine particles of ash circled around the main force of his strike. Half of the soot landed on my face and went directly into my lungs when I breathed in.

"Ack!" Gasping, I stumbled away. My eyes watered, and I coughed until at least one lung rattled loose.

"Sorry." White Feather wisely had his arm over his mouth while he searched the ground with his feet.

The beast scuttled across the top of an adobe brick. "There!" I wheezed out.

White Feather quickly stomped on the chunk of adobe.

"The tail!"

The stinger jabbed wildly from underneath one side of his boot even as he ground the scorpion into the dust.

The hair on my neck prickled, a shock that was almost electrical. I spun around, but there was nothing visible at my feet or in the trees. "White Feather," I whispered.

He lifted his foot and then smashed it down again. "The fire must have disturbed it."

"White Feather," I said more urgently and louder. "There's...someone here." It was impossible to take in the landscape all at once. Could Sarah appear in broad daylight?

White Feather finally noticed the change in the air, but instead of searching with his eyes, he put his hand out to probe the wind.

"Be careful!" The skin around my face tightened as though drying in a breeze after a swim. It quickly escalated to a feeling of tiny ants biting hard. I hightailed it to ground not covered in ashes.

Silver came from Mother Earth and was my tie to her. Clutching my bracelet with one hand, I anchored myself.

White Feather remained inside the house, standing against an enemy neither of us could see.

"White Feather!"

His head came up fast. "Stay back! It's coming from the fireplace. I tried to block it."

He must have failed, although now that I was touching Mother Earth, the prickling sensation wasn't nearly as painful. "What is it?"

"It's wind. But I couldn't block it." His voice choked as though something had hit him hard in the gut.

I swung my backpack around on my way to him, hunting for backup pieces of silver, an explosive spell and...just as I reached him, the biting sensation on my skin stopped. I wasn't sure if it ceased because White Feather was blocking it or if it stopped of its own accord.

"White Feather?" My hand on his shoulder brought him in contact with silver.

He shook himself and blinked. "Something controlled the wind. It wasn't that strong, but the wind went right past me as if I wasn't even here. I pushed it away from you, but then it hit me..."

He didn't finish the thought. Worried, I prompted, "And what?"

"It stared me down." He lifted his hand, testing the air.

I trailed my fingers down his other arm, capturing his hand in mine. It wasn't romance, it was protection. My silver ring linked across the back of my hand to my bracelet, which contained more silver. The silver had kept Sarah at bay.

Even when nothing came at us, we remained on guard. My silver was quiescent; not cold or hot.

White Feather flexed his fingers, but he didn't lower his hand. "If Sarah had anything to do with that wind, she wasn't your normal wind witch. Whatever that was, it didn't respond like wind should. It reminds me of Tara's spells when I'm training her. Her experiments have a tendency to explode in all directions and ricochet. Her spells have the same lack of focus as that wind, a scattered magic that hasn't coalesced."

"You're training your sister?" Tara was at that tenuous teenager time; hellbent on experimenting with sex, magic and everything else that would upset White Feather and her family. She had needed training for quite a while.

White Feather grunted. "Her spells are sloppy, usually contaminated and she mixes too many things at once. Sometimes there's--it's like a big fart in the room. Half the time it smells, the rest of the time, the magic explodes."

If we hadn't been standing in a blown-out house with a possible dead body and bad magical vibes, his description would have made me laugh. "That sounds like witch training all right. I thought she didn't want big brother's help in finding her life's direction?"

"She doesn't, and she's fighting me every step of the way. Her talent is nothing like mine. She spells things partway, and my techniques don't necessarily work for her. She ends up screaming and crying like an idiot."

"Hmm. You aren't still trying to pick her dates for her too, are you?"

His response was a growl in the back of his throat.

"I'm telling you, she'll stop dating shifters when you quit trying to stop her."

His hand tightened on mine in an echo of the growl. He obviously had no sense of humor on the subject.

There was no winning that particular argument so I moved past it. "The offer is still open if you want me to take a shot at training her. My magic might be closer to her talent."

His shoulders were tense enough to have been carved from granite. "The point I was trying to make was that even a spell gone wrong doesn't feel as contaminated as that wind. It was unfocused and...hungry. I swear I smelled blood as if a beast had just gutted a kill." He leaned forward to look down into the fireplace, but the ashes near his foot shifted. We both retreated, fast.

The scorpion that emerged was easily as ugly as the first one. It scuttled toward the hole and dove over the side before either of us had a chance to react.

"Mayan curses! Did she keep those things as pets or what?" I tugged on his arm until we were outside the perimeter of the house.

"The place was crumbling. It was probably full of them and now they've been misplaced."

"Shouldn't they have died in the fire?"

"The mountain nights are cold. Maybe they were attracted by the burning embers and new crawl space." He kicked a black line of what I had assumed was ashes. It shattered.

"Melted sand," he said. "This fire was hot."

My silver was still quiet, but that wasn't as reassuring as usual. "Let's go. I don't like this place."

He brooded a few seconds longer before finally stepping away.

I really hoped he didn't return here and explore on his own. The strange wind obviously had him worried, and I didn't blame him. Unfocused magic didn't usually smell like fresh blood. It wasn't usually hungry either.

Chapter 5

White Feather dropped me off and, completely preoccupied, immediately headed home. That left me with plenty of opportunity to work on a new spell that had at least some potential to help.

I had wanted to duplicate White Feather's ability to gather information from his surroundings ever since I'd seen him use wind to do it. Of course, such a spell had to be adapted to earth in order to work for me. Given what I'd just witnessed, using earth elements might also be a sneaky way to discover what was riding *in* the wind that was bothering White Feather.

Two birds with one spell, and I loved working on such challenges. Mixing potions was one of the joys of my job. No, not because of the power, but because of the sheer creativity. Herbs were basically pre-packaged, ready-to-use spell ingredients. Mother Earth did all the magic. All I had to do was collect and concoct the right combinations, or in this case, tap into the information she stored.

Silver was the first element for the spell because it was my strongest connection to Mother Earth. Next, I pulped cholla and pear cactus and pureed everything with several drops of essential oils from mesquite, creosote, and juniper. The idea was to have enough plant oils to link across just about any desert distance.

As soon as the spell was assembled, I headed out to Tent Rock. It was rumored to have once held a large pool of earth magic used by a long-ago disbanded witch council. The council had probably never met there, and if there had been a magical pool, it was unlikely to have been sucked back into Mother Earth when the ancestral witches disbanded.

Rumors aside, Tent Rock was a beautiful, secluded area, and it was obvious the desert magic ran strong through the canyons and mystical tent formations.

With the sun drifting low in the mid-afternoon sky, the wind-scrubbed formations rippled with pinks, browns, desert yellows and whites. After hiking a mile or so, the canyon walls closed in.

I crouched to make it under a fallen rock that rested across the tops of two larger boulders. This was the perfect area to set the spell, but to test its potency, I required a target.

The canyon widened and then narrowed to a bare crack before spitting me out at the bottom of a long trail that angled straight up. The tent domes here had morphed into tall spirals reaching to the top of the canyon walls.

Air was in short supply as I climbed the suddenly steep trail. Around me, tented rock guardians watched. Bands of color marked my progress; their robes were darker reddish-browns and then lighter grays, yellows and whites as their teepee-like bodies thinned to a point. At the apex of one or two, a single boulder balanced like a giant roving eye. The tents released whispered messages by skittering pebbles and sand across the sides of the sandstone.

Ahead of me, on the side of the trail, I finally got lucky and spotted a couple resting from the hike. Good. I wanted to test the spell against something mobile.

I stopped to catch my breath, making careful note of the guy's shaggy brown hair, bright blue t-shirt and grayish-green backpack. The spell might not convey anything as specific as colors. I might only get an impression of a human—or nothing at all.

The guy picked up a rock close to where he sat. He brushed his treasure off and showed it to his blonde girlfriend.

Whatever she said was lost behind the sandwich she was eating. Her elfish style haircut was held in place by a white sweatband across her forehead; very sporty. She stretched long tanned legs and laughed as he placed the stone in his backpack. Maybe she was ecstatic because she wasn't the one carrying a backpack full of rocks.

Not wishing to be seen or at least not well-remembered, I turned back down the trail.

The hikers had a bit of a climb to the top, and since the only other way off the flat ridge was through a clearly marked no-trespassing Indian reservation, they would both likely stay within range of the spell. They would either go up the remaining distance or hike back down.

Down was a quick jog that filled my nose with the smell of chamisa, juniper and baked rock as I squeezed into the lower canyon and scooted through the vase-like formations.

I hiked off-trail as soon as a side canyon wandered off into an open undulation. Sheer rock walls encased me, and the world was quiet except for shifting sand mixed with wind whistling its way through the rocks.

The canyon walls protected my privacy. No one was likely to see me. If they did, I was just meditating.

I set my supplies on a boulder next to a pear cactus proudly bearing bright red fall fruits. Pulp from one of the fruits made a nice addition to my spell. Once everything was ready, I painted the essential oil mix under my turquoise bracelet and on my fingertips.

Maybe this first time I'd only feel a tingle from Mother Earth, acknowledging me. If the spell worked extremely well, maybe there would be some sense of the hikers.

"Okay. Let's find a hiker." Inhaling Mother Earth and connecting to her through my silver was immediate. The heat through my hiking shoes was as welcome as the sand beneath me; all Mother Earth.

The smell of essential oils was really quite strong. Not only did my wrists tingle, so did my nose and eyes. I couldn't tell if the results were from magic or just the antiseptic properties of the plant oils.

There was no discernible message from Mother Earth.

I placed my hands carefully on two fruits still attached to the cactus and focused on the trail, on the juniper essence and the soil that connected it all. "What is in your world?"

The result was more and less than I bargained for. Nausea hit first. There was the feeling of Mother Earth, only it was through a vast swimming pool, a squishy floating mess. My senses felt dulled, surreal. I reached harder, diving to the bottom of the pool where hard packed earth existed.

The unfamiliar morass was suffocating. I lost my original grounding. Trying not to panic, I clutched my silver chain with one hand and linked directly to Mother Earth.

Mistake.

Bam! The world exploded.

"Aaaaeee!" I jumped away, half blinded. Tiny daggers pierced my skin and red fruit oozed across one hand and arm. The entire front of my shirt dripped pink from exploded pear fruit. One of the cactus pads had snapped off and lodged in my arm.

"Moonlight madness!" Had I fed too much Mother Earth into the plant?

Stumbling about like a one-eyed witch who had fallen into her own caldron, I managed to locate a stick to pry the cactus pad out of my arm. The pain was screech-worthy, but it came out a moan that would have done Sarah the ghost proud.

Once the pad wasn't hanging from my arm, the pain subsided enough for me to stop whimpering, but the bottle of essential oils had erupted along with the cactus. My eyes watered from the stench. I wiped at my forehead, dislodging another chunk of pink fruit from my hair. Great. If anyone discovered me now, they'd run screaming to report the beginning of the zombie apocalypse.

I pulled my water bottle from my backpack and hosed myself down, sitting on the boulder to keep from falling. Dizziness rocked my world. The sand gibbered at me, a million voices without distinct words.

"Hell...hello?"

The voices murmured, scouring the sides of the hollowed canyon walls; hitting, bouncing, echoing. The second time around, or maybe it was already the third, the rocks rumbled underneath me. A vibration that might have been hiker's footsteps echoed through the canyon. There was a faint sound of a throaty laugh from far away.

Mother Earth had a voice, and I was accustomed to listening to her, but this was a new experience.

When the sand at my feet shifted, the silver on my wrists tingled in response. The shape that formed in the sand was almost a perfect square, but the last side didn't complete. It remained an open box. The ripples of sand reminded me of the lines around Sarah's house, and the faint outline of a scorpion in the center of the open rectangle convinced me of the warning--if only I knew what it meant.

As quickly as the design was there, Mother Earth let go, and the sand shifted as though the picture had never been there.

The air stilled as though taking in a breath.

I didn't wait for it to exhale.

Further intimate discussions with Mother Earth did not appeal to me at the moment. I grabbed my backpack and scurried out the lower exit as fast as my wobbling legs could manage.

Chapter 6

Lynx could have easily hidden in the shadows of the desert instead of waiting for me on the porch. If the kid knew anything, he knew stealth. His shifted form was that of a feral bobcat, even though he had chosen the larger cat as a name for himself.

Lynx still did many an odd job for me, but he wasn't on my monthly payroll anymore, not since we had a bit of a misunderstanding. Independence fit him and made our relationship easier, although I couldn't quite erase the younger, half-starved waif I had first hired in a dark alley a few years ago.

Like the often insolent teenager he was, Lynx lounged sideways across the metal chair on my porch, the one not lined with silver. It was unlined specifically for him, and in case I ended up with any clients who happened to be shape-shifters.

I parked the car and trudged up the steps. Every pore in my body hurt.

"Man, what happened to you?" He blinked rapidly as he assessed my ruined appearance. His eyes then darted around the yard even though it was quite obvious nothing had followed me up my dirt lane driveway.

"Do you have some sort of sixth sense to stop by when I've been in an accident?" I asked.

He shrugged. "Nah. You look like you bin wrestling with some big bad dude a lot of the time. The guy that got you today musta been a real bad ass."

Resenting the comment was pointless because it was too accurate. My hiking pants had started out khaki-colored. They were now spotted with pink and smears of greenish black oil. My arm was in worse shape. Dried blood decorated the red patches where cactus needles were still lodged.

I unlocked the front door and limped inside. "I don't have any food."

He snorted. "You gonna put on weight if you eat your whole plate every time White Feather takes you out."

"Yeah, so?" I wasn't about to tell the kid that the reason the restaurant leftovers in the fridge had petered out was because White Feather hadn't been inviting me out lately. "Witching is hard work. I need the extra calories."

"You better change those calories to something that will grow skin back." He eyed the fridge longingly, despite my assurance that there were no leftovers.

"Have a soda."

It was only recently that he bothered to wait for an invitation. He only did so now because he finally had his own apartment for the first time in his life. It made him realize that the threshold of a house was meant to establish a line of personal belongings instead of another lock to be picked.

He headed for the fridge. With his body behind the door, he asked, "Why you always have carrots and no Cheese Whiz?" Giving up, he reappeared with two sodas, a diet for me.

Gratefully, I popped the top and took long hard swallows. "I need a shower."

His smirk wasn't quite hidden by the can. "Yeah, you better get cleaned up before White Feather comes by." His nose twitched.

The essential oils smelled bad to me; to his more sensitive nose it must have been a real treat. "You have business?" I asked. Lynx had always been difficult, and once his disguise had been broken, he went from twelve to seventeen overnight. With it came even more attitude, but better hygiene. His garbage-can-unkempt black locks were now a respectable buzz cut. Instead of a pathetic street urchin with dirt smeared on his arms and face, he could pass for a twenty-year old college student.

The only thing that hadn't been cleaned up was his smart-mouth. Luckily, his underground network didn't mind his mouth or appearance. He was my ticket to anonymity and jobs.

"Guy wants the antidote to the evil eye."

"Does he know who hexed him?"

His mouth twisted, Lynx's version of a smile. "Says he doesn't know, but he ain't lily-clean; probably brought it on himself."

My eyes narrowed. Part of the reason I paid Lynx was because I didn't want clients too far down the totem pole. It was not judgmental; it was survival. Some people equated killing those they hired with payment for services delivered. "You know him well?"

Lynx gave a half shrug. In his line of work, keeping his mouth shut kept him alive. The trust that resulted kept him in business. "He ain't real bright. Gets into trouble 'cause he takes on jobs and isn't real good at results."

"Hmm. Tell him it's triple the price if he doesn't name the person. If another witch directly hexed him, I can block the spell, but she can easily throw another one at him."

"You take the case?"

The problem with the evil eye was twofold. Half the time a client was having a streak of bad luck, there wasn't even a spell involved. When it was a spell, it was often a general curse that resulted in nightmares, flat tires, or broken appliances. If a witch really knew her stuff, she'd go after specifics—a vain guy might find the seams of his pants splitting in public or he'd develop a stench he couldn't lose.

"Tell him I can sell him a standard package to ward off bad luck if he wants to go the economy route, but a good witch will know ways around it. If he wants protection from a specific spell, I have to see the damage. The price may change depending on the witch involved too. I don't need a turf war."

Lynx nodded. His ears flicked toward the windows then, a pretty cool trick for a human. "White Feather," he declared even though White Feather's Prius was very quiet and no car was visible yet.

Since his hearing was better than mine by, oh, the skill of a bobcat, I didn't argue. I wasn't too keen on Lynx being here when White Feather showed up. He would quickly sense the change in our relationship. Of course, since White Feather was a known entity, Lynx wasn't going to leave without me telling him to, and suggesting it would raise even more suspicions.

I gave up without bothering to find a viable excuse to make him go. Hurrying into the bathroom, my ruined clothes went straight in the trash. My silver went under the sink in a special Navajo basket.

I showered quickly, washing off as much cactus, oil and dirt as possible. A pair of tweezers removed most of the larger cactus spines, and hopefully the sound of the shower running covered up my curses and whimpers.

A few spines were too embedded to remove.

With my arm stinging and throbbing, I threw on fresh clothes and grabbed my favorite silver and turquoise bracelet. It went on the uninjured arm. My grandmother's matching necklace was sadly no longer a part of my collection. Since I thought of it every time I wore the bracelet, it was still with me in important ways.

By the time I made my entrance in the living room, Lynx had already let White Feather in.

White Feather stopped mid-pace when he got a good look at my face. "When did you get sunburned?" His green eyes narrowed. "You haven't been exploring over at Sarah's cabin by yourself, have you?"

"No, I was working on a spell, and I think I insulted Mother Earth." The "sunburn" was more a combination of hard scrubbing and the remaining stain from red cactus juice.

My explanation didn't make him any happier. "Looks like it hurt."

"Don't worry. People pay to have their skin exfoliated. This didn't cost me anything," I joked.

Gently, he touched the side of my face. "Tara is in the car. I wanted to introduce her to you in case you had any training tips that might stick. Now might not be the best time, although if she meets you today, she might realize that witching is dangerous."

There was a snort from the doorway. Lynx had helpfully opened it when he heard someone on the other side. His tail, if it had been out, would have been twitching. Since he was in human form, he settled for flicking his eyes between players.

I peered around White Feather, and nearly gasped aloud. I had seen a picture of Tara, but the real deal was covered in so much makeup, I couldn't have picked her from a lineup. Her hair was dyed a deep black on black, her lips were painted with black lipstick and her face was powdered white.

"What, no tattoos?" The girl looked like the walking dead, the worst of the worst groupies.

"My body is a temple," she proclaimed, her palms out as though offering herself. "I will put no spells or marks upon myself until I know the purest of them."

White Feather snarled impatiently, "Adriel, this is Tara. Tara, you can drop the dramatics."

"Come on in," I said.

She tromped across the threshold. Although she strove for casual disinterest, her eyes missed nothing. My mundane living room was bound to be a disappointment. The garlic and silver protection was hidden underneath the door frame. The crucifixes were in plain sight, but most of the New Mexican population was Catholic. As decorations, they were not out of place over the fireplace and kitchen window.

The dried grasses arranged in a large Indian pot, a basket of pine cones and some other dried herbs all had witch purposes, but from the sudden slump of her shoulders, it was obvious she dismissed me, the room and any hope.

The only item of interest was Lynx, where her eyes lingered for a moment before she asked me, "Well? Did you want to question me to see if I am worthy?"

White Feather's lips thinned.

Before the situation could deteriorate, I asked, "What kind of questions?"

"Jason says you can test my potential. Like you know more than he does or something."

"Jason." I almost laughed. Jason was just too ordinary for the magic White Feather encompassed. When we met, I had used Merlin and he had used White Feather. His name had stuck. "White Feather, why don't you leave Tara here for her first lesson. You can pick her up in an hour or so." I did not add that dinner afterward would be a wonderful diversion. After all, Tara would be with us, and having her along was not likely to make for a fun evening.

"She knows that nickname?" Tara glanced at him in surprise, sounding impressed for the first time.

White Feather's head jerked from Tara to me. "Maybe this isn't such a good idea."

Lynx's eyes positively lit up with curiosity, and I was almost certain his ears grew slightly so he wouldn't miss a thing.

"We have to start somewhere," I said with a shrug. "Contrary to popular belief, I can't test her potential by waving a wand."

White Feather sighed. "Okay. I need to check on the house anyway. I'll be back in an hour." He opened the door and then hesitated, but couldn't think of anything else to say.

"Lynx?" I said.

"Huh?"

"Don't you have to be running along also?"

He shook his head. "No. I'm good."

"*Lynx.*"

He grinned. "Yah, yah. Yankin' your chain." He sauntered to the door where White Feather still lingered. He cocked his head sideways as though listening to something the rest of us couldn't hear. At the last second he turned and pinned Tara with his stare. "She's good, man. Don't mess with her. I need the business, and she gets into enough trouble without you blowing anything up."

He was around White Feather and across the porch before I could reply. Tara didn't know Lynx so probably wouldn't recognize the backhanded compliment or the fact that he moved with a grace and scurry not known to most humans.

I caught White Feather's eyes. With great reluctance, he finally pulled the door closed.

Not wanting to think too hard about possible consequences, I plowed ahead. "Let's go to my lab. I'll show you around."

Tara followed me, stopping at the doorway to the lab.

I invited her in, a formality, but an important one. The lab was marginally more impressive than the living room. There were ancient leather bound books, glass jars filled with herbs, pieces of wood, lots of stones, and pottery.

The concrete floor had two drains for hosing away messy chemicals. There was a dual burner with a protective hood next to a sink on the far wall. Three locked cabinets and shelves wound around the outer walls of the room. My computer and various books lived on one table; another long table on wheels served as a work surface. The windows were up high, not at normal levels where prying eyes would have an easy way to spy.

Tara said, "You don't have any goats. I checked when we drove up."

"Uh, no. I had chickens for a while, but the coyotes got them."

"Where do you get your goat heads then?" She perused the labels on my jars as though hoping to discover one hiding in or between the bottles.

"Goat heads?" I repeated cautiously.

"I want to learn the spell for turning men on," she said. "The aphrodisiac. I *know* it requires goat heads in the formula. I don't know if it is the entire head or dried pieces of it or the blood or what. But that's the spell I want to learn."

Tempting as it was, I did not cry. "You are what? Sixteen, seventeen years old? You don't need a goat's head to attract men. Trust me."

She nodded emphatically. "That's in the spell. If you don't know that, you can't be much of a witch."

I considered telling her the truth, but a little knowledge in the mind of the wrong person could be fatal. Whatever she had read must not have mentioned that "goat head" was just the common name of the garden weed known as a "puncture vine." I didn't want her killing any man by overdosing him, so I just moved on. "Have a seat." I took the stool and left her the low chair by the computer. "First things first. I need to know what's in all that makeup you're wearing because some chemicals will react with what we do. I don't want to figure out after the fact the reason your face ignited."

"I'm *not* taking my makeup off. It's part of who I am."

My arm hurt, my head was starting to throb, and I was about out of patience. "The black stuff—around your eyes and on your eyebrows—if it contains charcoal, it will dampen the effects of any spell."

She tossed her hair.

"Charcoal absorbs," I lectured. "For some spells that means complete negation. It might be why you've had trouble creating spells." It was also the likely reason she couldn't attract nearly every guy she wanted. But she was young. Stupidity like hers could usually be overcome.

Now why I had taken on this job, that was another kind of stupidity, and it probably couldn't be cured. I stared across the lab at my defiant...apprentice? and nearly dropped my head to the table. I'd rather teach Lynx magic, and he had the attitude of a cat.

Too late now. "Let's try a witching fork." I rubbed one end with an herb. Done right, she should be able to trace it to the jar from which it came.

White Feather had already taught her the basics. She marched the fork around the lab like a trained soldier, pausing at each jar. She understood the technique and tried to compensate for it mentally. If she had an affinity for magic it was well concealed behind a morass of emotion that was as thick and dark as her makeup.

I went to my workbench and retrieved two willow branches. "Okay, here. Let's try raw magic." Willow was naturally tuned to water. If she had ever seen a pair, she might know it, but she couldn't be sure I hadn't respelled them.

I handed her the sticks. "Follow them."

"To what?"

"Let the magic lead. Follow them."

She accepted the rods tentatively. Her fear of failure had her gripping the handles so hard the sticks couldn't have led her to water had the faucet been gushing.

"Relax your grip. Feel for vibrations." I turned her away from the faucet to the inside of the house. The sticks would go to the closest source. "Do you know how to center?"

She nodded, again putting in enough effort that any possible magic would be repressed if not extinguished outright.

"Magic is a living, breathing entity. Don't smother it with enthusiasm." I paced away, giving her space. "Where can you go?"

"What?"

"What place do you know well enough that you can visit in your head while still standing here? It's like yoga. Sleep without sleep."

"I don't...I don't have any place."

Okay, she didn't know how to center herself. "Your room at home. Walk into it and list every object."

Again the furrow of concentration. By the time we were done here, her makeup would be permanently creased. "Out loud," I instructed. "Close your eyes. It's dark and you are in your room to retrieve an object from your desk."

She blinked at me. "My desk is on the other side of the room. My bed is in the center."

"Turn the light on."

Reflexively, her right hand relaxed as her mind thought of reaching up. The stick in her hand swiveled toward the faucet. Predictably, she tightened her grip.

"Uh-uh. Let it go where it wants. You're busy in your room."

She stared down at the stick in her hand. "It moved."

No matter how hard White Feather had tried, Tara had not believed in magic. If it had ever moved for her, she had never believed.

I smiled. Her mouth gaped as though she had just witnessed a miracle. "List the contents of your room," I said softly.

We went through several iterations, but the girl was seriously stressed over the whole magic thing. When she finally got both sticks to swivel simultaneously in the direction of the faucet, I was almost as happy as she was. Unfortunately, she forgot to breathe, which became evident when she suddenly staggered sideways and hit the bookcase.

"Easy, take it easy." I shoved the stool under her. "Put your head down. I think you're getting a handle on it."

She leaned over, her head in her hands. "This is hard."

The problem, of course, was that it wasn't. I'd never seen a witch or even a normal nearly pass out from trying so hard. "Yes," I lied, "it is."

She glared at me through the curtain of her hair. Maybe she sensed the lie, or maybe she hated showing weakness because she said, "You know my brother will never date you."

I blinked. "What?"

"I know that's why you're helping me, but it won't matter. Even if you teach me." She waved one of the willow sticks. "After Claire, he won't ever date anyone again that knows he's a warlock, no matter what."

At the name of another woman, my heart jerked to an uncertain stop, as frozen as the rest of me. Then it pounded hard, sending blood up my neck, flushing my cheeks. By the smirk on her face, it was obvious she was satisfied with stabbing me. The little bitch could be lying, but she probably knew it wouldn't be easy to ask White Feather about it.

"Be that as it may," I managed, "we teased a little bit of talent into showing today." I indicated the sticks with the wave of my hand. "Take those home with you. See where they lead you. Next time you come, tell me what they are set for."

Petty, yes. I could have told her they were set to water, and she could have practiced. But this way, she couldn't cheat by forcing the sticks to lead when she wasn't centered and relaxed properly. And if she didn't discover what they were drawn to, I'd know she hadn't been brave enough to practice—or that she had failed.

I smiled for real. She could push me if she wanted to, but she had better know that White Feather's sister or not, bitchy could be a two-way street.

I turned my back on her and led the way out of the lab. Reciting the ingredients to a basic spell almost kept me from gnashing my teeth while we waited in the living room for White Feather to arrive.

Chapter 7

The first car to roll up the dirt driveway was not White Feather's Prius. It was a white Mustang.

My jaw dropped when Lynx climbed out. I knew that one of his more unsavory cohorts had sold him a fake ID, because Lynx had rented his first apartment. He wanted a house, but couldn't pass the tougher scrutiny into his background or earnings.

There was a part of me that wanted to help him with a house deal, but the more intelligent part of my brain recognized he was not a good credit risk. Despite a steady income from the underground, the kid knew way too much about abandonment. He was a survivor, first, second and last. He was not capable of placing any other person—and certainly not their money--above his own survival, not after living on the streets for so long.

Scrutinizing the pristine car and the kid sauntering up my porch steps, I was stunned at what a fake ID could do for a person these days. What did he want with a car anyway? When he needed speed or stealth, he went bobcat.

Then again, he was entering the world of grownups, including the normal world. The Mustang indicated that he was entering on better terms than I had when I turned eighteen.

He paused to wait patiently for White Feather, who drove up and parked next to him.

Since I was being nosy and making no attempt to hide it, I opened the door before either could knock.

"Hi." I raised an eyebrow and tilted my head toward the Mustang. "Nice wheels."

"Thanks."

If he knew I was choking back questions like, "When did you learn to drive?" and "Where did you get a car like that?" he didn't bother to assuage my curiosity.

"How did it go?" White Feather asked, replacing my worries with his own.

Lynx smiled at Tara. "Bet it went okay."

Tara nodded. "Can't complain."

"Told you she's good. You ready for some chow?"

She smiled. "Anything. I'm starved."

Lynx, in a gentlemanly manner I had never before witnessed from him, took the door from my limp fingers and held it open for Tara. They both walked out.

White Feather and I stared after them, speechless. My mouth moved, but no sounds came out.

After the dust settled in the driveway, he faced me. "I thought you said if I didn't tell her who to date, she'd pick better dates."

"Didn't they just meet?"

"Far as I know."

"How could they—what just happened here?"

"I think *Lynx* just took *my sister* on a date."

I tried to think of a silver lining. "It could be worse."

His eyes widened. "He's a shifter."

"She's a witch," I said. "Probably. She should be able to handle herself and, well, it is Lynx." On second thought, that really wasn't a huge reassurance.

"Are you trying to tell me that he isn't like every other guy out there, more than happy to take advantage of my little sister?"

"She's not that little! And neither is Lynx. I don't think I know how to handle this."

He indicated the still open door. "I think it's been taken out of our hands."

There was that.

I had obviously missed out on several conversations, including the one I should have had with White Feather about his past relationships. It took superhuman effort to keep from blurting out questions about the mysterious "Claire." There was no point in coming across as a jealous shrew. If I couldn't figure out who she was on my own, maybe I'd hire Lynx.

The very thought made my eyes water. Hire Lynx to look into my private business? Was I losing my mind???

White Feather misread my upset. "It's just food. It can't be that bad. It is Lynx."

I nodded. "Right."

He let out a huge, pent-up breath. "I brought something to show you, although I was planning on waiting until later. Since Tara left, now is as good a time as any."

"Okay."

"It's...ugly. Maybe this isn't such a good idea."

"Can't hurt to look." In my opinion, it was past time he asked for my professional opinion with whatever was going on.

He stalled. "That arm doesn't look good."

I lifted it. My entire forearm was puffy. "Cactus needles. They'll work themselves out."

His eyebrows drew into a frown, but the arm couldn't be helped at the moment. Reluctantly, he led the way to his car. From the passenger side, he extracted a clear plastic bag from the glove box. It was labeled, but I didn't need to read it to know its contents.

Charred, human bone. An aura came from it that reached me all the way to where I stood near the hood.

"Gordon did a quick search with a cadaver dog at the site this afternoon. He found three fragments like this one, probably the same person. Gordon is running tests, of course."

The aura was a spiteful, hateful wave. I had feared Sarah and her ghost. This aura was even stronger and more defined. My skin crawled now, just as it had then. "I think it's Sarah."

White Feather didn't respond. He stared down at the bones, fingering the side of the plastic. His focus bordered on fixation.

My eyes widened. The damn bone—or the aura--was beckoning him. I swooped in and snatched the bag. My arm jerked with pain. It felt as if someone had just rubbed sandpaper across the embedded cactus needles.

I dropped the bag and leaned over, suddenly needing more oxygen.

"Hey," White Feather protested. "That's evidence!"

When he leaned to retrieve it, I kicked it aside. "Don't touch it! Don't pick it up without silk!" My kick did little to move the bag. He easily scooped it up.

"This is crime evidence, not a football!"

"White Feather." Still bent over, I held up a flat hand to indicate I wasn't the threat. "Drop the bag."

He looked unreasonably hurt. "My brother expects this to be returned intact. You can't go around destroying evidence."

"It's contaminated, White Feather. You need to put it down."

"It's in plastic. It's fine." He wasn't letting go of the bag.

"It's toxic. That magic is not contained by that plastic bag." Even though I was no longer touching it, the vibes stabbed at me with malicious intent. We needed some silk or more silver. Or a miracle.

"Don't be ridiculous. I knew I should have left you out of this."

I removed my bracelet. "Here. Put this around the bone." My heart stuttered a protest. My bracelet had years of accumulated magic associated with it. Direct exposure to the bone could ruin it.

White Feather glared at me in disgust. "I need to check the house." He slammed the passenger side door and headed for the driver's side.

"White Feather!" I grabbed his arm, but he didn't slow down. "Wait!" The sandy driveway provided zero leverage. "Don't you want to know if it belongs to Sarah?"

He kept the bone protected with one arm. "We can't prove it without something of hers."

"I have something of hers, remember? I can do the test!" My grip on him was hampered by my bracelet so I let it drop to the ground. The result was instantaneous and disastrous.

The full force of the aura hit me. The smell of burned sulfur and rotting meat knocked me off my feet. "White--" But it was only a choking noise. My lungs compressed, hungry for oxygen as though they had collapsed completely.

Half on the ground, I floundered until my fingers found my bracelet. It took a second or two, but my lungs expanded. The stench of sulfur lessened enough for me to breathe. "White Feather! I can do the test."

He blinked, but instead of looking at me, he stared at the spot where I had been standing. "Do you really have something of Sarah's?"

"I told you so at the cabin, remember?"

His hold on the bone didn't lessen, but his hand dropped from the car door handle.

I stood, relieved.

His gaze remained focused somewhere behind me. The green of his eyes was dull, faded. He didn't seem to know I had fallen or that I had gotten back up. He stared at the house without blinking.

"Oh my God." I hadn't reached him at all. The aura, whatever it was, had living ears. It had attached itself to White Feather, and it wanted to know what I had that belonged to Sarah.

Chapter 8

That bone was not coming into my house. Given all my protection spells, I wasn't sure it would even be possible. My house had enough wards against evil spirits, other witches, and bad auras that sometimes I worried I'd be kept out if my mood was sour enough.

"I do have something of Sarah's." My feet pedaled slowly toward the front door. "Let me bring it out here."

White Feather blinked. "What is it?"

"I have one of her spells. Wait here." I sprinted madly for the porch. My mind gibbered, *not White Feather, not White Feather*. How could he let this happen? He was a warlock. Of considerable power! How had it penetrated his defenses?

What if I couldn't save him?

"It's an aura! He's not dead. He's there, he's under there." I slammed the front door closed and locked it. It was rude, but there was no point in counting on spells when the mundane would do. Whatever that thing was, it wasn't worming its way inside my home.

Some evils had to be welcomed, some merely had to be accepted, some were insidious. A few complex ones triggered after certain conditions were met, stealing control so stealthily no one noticed until it was too late. Almost certainly that was what had happened to White Feather. He had associated the bones with nothing more than a harmless bag of evidence from his brother. "Mayan *Sacrifices!*"

Searching frantically through my herbs, I dropped one bottle, but managed to save the other. Was that my heart thumping loudly, or had a car engine just started up? "Don't go!"

I snatched up a red silk scarf, but stowed it under my shirt where it wouldn't be noticed. If he had driven off, I would trail him to the ends of the earth.

With one foot already outside the lab, I hesitated. Should I take Sarah's spell? How much damage could that aura cause?

A lot, considering it already partially controlled White Feather.

Was the aura Sarah? A powerful ghost could cling to something such as its own skull, but scattered and burned bones?

No matter. If the bone was Sarah, her spell would only make things worse. It wasn't possible to fake a witching fork…then again, why not? Tara had done a pretty good job of faking results. And if I held the fork, White Feather wouldn't know whether the fork really pulled to the bone or not.

"It's an aura. It can't think. Right?" But it was an aura tied to a *bone*. Ugh. That was as bad as a blood aura. It had power.

I dashed into the bathroom and looted the Navajo basket. My special bracelet that looped to a ring held several special carvings, including my favorite protection, a medicine bear.

I sped back outside.

White Feather was wary in a half asleep kind of way. "Why did you lock the door?"

At least he had noticed. I waved my left hand in front of his face. He was definitely more alert because his eyes not only tracked my hand, they narrowed suspiciously.

"Bad magic," I panted. "You need to put it down." There was no point in concealing the facts from the victim. Without warning, I pushed my hand under his nose, doing my best to get the sage airborne. "Breathe deep!" Sage tea would have been better, but he probably wouldn't allow me that much leeway.

Instinctively, he grabbed my wrist, coming in contact with my silver. "What are you doing?"

"Don't reach for your wind. I'm not sure what will happen if you do that." At the cabin, his wind had only added to the danger. Silver, on the other hand, had blocked. "Drop the bone, White Feather."

White Feather frowned and then lifted the bag higher as though he hadn't realized he was holding it. Now that he was in contact with my silver, he reflexively shifted his grip to hold one end--like anyone might do when exposed to something obviously dead and disgusting.

"Put it on the ground."

He tilted his head, but then clutched the bag tighter, wrapping his fingers around it again.

He wasn't free yet. "Just so I can see if it belonged to Sarah." My soothing voice squeaked at the end.

I felt it then. An ill wind, an outright attack. The aura didn't trust me, even if White Feather did. I panicked. I wasn't prepared to fight wind. It pushed at me, threatening to choke off my air supply with sulfur and stink.

Raised hands, even those with silver, were not much protection against fetid air. I gagged in a useless struggle to find fresh oxygen.

Before I could circle around or consider more than a gasp of a warning, White Feather blinked. Wind was his forte. His mind might be in a fog, but the twisted abuse of the wind penetrated whatever haze gripped him.

"Adriel, watch out!" He parried, shoving the wind away from both of us. The bag fell from his fingers, either because he felt the sickness or because he wanted his hands freed for a fight.

I dove so fast, a tornado couldn't have stopped me from falling on the bag like it was a bomb.

Three feet above the ground, the silk under my shirt rammed into the aura. "Ooof." White Feather's wind pressed against me, blasting the ill wind away, but unintentionally holding me down. The silk was as firm as a metal shield, hard against my stomach. I hung in midair, compressed from both sides, barely able to wave an arm.

Mother Earth wasn't available to me from three feet above the dirt, and even if she had been, the closest path was directly through a dark, evil aura.

"Mnng!" My vision went dark.

White Feather finally finessed his attack, blowing away the aura underneath my body.

The aura dispersed. As graceful as a sack of groceries, I flopped onto the bone.

"Ugh." Somewhere along about the fourth shake my head cleared.

White Feather spoke, but the buzzing in my ears left me deaf. When my fingers finally responded to my commands, I extracted the silk scarf from under my shirt and wrapped it carefully around the bagged bone. I admit, I muttered a prayer, not only for the dead, but also for the living, all in one breath.

"What the hell was that?" White Feather flexed his fingers, searching for the enemy.

I stayed on the ground, resting, while he searched his memory. "Bad magic."

"It yanked on me."

It had done more than that. "Your wind? Or you?"

He didn't answer right away. He crouched down next to me. "What just happened here?"

I sat up, holding the package. "You remember the evidence your brother gave you?"

"The bone."

"It took a liking to you."

He frowned. "I brought it over here to show you. And then...How long have we been out here with that thing?"

"It had you under the influence. I couldn't convince you to put it down." I spit some of the dust off my lips.

White Feather helpfully set me on my feet.

"I'm not sure it had any definite plans, but it seemed to want to be a part of you. Aztec sacrifices, you had me scared." Truth be told, I was still scared.

Rather than releasing my arm, his fingers gripped harder. "It was a dream. You wanted to take my treasure. It wasn't a bone."

"Oh, yes it was." I put one hand on his, letting us both benefit from the silver.

He glanced down at the bag still in my other hand. "Can you put it down?"

I happily leaned over and set the package down. White Feather's power tingled against my fingers. He drew me closer to him, away from the package. "Dammit. I knew I shouldn't have involved you. That thing is dangerous."

"I have a way to tell if it is Sarah, but I'm not taking it into the lab."

"Taking it anywhere is a bad idea." His wind stirred, circling like static electricity.

"I'm not sure using wind around it is a great idea." Without conscious thought, I grounded to Mother Earth. The solid earth was very reassuring. She was a flow, a heartbeat carried through my blood, a rhythm of earth.

As suddenly as White Feather relaxed, he tensed again. "What--?" I found myself unexpectedly sandwiched between him and his car, about to be flattened again.

The danger had to be coming from the bag.

I squeezed around White Feather's protective arm, but it was too late. The bag was halfway across my yard, running hard into the desert. "The cat!" I yelled.

"It's a cat?"

A brown streak with a bright red scarf trailing around the side of its head scampered into the trees.

"Come back here!" As if it would listen. The cat wouldn't deign to touch the tuna and water, but one old, disgusting, evil bone, and it was suddenly my best friend, coming right up to my very feet.

I slumped in defeat. "It's gone."

White Feather split his attention and confusion between the now empty desert and me. "What would a cat want with that bone?"

"That motley feline has something to do with Sarah. It was here when she was."

"She had a cat?"

"I don't really know. That cat could be friend or foe." For all I knew, the cat was more connected to the aura than Sarah. "At least I don't have to worry about bringing the bone into the lab anymore."

"The bones. The dream. That damn wind again!" His fists clenched.

"The same one from Sarah's cabin?"

He powered his breeze around us both, guarding now as he hadn't done before. My toes tingled. I breathed in the heady magic of it. "Take it easy. I think it's gone now."

"It's almost as if it's following me. Or someone is using wind to find me. Maybe it's really following Sarah?"

"Something was at the cabin. Do you think...can wind really track you?"

He let his power settle, but he was far from serene. "Wind isn't alive. Not exactly. And this wind is hungry. There was that same smell, but at the time, I thought I was smelling the bones." He shook his head. "Most blackened bones don't smell like gutted kill, blood and offal."

"Silver," I said. "It helped me. Maybe I can help you block this thing, whatever it is. Let me try something!"

White Feather wasn't nearly as excited as I was, but he followed me inside.

I raided my stash of fresh silver and sized a piece around his finger. "Gold would be stronger, but I'm totally out at the moment. I'll design something more permanent, but for now, I'll fashion an alarm." My experiments with wind needed to move up on the priority list. It was obviously a weapon—and White Feather wasn't the only one wielding it.

White Feather watched as I braided the fresh silver and then fashioned a circle, melding it without losing the design. Most clients wouldn't get even a rub from my grandmother's silver, but White Feather was special. A single leaf decoration from my own bracelet, embedded in the fresh silver, would go a long way toward protecting him.

"What exactly will this spell do?"

"Warn you mostly." I set the silver aside to cool. "Silver is a natural blocker. A determined witch could overcome it, but hopefully, once you're warned, you'll be able to take steps of your own."

He reached for the ring. "Let's see if this fits."

I was skilled with jewelry since I fashioned so much of my own. It slipped over his finger perfectly. He yelped, surprising us both.

"Ow! Hot!"

He yanked it off, dropping it on the table. "Better wait for it to cool."

"Moonlight Madness." I picked up the ring. It was cool to the touch. Either the stricken look on my face or the fact that I didn't immediately drop the ring told him all he needed to know.

"I need to create a different spell," I choked out.

He stared at me without asking, but I told him anyway. "The heat is the warning. Except that in this room, you should be shielded. There's no wind. There's nothing in here which means--" I didn't finish. I couldn't.

"I'm contaminated." His face drained of color.

My own face felt pasty. "There's some type of spell on you. Probably from whatever that thing was in the bones." And had I not used my grandmother's bracelet with the old, experienced silver, we might never have known. Freshly spun silver was untainted. It would pick up new spells *as they occurred*, but it wouldn't trigger for an established spell. Thankfully, old magic, like that in my bracelet, was stronger and smarter than new silver.

"You're," I swallowed bile, "going to need some purification."

"I'm leaving. My being here is putting you in danger." White Feather made for the doorway.

I ignored his suggestion. "We can cover the basic purification and warding." The spell could have come at him through dreams, food...I nearly refused to contemplate voodoo and blood spells because whatever had been in the bones wasn't even alive, but this was not the time to be stupid. "It would help if we knew the witch. Sarah didn't seem that strong."

White Feather had to stop or walk out with me still talking. He stopped. "Maybe she gained power through her own death."

I gathered sage, corn pollen and other necessary ingredients. "Can ghosts still cast spells? That shouldn't be possible."

"It is, at least with some magics. Ghosts have an affinity to air currents because that's what they can control best when they cross over. A wind witch in particular might be able to impart some sort of spell."

"Really?" The possibility would have been a lot more intriguing had we not been talking about a malicious ghost. "I need to beef up on my research."

White Feather didn't come back into the lab, but he didn't leave either. "Grandfather wasn't quite ready to cross over when he went. Let's just say he's been heard from now and again."

I almost dropped a beaker of holy water. "You have a ghost in the family?"

He sighed. "Two actually. It's a long story. And you keep insisting that Sarah wasn't a strong wind witch. I don't know what to think, but it's better if I track this down myself."

With him under some sort of influence, that was a particularly dangerous idea. My heart didn't like it, nor did my head. "You can fight it with wind if you want, but it won't hurt to use every skill we have. Many things counter wind and wind spells. Water. Fire. Earth." I forced my voice to remain calm as I added holy water to the protection and twisted the elements together with a leather braid.

In addition to the silver, I needed an arrowhead. It might interfere with his magic, but desperate times called for desperate measures. Thankfully I hadn't put away the arrowhead from the other night. It was still on my kitchen counter.

Unfortunately, White Feather followed me to the living room. He wasn't inclined to wait for me to finish the blocking spell.

His hand was on the doorknob when I said, "Try this, White Feather. Hold this in one hand and put the ring back on." I braided quickly. "The arrowhead may interfere with your own magic, but give it a shot."

I felt his wind before he moved. The anger in it brushed along my arms, threatening. Something in the kitchen fell over, probably the roll of paper towels by the sink.

"None of this is safe!" The green in his eyes darkened to the black of the sea.

"You can't fight this alone."

"Yes, I can!"

I held the braid out. "Loop the leather around your wrist. Let me embed the arrowhead in the ring, and you can test it again."

I left him standing there, the braid on the counter. "I know how this feels, White Feather. I've been stalked before."

He glared at me, an inferno about to explode. But he had been there. He remembered. For a second, sympathy flashed, but it was quickly replaced by anger. Still, one fist unclenched enough to reach for the braid.

Chapter 9

I took my time on the ring, hoping that giving White Feather some space would make him more receptive to my help.

The obsidian arrowhead was too large for the ring, but instead of carving it smaller, it occurred to me that turquoise would provide even better protection. My hand hovered over my bracelet again. Not only was turquoise a healing and purifying stone, it would strengthen the good and dispel the bad without interfering with magic. Only for a family member would I donate any of Grandma's turquoise. Or for White Feather.

I pried the turquoise out of its setting and chipped a chunk from the bottom where it would be least noticeable. Turquoise was perfect for causing spells to slide off and away. It soaked up evil, detoxifying it.

It took careful carving to form an arrowhead from the turquoise, but the shape as well as the mineral had to be perfect. Embedding the turquoise in the silver ring was easy.

I cooled the ring in holy water before returning to the living room.

White Feather paced across the small space like a caged tiger.

"I've one more ingredient to add to the leather band I made you." It came out more a question than I intended.

White Feather saved his glare for the band around his wrist as he untied it. He watched without comment as I embedded the leftover turquoise dust in the leather.

When I was done, I offered White Feather the ring.

He took it, his eyes hooded. "Aren't I the one who is supposed to give you a ring?"

It took me a minute, but I finally got it. "I...what?"

He rewarded me with a weak smile that reached all the way to his eyes-- and my heart. "I'm not accustomed to accepting help." He spun the ring around the tip of his finger. "Thanks."

My face flushed. "Me neither, not really."

He put my hand on top of his and slid the ring on his finger, still holding my hand. The silver was warm, but wearable. The arrowhead was spelled, earth to earth. Hopefully it was strong enough to absorb the taint lingering around him.

"If it heats up, get yourself into water. A swimming pool, shower, whatever is closest."

"Or fire. Or I could dig myself a hole in the ground."

"That would work, but it might be easier to stay alive if you chose a different option."

Neither of us laughed. Whatever spell had been used was subtle enough to cross the threshold of my home without detection and strong enough to not be completely blocked by the adobe. Of course, I always welcomed him in, which would make it much easier on a stowaway spell.

"If someone comes after me, I'll give them their money's worth." He squeezed my hand hard.

"Be careful, White Feather. Whoever is messing with this isn't just using wind. They're trying to access *you*." And whatever aura was out there had partially succeeded, at least when Sarah's bones had been involved. We needed to break the link. Yesterday.

The slope of his shoulders echoed the weight resting on my own. He reached for me, but then dropped his arm and took two strides to the door instead. "I'll call you later."

I wanted to scream out my fear, but there was no time to waste on self-indulgent luxuries. Welcome or not, I was going to save his hide from whoever had marked him, be she dead or alive.

When the door clicked shut behind him, I locked it and immediately began to plan.

Chapter 10

My first chore was to eat because no witch does her best work on an empty stomach. I grilled a cheese sandwich and then read about cats, possessions and spells. Using extremely dangerous magic, a cat could be possessed by a living witch. Even possessed, convincing a cat to cooperate was difficult because cats had natural protections against magic--and a mystical ability to ignore orders or coercion.

They couldn't be spelled or trained to cooperate. On rare occasions they could be cajoled into helping, but they were capricious.

Ghosts were easier to handle. They could be forced in and out of realms and, as I suspected, their bones could serve as a control. They could be called using personal objects or drawn to the living by unrequited desires. It was almost unheard of for a ghost to draw power from the realm of the dead *on its own*, but it could be forced as a medium through which some nasty stuff could flow.

"Aztec curses."

At midnight, more confused than before, I showered again and went to bed.

Sleep didn't provide any answers, but it did help me to prioritize. Whether the cat had anything to do with Sarah or not, we needed to find out if Sarah was haunting White Feather. He probably wouldn't be pleased with my interference, but it was imperative to know one way or the other.

Gulping fully-caffeinated tea, I slogged into the lab at daybreak.

Sarah's spell was my last link to her unless Mat sold me the other spell. Preserving at least some of the spell was crucial. Hmm....maybe a silver toothpick through the cork?

No, the spell would rub off on the way back through. A hook would get stuck...Silver with a little crevice to hold some of the spell?

I coated a thin steel pick with silver and notched one side an inch from the tip. It should be enough to capture bits of spell and aura.

It took some finesse to insert the pick without the jar spinning away from me. Extracting the pick without popping the cork wasn't all that easy either.

Once out, there was no sign of any chemicals nestled inside my specially crafted indentation, but aura and spells weren't always visible to the naked eye.

I spelled the witching fork with the invisible aura, packed my backpack, ate breakfast and debated calling ahead.

He couldn't say no if he didn't know I was coming.

I was ever so slightly nervous over whether he would accept any more help from me. If he refused, did it mean he was under a spell? Or that he was just stubborn?

I had only been to his place once; it had seemed to be an introduction of sorts, a stop on the way to bigger and better things. Until bigger and better had dwindled to phone calls and emergencies.

My hands were not sweating from gripping the steering wheel as I drove. It was a nice day and not hot enough for sweaty hands.

White Feather, true to his nature, had designed his home off-grid, completely powered by solar and wind. The solar panels were mostly for show because he generated enough wind to charge the storage batteries whenever necessary.

Backpack in hand, I was barely out of the car when White Feather barreled out the front door. "Adriel!" His wind reached me before he did. "Are you okay?"

"What? Yes. Yes, I'm fine."

He halted on the walkway. "You're sure? No ghosts? Or spell-demon cats, dogs, whatever?"

I hadn't expected such concern over me arriving unexpectedly at his front door. "No, I swear I'm fine. I brought my witching fork to check your place for traces of Sarah."

He settled back on his heels and rearranged his train of thought. Finally he said, "Not a bad idea."

I joined him on the walkway. "If Sarah has anything to do with whatever has spelled you, I want to find it."

He leaned in and kissed my lips lightly.

I blushed, caught off-guard by the warm welcome. "I would have called first, but..." I could hardly tell him I planned to check for Sarah come hell or high water.

"It's a good idea to hunt for her," he said. "The ring is warm, all the time, even on home ground."

I touched the silver band. It radiated a steady heat, not enough to burn, but a constant warning.

White Feather led the way inside. Like many newer Santa Fe properties, his house was brown adobe with lots of tile. Not only was it possible to see from the living room into the kitchen, with a breeze White Feather could easily check down the wide hallways and into the bedrooms.

The tiled floors were generously decorated with Navajo wool rugs. His home was everything mine was not; large, open and expensively furnished. The colors were similar to mine, a mix of desert earth browns with generous splashes of the deep blue of the sky.

Before I was halfway into the living room, a bright pink purse on a side table caught my attention. I cut my eyes to White Feather. He didn't notice my sudden tension.

Okay. This was too obvious to simply ignore. "New purse?"

"What?"

I pointed to it.

He rolled his eyes. "Tara. She left it here after a particularly bad training session a few weeks ago, and then forgot it the next three times. I need to drop it off."

"Oh." I relaxed, but threw an inward curse at Tara for causing jealousy about some Claire person that may not even exist. I set my backpack down on one of the six woven fabric chairs. The arms and legs were sturdy oak, carved with gorgeous detailed patterns, ones I'd love to investigate someday.

Six was a magical number, and White Feather was a warlock. Either the number of chairs was significant or the way they were aligned was protective, magical or both.

White Feather said, "If Sarah is the reason for my paranoia, and she's only a ghost, I'll give her a send off she won't want repeated."

I pulled out the witching fork. "You can get rid of a ghost easily?"

He smiled, but his eyes held steel. "A specific ghost, yes. Especially if there's an object here tied to her. If not for Grandfather, I would have purged for all ghosts after you told me you saw one."

"Ah, your grandfather might not like it if you purged him." I walked the perimeter of the living room. The fork didn't vibrate even slightly.

Working my way into the kitchen, I held the fork high, low and in-between. The bar at the side of the kitchen held one of White Feather's inventions, a beautifully detailed electric train powered by concept windmills.

On my last visit, he had demonstrated how the train delivered whole coffee beans to a grinding station and then paused with one of the cars positioned under the chute at the other end. Once filled, the train took the freshly ground beans up a hill and dumped them into a chute that fed either the espresso maker or the coffee pot.

The train completed the circuit past a detailed forest backdrop where it collected green beans from another hamper and deposited them at a roasting station. White Feather had carved each car from a different type of wood.

I gave the train a friendly pat. "I love your train." The witching fork didn't quiver the least bit near the train. Relieved, I looked at him for permission before going down the hallway.

He nodded, looking slightly amused.

I had never been in his bedroom. It was as neat as the rest of the place. It was more suggestive than any other room too. The tingle in my hands and toes was not from the witching fork.

White Feather's desk was pleasantly cluttered; model windmills and parts sat alongside papers and a laptop. No less than four computer screens stretched across the desk. One of them displayed a graph of windmill speeds and battery charge level stats.

I approached the handmade dresser, a design that quite obviously followed the pattern the wood had supplied. Rather than a perfect rectangle, the dresser was tall, more like a very large tree with drawers. The wood was a stunning mix of reddish browns, too dark for oak. I couldn't resist running my fingers across its smooth surface.

From the doorway, White Feather said, "It's mesquite. Grandfather made it."

I jumped and dropped the witching fork. "Whoops. Must be where you inherited your talent for wood carving. It's gorgeous."

He smiled. My heart stopped. Being in a bedroom around White Feather was a whole new level of temptation. I stooped to retrieve the witching fork. "I'm not getting anything at all. I thought for sure there would be a reaction."

White Feather had used wind at Sarah's cabin and some type of force had responded. He felt something the night Sarah appeared at my place. Then when he brought Sarah's bones, a malignant wind had appeared again.

But now, the witching fork was silent.

"Let me try." He reached for the fork.

We had merged magics before. "Are you sure? If she's attracted to your wind, it could be dangerous."

"Better on my territory than hers."

He was right about that. I waited while he added his wind to the spell already set.

"Try it again."

I detected no change, but knew the spell was stronger with his magic added. Together we paced the room, not avoiding the bed or anything else. Working with him was heady stuff. I was wildly attracted to him even without our elements colliding; add the suggestion of the bed and my magic, and it was all I could do to keep my hands off of him.

Our bodies brushed as we moved from the bedroom to the master bath and back out. He put his hand on my shoulder and let it drift to my lower back as we walked down the hall to the guest bath.

Things were vibrating now--everything except the witching fork. We entered the guest bedroom like dance partners, matched step for step, our magics still merged through the witching fork.

He opened the window. Without any help from me, he spun the essence on the fork outside, exploring the perimeter of the house.

"She's not here." His hand captured my fingers. "Not inside or anywhere near the house."

"You're right. So what here is causing problems?" There was my magic, his magic and a lot of hormones in the room. There was definitely no Sarah. He kissed me. The brush of wind he had sent outside wafted back in around us, swirling with the breeze from the open window.

He drew me in from the waist. I met him more than halfway, fingers splayed across his chest, ready to explore.

"Son of a--" he swore and jerked away. Even as he pulled his hand away, I felt the heat from the ring. My grandmother's bracelet, part of the same silver, reacted in sympathy, flashing red-hot for an instant.

White Feather yanked at the band around his finger. I stared at the witching fork in disbelief. The wand remained completely dormant.

White Feather ripped the silver ring off. I snatched it before it hit the ground. Even with the ring in one hand and the witching fork in the other, there wasn't a twitch from the fork.

The skin on my face was suddenly dry and tight, stabbed by a thousand needles. The presence from Sarah's cabin was with us in the room, but according to the witching fork, it wasn't Sarah.

Chapter 11

My heart pounding, I spun on one foot and slammed the window closed. There were no trees or soil under me, but the foundation of a house did little to prevent my silver from reaching Mother Earth.

White Feather stopped breathing. He drew me close, my back tight against his front. "Shh," he whispered in my ear.

I tried to ground us both as I had at the cabin, hoping to keep whatever it was away from him.

The length of his body was hard against mine, but his magic was gone. Completely shut down. I reached behind me, anchoring my hand around his arm, but even then, there was nothing but a man tensed and ready to fight.

We stood, both of us holding our breath. White Feather took a quick sip of air, but held it again. Puzzled, I followed his example. From his tight hold on me, it was obvious he was angry, but he had tamped down so completely on his power, his warlock aura was invisible.

How could he do that? My power was strongest in my home, but...yes, perhaps more under my control than anywhere else.

The tiniest of breezes touched my hand through the closed window. Needles stabbed. My silver flared hot across my wrist. I looked down at my hand expecting blood, but instead realized that I still held the witching fork with Sarah's aura.

"Moonlight madness!" I held the fork up, gaining White Feather's attention. Sarah's aura seemed to attract the ill wind; it must be linked to her somehow. Every time White Feather used wind around Sarah's essence it drew the prickling wind like a magnet.

White Feather grabbed the fork and shoved the window open. I would have worked the screen free, but he tossed the fork with such force, the screen blew outward.

His anger rocketed the screen and fork away as though propelled by a mini tornado. A strange, almost dead calm engulfed us while the witching fork spun away end over end.

White Feather drew his power back then, but it was too late. A vacuum sucked up the witching fork as if were the best of the Halloween candy. It splintered into tiny pieces, lost in a swirl of wind.

Instead of a satisfied burp, the hungry zephyr bounced as it tested the air. A tendril, like an arm, funneled our way. The main rotation touched the ground and started growing.

White Feather cursed. He clamped down completely again, but the wind circulated in bursts, sucking in dirt and sand. When the dirt devil had enough momentum, it began to move toward us.

"Go!" White Feather grabbed me around the waist and propelled me into the hallway. My eyes remained fixed on the tunnel of wind, wondering if it would do any good to pull at the earth elements joining the fray.

With me in tow, White Feather rushed down the hallway and into the master bedroom. "Time to hide."

"Hide?" I squeaked. "How do you hide from the wind?"

"That thing, whatever it is, has never responded to me. I can't control it." White Feather braced his arms against the dresser. It slid sideways, revealing a narrow hallway lined with tree roots.

There wasn't time for White Feather to explain, but I needed no urging. The wind outside had risen to a roar.

The moment we were both tucked inside, he slid the dresser back in place. White Feather's harsh breaths punctuated the darkness next to me. I worked to quiet my own breathing.

I wasn't certain where we were, but magic radiated all around us. You'd have to be dead to miss it. The beat was Mother Earth, but more than that, it was the lifeblood of the desert, earth and forest.

My silver sang as it joined the choir of sand, soil, water, and that which had turned into the magic of a bountiful tree. I molded myself as close to White Feather as possible, surrounding him with my magic, happily burying us both in the earth around us.

"Grandfather came to this spot on his vision quest." White Feather's voice was barely audible. "He found a stand of mesquite with a single oak and a cedar tree. He added other tree roots as he carved and infused his own magic here."

"Incredible." My skin tingled from the warmth of it. "I thought your grandfather was a wind witch?"

White Father gave a low chuckle. "I never said that. I said he trained me. And this was built by my grandfather on my mother's side. My grandfather on my father's side trained me."

"Wow." No wonder White Feather commanded so much power. He came from two strong lines. I was in awe, not only of the magic around me, but of White Feather. His house was built around a sacred, magical place. That made him a *guardian*.

"His talisman was the forest."

"That would have been my first guess." As magicals went...well. Not only did he tap directly into an element for his power, he was a keeper of another, completely different power.

There was no escaping it. The roots of the tree beckoned me. I traced the silky, craggy surface with my fingers even though it was too dark to see its beauty.

Like a mini landscape, there were ridges, valleys, wonderful bends and alleys. I envisioned the copse of trees as if it still stood in front of me. "The trees must have been closely knit, sharing water."

White Feather guided my hand. "The cedar was bent over from strong winds. The mesquite not as much."

I felt the carving of a wing, the smooth wood like a balm on my fingertips. Knowing White Feather's grandfather was of the forest, I guessed an eagle or a hawk. The sleek edges indicated Mother Nature had designed the wing, not man.

"Owl," White Feather said, spreading my hand across the polished, burled face of the bird. He moved my fingers to another large carving in the mesquite. "His mother's strength was the bear."

The next section was flat and long, ridges notwithstanding. "Wind," he said.

"It's gorgeous." I inhaled the soaking magic of the cedar, letting the magic wash through me.

Just past the doorway, we traced another carving, one where sharper cuts indicated it had extra help from his grandfather. Parts of the face were from nature, but the chin and eyes were gently etched. Hair flowed like a waterfall down into natural carved robes.

"My grandmother."

There was a pulse through my fingertips. Walking the trail of his ancestors was a power completely separate from that which was forest, roots and trees. It was his essence, it was his heritage.

White Feather brought my fingers to his lips. Gently he kissed them. In this time and place, it was not a mere romantic gesture. It was a question; it was a promise. Whether I answered or not, White Feather had made a pledge to me. It was the equivalent of a vow in a church, but it was not complete because a vow required a response.

My heart beat furiously. "I--" Words failed me.

He moved my fingers to my lips. "Shh. You don't have to answer." Faint regret edged his voice. "I've been a complete idiot. First I get marked by some rogue spell. When you show up to help, I invite an ill wind down on us. I know better than to fight wind with wind."

For a scant moment, there was nothing but silence. Of course there was only one answer, and it wasn't words that I lacked, it was courage. How could I live up to any promise I made him?

Surely, I would fall entirely too short.

Nevertheless, I turned his hand to my lips and kissed the palm of his hand.

Chapter 12

Time stopped. I should have been contemplating a spell in case the roof of our haven suddenly blew off. But at the moment, the wind outside had no meaning.

White Feather crushed my lips with his own. It was the same promise, only this time there was no question. I answered it anyway.

Magic swirled. White Feather's wind flared for only an instant before he yanked back as though burned. "Now would not be a good time for me to be visible. Not even here. Especially here."

It was impossible for me to stop. I reached up, my hands on either side of his face, and offered him another kiss, a promise, perhaps a rash one. I had been kept away from him for too long.

He did not resist. He traced my lips with his tongue, pressing me against the hard wood wall. Our tongues tangled, and he nearly ripped my shirt, one hand under and one not. My whole body responded with a rush--as did White Feather's wind.

He cursed vehemently.

I panted out a half laugh.

"We need to...that thing has my scent. I'm not inviting it in here."

He was right. The magical protections might be the strongest I'd ever felt, but there was no point in advertising the shelter to the enemy.

My hands trailed down his arms, lingering long enough to knead his muscles with great longing.

He gave my ribcage a tight squeeze.

With regret, and a huge sigh from me, we eased apart. "That wind can't last forever," he said.

"I'll check."

"No, you won't."

"You can't go out there. If you search ahead with your wind, you'll be detected. It doesn't know me. And even if it does, it's not gunning for me. It's attracted to you or something that links you to Sarah."

The grinding of his teeth was very audible in the quiet. "Not going to happen. If I don't go out obviously fighting, I'll be safe enough. I don't hear anything still storming out there."

I wouldn't know; I had only heard his heartbeat and mine. "I'll check and then--"

"You are not going out there alone."

No way would I allow him go alone either. "Stay linked to me," I urged, giving up the argument. "I can't conceal us completely, but I can reflect Mother Earth. We're a blank stretch of sand. We're nothing but a bit of this mesquite."

"Don't use too much of this place. It's imperative that it remain hidden."

I nodded, but he couldn't see me. "Of course. I only borrow the tiniest bit of essence." I removed his ring from my finger and returned it to him. "Take my bracelet too." As long as I was sharing, I tore open the sage packet that was around my neck. "Put these leaves in your pocket. We are nothing but plants and soil. No threat, no power."

He didn't argue.

It was easy to borrow from the roots. I was on solid ground as far as magic was concerned. Tying the pieces from the roots to the sage and silver was as natural as breathing for me.

When I was ready, I gave his fingers a quick squeeze. "Okay. Let's do it."

Chapter 13

In the quiet of the retreat, the tornado hadn't existed. The lack of noise had fooled me, creating the illusion that the wind had dispersed as soon as we disappeared.

White Feather's room was nearly untouched, but the computer monitors were all black. "There's a shutoff on the windmill and the feeds," he said.

I hoped that was good news, but as soon as we stepped outside the bedroom door, my hopeful relief turned to nausea. The entire back of the house, including the guest room where we had stood, was sheered off. The walls had been crushed and scattered as rubble.

My mouth gaped. A gentle breeze and sunlight bathed my arms. With no walls, it was easy to see into the backyard where White Feather's lab had once stood. Like Sarah's house, a few pipes remained, one not even twisted. Unlike her house, White Feather had a concrete foundation under the lab. It was now almost as pristine as the day it was poured.

White Feather cursed, but kept his magic completely quiet. I pulsed the gentle smell of earth around us. He muttered, "No need. It's gone."

"The wind?" I wasn't sure if he meant the wind or the house.

"The wind, half the house, the lab. The windmills, the solar panels." He rubbed his chin. "Most of the kitchen."

"Oh...no." I squeezed White Feather's hand tighter. The windmill was lying halfway down the hillside, at least one blade snapped. A slight stirring moved the air. Was it an innocent breeze?

I took no chances, countering with more of Mother Earth, letting it trickle through my silver, running like a current.

"The storm was winding down by the time it hit the power sources." He turned back to the kitchen. Part of the room was now open to nature. The living room was strangely intact except for the large picture window, which had shattered outward. My backpack still rested on one of the six chairs, untouched. Tara's purse had fallen off the end table.

I frowned at the anomaly.

White Feather gestured at the chairs. "More of Grandfather's protection. Not much magical can get past that circle."

"Your bedroom is protected by the furniture too, isn't it? Your grandfather was a force to be reckoned with."

"He studied things. The paths of water and wind fascinated him."

"They're pretty fascinating, all right." My eyes followed the path the wind had taken. The destruction had gone around the living room, blowing garbage into what was left of the kitchen.

"The train!" I cried, rushing forward. The counter where it had been was under the fridge. Part of the ceiling had fallen, resting on what was left of a wall.

White Feather grabbed my wrist. "I can rebuild it."

The tiniest echo, or maybe it really was an innocent breeze, brushed past. There was no excuse for my distraction. I flared my magic again, hiding us.

White Feather tensed. He pulled me close, his free hand at his lips in a shushing motion. Slowly, he tugged me toward what had been the guest room. I matched his stride, careful not to crunch debris. I wasn't certain it was possible to be quiet enough to fool wind, but I mimicked White Feather's example.

By the time we reached the sheered off hallway, I was strangely light-headed, which was odd considering we hadn't moved very fast or very far.

It wasn't until White Feather released the spell he had cast that the air was suddenly fresh again.

I took a deep breath. "What was that?"

"Shh."

We sat tight, the seconds stretching to minutes. Thankfully, my silver remained dormant.

Finally, White Feather relaxed. "It's gone. Whatever it is."

I shivered. "What did you just do?"

"Displaced the air. I created a bubble around us, but a layer after that was devoid of oxygen."

"You separated the elements of air?"

"If it had been Sarah--a ghost--it wouldn't have worked. Ghosts don't need to breathe. I learned it for other reasons entirely, but it seemed to fool whatever was searching, at least for the moment."

"That thing was not Sarah. The witching fork never twitched. Whatever it was might have been looking for her."

"It was far more dangerous than any ghost. That wind didn't just snag that witching fork away. It grabbed the gust I threw and intended to bleed me out. It's tired of waiting around for its next meal."

My voiced cracked when I said, "That's not good. Maybe you should leave this place for a while."

"No. I'm not leading it anywhere else. That thing has tasted me twice now. It may have found me through Sarah, but it acts like there's a very strong link to me. Maybe it's only my wind; maybe it's something else." He squeezed my shoulders, but it wasn't the answer I wanted. "I've stayed in Grandfather's retreat before. It's perfectly safe."

I turned and embraced him, pouring all my worry into it. I couldn't force him away, but he wasn't the only one with a few tricks. The man needed a silver barrier, every protection spell invented and a lot of luck. I might not be able to manufacture luck, but I could certainly help with the rest.

Chapter 14

Warding White Feather's house kept us busy long into the night. I wanted to stay with him, but he had withdrawn again, leaving me worried and dejected. From the set of his chin, he wasn't thrilled either, but the reasons were probably not the same as mine.

I headed home, but even after the long night, sleep was impossible. I dozed on and off until dawn, but couldn't shake the image of White Feather's nearly destroyed house. I knew the devastation of a lost home; I had lost mine to a rogue spirit trapped in old Aztec gold. The relief at being alive was quickly replaced by despair from the destruction. The sense of hope was tempered by a huge fear that the thing would return to finish the job.

White Feather's cell phone worked fine so checking on him was only a speed dial away, but I'd rather he be locked safely here with me.

Up early, I was about to tackle wind research when Lynx interrupted with business. Just like old times, there was no car, just a knock at the front door. As soon as I opened it, Lynx blurted, "He's good for it. He wants a meet."

Several seconds passed while I processed his statement. It took a while before a ragged piece of memory finally broke through the stress of the last few days. "The evil-eye client?"

"Yup. He tol' me all about his bad luck, how he's sweatin' all the time, and how business ain't good. Even better, he paid cash, and he paid triple because he still claims he doesn't know the witch that did him."

"Hmm. Not very specific. I can sell him a standard protection ward." I didn't want to mess with a new client right now. A basic spell might be enough to calm the guy down, and if he was just having a run of bad luck, the talisman might solve the problem without further involvement. If he turned out to be one of those needy types who wanted spell after spell, this would push him off until I had more time.

"Guy wants a meet. I set it up for Sunday since he paid triple. He suggested Hyde Park, by the lodge." Lynx made his way into the kitchen, ignoring my frown.

"How'd you know I would take the case?"

Lynx gave me his best Cheshire cat grin, not perturbed in the least. "Doesn't matter. You don't take it, I find someone who will."

"Business as usual." I seriously considered letting the client go, but well-paying customers were necessary--especially if I wanted the luxury of researching off-the-wall spells to help a guy who would rather I stayed clear.

I accepted the money, knowing that Lynx would already have deposited anything the client had touched.

"Dawn, at the rear of the lodge, near the hiking trail," I instructed. "The front is too open to the road, and people driving by will assume something nasty like a drug drop."

"Dawn ain't nobody gonna see you in the front or the back. Drug drops are done at night. Ain't no dopers gonna bother to be up that early."

Lynx's knowledge was one of the reasons I valued him. Lynx's knowledge was one of the reasons I feared working with him. "Dawn anyway and in the back."

"You the boss."

His acknowledgment would have been more respectful if he wasn't digging through my kitchen cupboards. He easily located my last box of animal crackers. I was tired, crabby and more than a little frustrated. Maybe that's why I made the mistake of trying to squeeze my money's worth out of Lynx. "I have a question."

"Sure." He nodded too, just in case I couldn't understand him around the cookies in his mouth.

Asking Lynx about anything to do with shifting was risky business. He was a shifter, and he was well-aware of my knowledge, but life in the underground was all about illusions. We never openly discussed shifting. We never openly discussed how my spells worked. Those topics were lines not crossed.

I bounded ahead anyway, convinced the reason was important enough. "You any good at talking to other cats?"

"I can talk to anybody, anytime, get anything. What you lookin' for?"

"No, I mean cats. Real ones. Small, about…" his eyes narrowed, but I plowed ahead. "I've got this problem with a cat."

"A cat."

"I think it's a house-cat type of cat, not a shifter, but I've only seen glimpses of it." He slapped the box of crackers down on the counter. His ears were flat against his head, an impossible trick for human ears.

"You think I'm like some kind of pet?" The contempt was almost a snarl.

"What? No! Lynx, this isn't a joke! I'm not some shape shifter voyeur, you know that! Look, I'm pretty sure the cat is alive, but I did see it the first time around a ghost."

He hesitated, halfway to the front door.

"I'm not sure if it's trying to haunt me. That could be the case if it really is dead, but it might be trying to convey some other information."

He turned around, his eyes glinting with cat. "Like maybe it's hungry?"

I shook my head quickly. "Well, that too. But it came with the ghost. It warned me, so I think it's alive. Could have been coincidence." I held up my hands. "But I've seen it when the ghost hasn't been anywhere around. That cat also stole something that may have belonged to the ghost. It wasn't food either. Why would a cat steal something?"

I dropped my eyes, unable to meet the accusation in his gaze. His stare burned into the side of my head while I studied my fingers.

"I don't know nothin' 'bout no cats." The door snicked closed, leaving me no chance to apologize or explain further.

"Hey," I shouted. "I wasn't trying to be ugly!" If I'd asked him to spy, kill, cheat or steal, he would have been proud. Imply he might have an affinity with a house cat, and he was insulted. Maybe I should have my head examined for gross-stupidity. Maybe I should do all my research by reading textbooks instead of asking moody bobcats what they thought.

Chapter 15

Mixing a spell for Lynx's latest client, a protection and generic warding spell, was quick and since I lacked specifics, easy. As soon as that was out of the way, I tackled more important spells. White Feather's ability to search the wind was currently a liability, but if I used earth in such a spell, maybe we could gain some critical information without any ill winds being the wiser.

It hadn't occurred to me to ask Matilda for advice because I'd associated the spell with White Feather. However, if she didn't know how to create a spell, she bought it from someone else to sell in her shop. If a spell existed for collecting information via air or through the earth, she would know about it.

I arrived only minutes before Matilda normally opened. She unlocked the door with the hand not cradling a giant cup of coffee. "It's early." She paused to yawn. "What happened to your arm?" She was already in shop-keeper form, her red curls floating with wild static. Only a witch would strive to add static to a hairdo.

"Spell accident," I mumbled.

"Ah."

No more needed to be said, really. "I'm looking for a spell," I told her.

"Of course."

"It's not a simple one. I've seen this spell done using wind, but I want to use earth."

"Anything using wind magic is likely a combo. You can't capture the power of wind in a bottle, but what are scents if not part of the air? Basic wind spell."

"I'm after something specific that can collect information and transfer the essence of it through earth. I've only ever seen it done with wind." I explained in as much detail as possible how White Feather gathered information.

She scanned her shelves, sipping coffee in big slurps. "There's only one I can think of and you're right, I use wind, but I don't sell them as wind spells."

"You make a wind spell?"

"Sort of." She checked the lock on the front door and then led the way to the back room. "For the right price, I'll work with wind. It isn't easy, because I'm a water witch, but I use vapor as a substitute, which I then integrate for fortune telling."

She opened several files on her computer. "My spell is more a merging. I use the power of the water as it changes. The person breathes some of the vapor, and then I interpret the vision."

She turned the monitor for me to read. "The bloodstone—heliotrope--turns the water red during the telling. The reflections impart all kinds of foretelling in the water and the vapor."

"Heliotrope? The healing stone?" While I worked easily with any earth element, healing wasn't my forte.

Mat winked at me. "If you didn't have such an aversion to fortunes, you'd have read the spell before. Bloodstone calls storms and everyone knows there are messages in the wind. I use it in fortune telling because clients pay through the nose for that kind of telling."

I focused my attention on her notes while she skirted around me to her safe.

"How in the world did you come up with this spell? It integrates earth, water and wind!"

"Because I'm brilliant?" She giggled and waved a hand. "I actually learned it was possible from talking to Abuelita."

"Ah, Granny Ruth." Granny was neither her grandmother nor mine, but witches were funny about names because names were power. All witches used one or more nicknames. My own everyday name was from my great-grandfather and not my actual birth name.

"I wanted to carry something from Granny in my shop for a certain client. If she didn't have the spell, she has every magic book ever written. If her books couldn't help, she knows every witch in town."

"And has their respect." Most of us were either in awe of Granny Ruth or afraid of her. Rumor had it that she had been a coven head back in the days when there was a council of witches. Of course, the nastier gossip-mongers implied that the reason she had all the grimoires was because she had stolen them from the other witches when the council disbanded. I didn't believe that since Granny shared the books with almost anyone who asked.

Mat continued, "We were discussing healing spells when Granny mentioned heliotrope is sometimes used to see the future. I took it from there, and I've been pretty happy with the results."

"Amazing. Do you actually hear voices in the wind?"

"Mostly I use the visions in the vapors, but when you're talking about past, present and future, wind adds other dimensions. I guess I'd call them whispers." She turned away from me and muttered a quick spell. The picture on the wall changed from an old western sheriff with his gun drawn to a sheriff lounging against a wooden post in front of an old building.

She dialed the combination to the safe hidden behind the picture. After swinging the door open she extracted a silver case and a shallow crystal bowl. There were several other valuable pieces of crystal inside; at least one Waterford, and two or three natural bowl-shaped geodes.

"This square crystal works best because it ties to earth, wind, fire and water. The heliotrope is strongest in late February and early March. If a client requests this kind of telling during another time of year, I'll only do it during a thunderstorm."

I returned my attention to her notes, devouring the information eagerly. "Audible oracles. This is very close to what I need." If I spelled it right, the heliotrope would mimic what White Feather did when he used the wind to gather information. "I'll have to use it differently than you do. It's a direct tie to earth for me so I won't need the water."

"I'd still recommend you use it when there's plenty of wind. During thunderstorms, it's like an open door. Without the portal, it isn't worth the embarrassment in front of a client if it fails." Mat extracted a deep green stone from the silver case. Drops of deep red shone from it.

When she handed it to me, I felt a tiny pulse, a throb not unlike that from my silver. The current warmed and then cooled as its strength ebbed and flowed. "Do you use the spell often?"

"No. Granny told me about it a couple of years ago, but it's not an easy spell. A lot of clients refuse to wait for a storm or the right time of year so they go elsewhere. Plus, mixing two types of magic is dangerous which means I charge a lot more."

I was well aware of the danger, but if I mimicked a wind spell, even a partial one, I might be able to discover what in the wind was bothering White Feather. "During a storm do you think the magic would be noticeable to someone looking for auras or wind spells?"

"The power is there for the taking. Who is going to be monitoring it?"

"Hmm." Someone or something had sought out White Feather. Maybe he had used his wind too often around something linked to Sarah or maybe his affinity to wind attracted...whatever was hungry. If that ill wind noticed me, I needed to be prepared. "Mat, you are a genius."

She smiled coyly and primped her hair. "I like to think so. Here, let me tell your fortune using the bloodstone. Without a storm, we won't get much, but you can get the idea. There's a bit of a trick to it."

"No way. Foretelling is too dangerous. I don't need a demonstration, I need to bond it to something I can control."

She waved an impatient hand. "I'll use myself as the focus since you don't want to tempt fate." She poured water from a stoneware jug. "I won't get much wind, but you'll be able to learn the technique."

There was no better teacher than experience, but in light of the strange things happening lately, I preferred to be in my lab with every possible protection before running anything to do with wind. "Mat, maybe it's better if we wait."

She opened the side window. "Honestly, I know you're afraid of your own future, but I've told you before, a good witch doesn't mix foretelling and fate magic! I have never once forced a future instead of telling a future."

"Seriously, Mat." I moved near the window, feeling the fresh air from outside. My friend had an enormous energy and aura even when she wasn't brewing a spell. What if something nasty noticed her bright, loud aura beckoning the wind?

Mat ignored my concerns. She glided to her chair and dropped the bloodstone into her crystal bowl. "Just watch."

The green of the rock faded into the bottom of the bowl as though it were a pond; murky, but quiet. Red specks danced across the top, forming a strong red line to each corner of the bowl. As Mat finished the spell, the red arced and merged with the bloody dots already in the water.

Voices suddenly teased my ears. It was the murmur of sand scraping rock, a throaty, almost triumphant laugh, then nothing. Maybe it was only the breeze brushing my clothes or the rustling of leaves along the ground, but the sounds coalesced like a thousand voices riding an electrical current, buzzing and clamoring.

I strained to discern individual words, but in a single heartbeat, the innocent breeze turned to frost. The sudden chill made the hair on my arms and neck stand on end.

"Mat!"

She heard the change in the voices seconds after I did, but she was more familiar with listening to the vibrations. "Danger? Danger of what?"

"Mat, be careful!"

My pleading distracted her. The red lines wavered. The voices remained just outside my hearing range, like muted whispers in the next room.

As suddenly as they began, the taunting sounds stopped. I would have searched, but I didn't know how. The wind wasn't like Mother Earth; it was more ethereal, leaving me in a dark space fumbling for a light switch.

Mat scowled at me, exasperated.

"Sorry," I said shivering. "That felt about as safe as if you were telling my fortune. Did you see anything?"

She shook her head. "That's the tricky part. I have to concentrate on the wind part, make sure it's perfectly formed before I involve water. If I do it the other way around, the vision tends to break up the bloodstone connection. It ends up like a painting with colors dripping everywhere."

"You definitely had the wind."

"Did you notice the formation? Shoot. It would have been a really strong vision. I better run my fortune again."

"Sorry," I repeated.

"Don't worry. I don't need the wind to check my own fortune. I was hoping for another romantic foretelling—that's what I saw the last time!" She grinned and wiggled her eyebrows.

I wasn't quite relaxed enough to match her grin, but I made a valiant effort.

She jumped up from the table. "I hate to part with this because I've already used it successfully with clients, but if you need it I'll give you a good deal on it."

Mat knew I preferred my stones pure. Her shopkeeper antics helped me find a real smile. "I'm sure you would, but I'll hunt down Martin, which will result in an even better deal."

"His prices have probably gone up since I bought mine!" She frowned, but then laughed. "Oh, let me know. This one has performed really well for me so it should be fine for you."

Matilda returned to her safe while I contemplated my options. Since Mat had used the stone, her aura would enhance the magic, which was tempting. Her spells were tied to water though, and that magic might hinder things. Using the stone would save me time. Then again, the time-saving game had ended up costing me in the past.

"I should be able to find Martin at this time of year."

Like a good saleswoman, Mat turned the stone to the light and showcased it before returning it to the safe. "If you change your mind, let me know."

"You've been a huge help," I told her. "Stone or no. I had no idea it was possible to use the earth to reach the wind. You deserve to be paid for such valuable advice, don't you think?"

"If you'd let me sell one or two of your spells in my shop, we'd be so much more than even. I'd owe you, in fact."

I laughed at her wide, wistful blue eyes. "No, thank you! I run a totally private enterprise, even though I love you dearly."

She grumbled good-naturedly all the way across the store, but we both knew it was theatrics. When she unlocked the door, I pushed it open. She blew me a kiss.

I nearly ran into a guy coming in. He was short, blond, and headed to fat, but young enough that he probably convinced himself it was all muscle. Before I could consider an apology, the guy with him, taller, and also in a white shirt and sports jacket, grabbed my shirt.

"Hey!"

With brute force, he shoved me back inside, his large bulk very effectively blocking the exit.

Chapter 16

Shiny black shoes and dark chinos whirled across my vision. I nearly capsized, but caught myself on the clothing rack. "What in--"

"Time for enlightenment, sister." Widely-set eyes made the guy resemble a giant frog. Unfortunately, he was strong for an amphibian. He yanked me sideways and shoved a black Bible with gold letters in my face. "This store ain't open for business no more."

I dug my feet in. "Let go." Silver flared hot on my wrist.

"We've got a special job for a witch!" The blond guy shook a hand in front of Matilda's pale face, but instead of a Bible, he waved a grill lighter. If, like Frog-eyes in front of me, he reeked of alcohol, he had better keep the nasty blue flame away from his mouth.

"Mayan Sacrifices!" I cursed.

"Get out!" Matilda shrieked. She lifted her arm to gesture or start throwing spells.

"Mat--" There were shelves of trouble and ignitable potions lining the walls. Some would burn like acid on contact. Others might explode with the least little encouragement from a flame. The two clothing racks in the center contained spelled shirts, shawls, and hats that would be instant kindling.

I ducked. No matter what my friend threw, I wanted to avoid it.

The guy twisting my arm used my momentum to shove me sideways. My shoulder thudded hard into the wall, and the top of my head grazed the shelf above. The dreaded sound of shifting bottles filled my ears.

I kicked his kneecap, hard. He dropped his Bible in a hurry. I shoved my fist into his stomach and grabbed a tuft of greasy black hair from the side of his head. My other foot should have helped me balance, but it hit the wall instead of the ground.

A bottle from above us bounced off his lowered head before shattering on the terracotta tile. Matilda shrieked, maybe because of the bright green liquid that splashed or because the blond guy propelled her toward the back room.

In desperation, Matilda grabbed onto the heavy cash register at the end of the jewelry counter.

Blondie howled, "Tie'm!"

My knee in Frog's nose knocked him sideways, but he wasn't out. I shoved him into the green pool of liquid praying it wasn't some kind of strength potion. His feet slipped, and he cleaned most of the green off the floor with one arm when he tried to catch himself. Unfortunately, he used the other arm to grab my foot when I kicked at his head.

"Aaaagh!" I screamed. Mat resold just about any potion made, but she was too far away to use them. Me, I had my choice, but I didn't know what any of them were. I grabbed a bottle anyway and in the process knocked two more to the floor.

Frog-eyes yanked my foot, dragging me down across the mess of glass and liquid.

Smoke drifted up from one of the broken bottles. I held my breath. What if it was a love potion, and I was suddenly overcome by passion? Wouldn't that make his day, to find a witch lusting after him?

I scrambled away, but he refused to let go of my ankle. Desperate, I rammed the bottle in my hand against his forehead.

His grip barely loosened. Dizziness assaulted me. I sucked in a shallow breath. One or more of the potions smelled really horrible.

"Spatunia and wort!" Matilda screeched.

Magic tingled across my skin right before something popped. The scent of hay filled the air. I wrestled my foot loose and would have kicked the guy again, but he had more than one head now. Two bodies half sprawled in front of me; one skeletal and one that looked like the Pillsbury dough boy. Both were wearing the original businessman khakis so it had to be an illusion.

I raised my silver to my nose and scrambled away on my knees. The smoke was quite possibly more dangerous than the man on the floor.

A large swath of petunias nearly stopped me. Another illusion?

The trail started from the mass of jars that had spilled and followed me as I tried to get away. "Moonlight madness!" I choked, scrambling faster.

Once on my feet, I noticed that the two bodies of Frog-eyes had merged back into one, but petunias were growing straight across the top of his felled body. "Flo...flowers?"

Matilda screamed. Blondie flared his lighter and the scarves across the doorway that separated the front of the shop from the back ignited. Mat was pinned under them with him waving the lighter in one hand and holding her by the throat with the other.

Dangerous as the possible fumes were, I hurtled myself at Blondie. There wasn't time for any real speed, and I was probably half his size.

On impact, all three of us flew through the doorway into Mat's living room. I grappled with Blondie for the lighter, but missed. He grunted when we hit the floor. All the air was forced out of my lungs when I landed.

The front door must have opened at some point, although I never heard the bell. Someone yanked Blondie from the pile. For half a second I thought it was Frog-eyes, but then I recognized Matilda's friend, Jim, as he popped the guy solidly on the chin.

Mat stumbled to her feet and raced to smother the flaming scarves with one of her flowing robes. "Adriel! Adriel, are you okay?" Mascara ran down her cheeks and her throat was red and bruised. Her beautiful red hair was singed.

"Oh Mat! Your hair!" Her hand went to it just as I smelled the awful stench of it.

"Damn...damn them." She turned to Jim, who held the blond guy in a headlock. Shorty's legs weren't doing much to support him.

Mat hiccuped. "Out the back." She gimped to her back door, and threw the bolt in a single motion.

Jim dragged the guy through and deposited him in the alley. "The other one?" he huffed.

"Put him out the front," I suggested. "Let them wonder what happened to the other." I stood to help, but had to catch the wall when dizziness unbalanced me. Still swaying like a drunk I used the wall to work my way toward the front of the shop with Mat. We paused in the doorway. "What's with the petunias?" I gasped out.

Matilda tried to laugh, but it came out a half sob. "I saw you spill the green potion, and knew it was for a flower. You're supposed to add water and say the magic word, but when the other stuff spilled on top of it, I figured at least one of the potions had water in it."

"Someone buys that stuff?"

She shrugged. "Guys buy it to impress their dates."

We stared at the mass of flowers covering most of the floor. Jim dragged the moaning body of Frog-eyes through the purple blossoms on his way to the outer door.

"It is pretty impressive," I said.

Matilda stepped over the petunias, checked to make sure no one was near the front door and then opened it. Jim did not drop the guy lightly. From the way his head bounced on the concrete, it would be a while before he managed another moan.

Matilda waved at the flowers and said, "It's only supposed to be a single flower. I wonder what else broke."

I leaned against the glass counter. "There was some smoke that messed with my head. Who in Mayan Ruins were those guys?"

"Religious fanatics. Damn their hides."

"You know them?"

She shrugged. "They caught me as I was locking up a couple of weeks ago. I got the door locked, but the fat guy slammed the glass a few times with his stupid Bible. He shouted a bunch of threats until a few tourists dialed 911.

"After that, I made a spell to keep them out. They've come by a few times, but the spell activates an illusion that the shop is closed and leaves an impression of a locked donut shop." She wiped at her face and realized she was a mess.

"Maybe you shouldn't have picked a donut shop illusion. Blondie looked like he was a bit too fond of donuts."

She rewarded me with a weak smile. "I didn't have anything in the spell to stop them if the door was already open."

I groaned. Her gaze focused above my head, no doubt contemplating an improved spell, one that wouldn't let them cross the threshold at all. I clamped my lips down on any criticism. Less serious fanatics or mischief-makers would have been fooled by her spell, forgotten the place and moved on.

Jim stepped back inside. He used Mat's still dangling keys to lock up. "Mat, are you all right?" He glanced my way, but his attention was on my friend.

"I'm fine," I said.

Jim grabbed Matilda's hand and rubbed her shoulders. She leaned against him in relief.

I found a sudden need to inspect the cut on my right hand with rather more attention than it deserved. It burned, but most of the liquid from the broken jars seemed to be on my shirt rather than the cut. "I gotta go." I stepped over the flowers.

Matilda reached out. "Oh my God, Adriel, that was awful. Are you sure you're okay?"

"Sure." Jim spared me another glance, but I beelined to the front door. "I'm going home to get cleaned up. Let me know if you want any help improving that spell." With her contacts it was doubtful, but her natural abilities leaned to illusion. In this instance, she needed something with a bit more heat.

A quick check outside revealed a bloodied Frog-eyes starting to come around. I pushed the door open and dashed down the street before he even thought about finding his feet.

Chapter 17

Bloodstone wasn't native to New Mexico, which was one of the reasons I hadn't studied it thoroughly. A local Indian jeweler might have a stone or two, especially since healing was one of the properties associated with the stone. The problem with worked jewelry was that it often carried any number of properties added by the artist.

There were numerous good suppliers for silver and gold, and I could dig up my own turquoise, but the best place to get untainted stones was Martin.

Unfortunately, big unfortunately, Martin was a freak. If I called to tell him what I needed, he'd probably be naked when I arrived, in all his wrinkled glory. He was sixty years old if he was a day and even though he had never lived in a commune, he liked to pretend he was into drugs, free love and flower power.

For a long time I thought he was an addict—got a little too much magic under his skin and couldn't stop drinking it in. My mother disagreed. Her take was, "He was always a bit 'touched' even when he was younger."

Touched or not, I wished he'd wear his damn clothes.

After a quick shower and change of clothes, I went searching for him. He lived in a teepee. No, not one of those impressive ones made out of deerskin that had professionally constructed poles and required a good-sized trailer to move around. His teepee was a ragged mix of cloth and leather that may or may not have been cured properly.

His trailer—and he did have one—was for his collection of stones, odd pieces of metal, and at least three railroad ties. He claimed they were from the original Santa Fe Trail. His rusted-out, lopsided, dented truck should have been scrapped twenty years ago. Maybe he kept it running by using some sort of energy-from-rust spell.

Martin tended to favor the older highways that paralleled the interstate. He parked and walked for miles scavenging for desert riches.

After driving north for twenty minutes and perusing a few side roads, I retraced my route and headed south of Santa Fe. When I finally spotted the ramshackle truck and its owner, I pulled over.

It was my lucky day. Martin had underwear on. One hand held a can of beer.

At least he was awake. His sign was out, advertising "natural stones."

Who in their right mind would pull off the freeway and buy anything from a dirty hobo in his underwear?

Grumbling at my apparent lack of sense, I parked for a fast get-away.

Martin lounged next to a weathered, plastic lawn chair. He belched and raised the beer in my direction as I approached. "What do you need the stone for?"

He wasn't as clairvoyant as he pretended. All I ever purchased from him was stones.

"Bloodstone for wind spells." Said force ruffled my hair, pushing it away from my face and swirling the dust that my car had stirred.

Martin burped a series of noises that could only be a love song to the desert toads. There was no way to know if he was lost in thought or if he hoped to appear mystical. "Not your usual." He touched a dirty finger to the side of his nose. "Could be dangerous. There's a lot of danger in the wind right now." He sucked in a large breath of air, gurgled and then spit the results. He finished with a swig of beer.

I tried not to gag. "Yeah?" Was it good or bad that someone like Martin had noticed an ill wind? It could mean that the wind was gaining power or given that this was Martin, it might mean nothing at all.

"I don't like this wind. Interferes with my hunting."

The sad truth, and perhaps the principle reason I disliked Martin was because he was of the earth. He had to be. He collected bits of it, skillfully selecting the stones that mattered. If they weren't pure, he purified them. Nothing I had ever purchased from him had the slightest contamination.

That his talent was even vaguely related to mine left me disgusted.

Martin finally sauntered to his old horse trailer and grabbed one of the cloth bags tied to a side rail. He fingered the contents.

I'd felt his power before, usually as a sudden sense of dirt, not fully decayed with a kind of dried out sandy smell. This time, there was another scent, probably rotted beer farts. I held my breath until he tossed me a stone.

I caught the flick of green, nabbing it with my left hand. Specks of red mingled with the deep juniper color. Scant rivulets connected the larger spots like rings in a tree. It was beautiful.

"I have others." He sorted through two more cloth bags before holding up a darker green, almost brown stone. It too had flecks of red; larger drops of blood. "Not too many people know about bloodstone and its air affinity. Usually, I get healers."

"Uh-huh." According to Mat's notes, the dark green was chalcedony, while the red streaks were jasper. In addition to healing, chalcedony had the reputation of curing the ability to see ghosts. I took that to mean it repelled them. The witch who had tested the chalcedony didn't believe in ghosts, thus when the haunts disappeared, he labeled the stone as a cure for hallucinations. As with any text, interpretation was up to the reader.

Jasper was not only the "rain-bringer" and healing element for blood diseases and hemorrhages, it also protected against venomous creatures and extracted poisons. "Which of these stones is better for wind spells?"

"For wind, I think the green," he said. "But this dark one has a stronger earth quality. Your earth link is already very potent. You don't want to crash the elements, just touch them." His fingers caressed the stone in his hand while his eyes roamed suggestively down my body.

He was beyond disgusting. My hand curled reflexively around the green stone. To my surprise, it responded. Clutched in my hand, a light brush of earth or wind squeezed out from the inside. I glanced down, but there was nothing to see. A grunt from Martin drew my attention back to business.

"Let's talk price, Martin. This specimen came from Wyoming? Or Texas?"

His beatific smile revealed very crooked teeth. "I liked it up there." Then he frowned. "But the ranchers, they weren't as kind as down here. Didn't want me roaming on their property. Kept moving me off. You're lucky I was able to get such a good specimen."

The ranchers here didn't want him on their property either, but the summer heat was more intense here, which meant they weren't out and about to ask Martin to leave when he trespassed.

"Don't get greedy." I opened my hand to inspect the stone again. A slight whiff of something rotted caught me by surprise. "Is this pure?" It was the same smell I had thought was Martin's body odor, but the rock shouldn't be tainted with it.

Martin's eyes darted back and forth. He straightened up tall. "Don't tell me."

I had expected him to argue with me, not be afraid. He dropped the brown stone from his hand. "Only a few know about its affinity for wind spirits, mostly the fortune tellers, but they don't need the stone to work their magic. Hardly ever gets used for that anymore." His shoulders slumped. "Damn. Of course it would infect this stone first."

"What would?"

His eyes rolled wildly. "We will have to purify it!"

"Martin, what in all of the moonlight phases are you talking about?"

"Why is it that when the contamination creeps in, you can't see it yourself? Can you smell it? I sure can't."

Had it been anyone other than Martin, I wouldn't have said it, but this was Martin. "Beer farts and donkey pee," I declared.

Without changing his gaze from the horizon, he chuckled. It started small and then grew louder. I'd heard him cackle before, but this was softer, true amusement. "The beer farts, you ain't got to worry about." He waved his hand and then reached over and took the stone from me. "The other, we can fix. I give this to you as a gift, not meant to harm, not meant for me to gain, but for you to find that which you seek and so that you can prosper. I give it to you freely, only the stone and no other."

I knew the spell he was activating, but I nearly hid my hands behind my back like a stubborn child not wanting to take medicine. He held the stone out. "Please?"

The plea upped the ante and added additional purification. He was asking for help freely given. "Okay." I put my hand out. "I accept your gift of the stone with no obligations or attachments."

He smiled. "Gifted, the spell can't follow. I'll have to purge the rest and make sure it hasn't gotten any further."

"Hmph." There were numerous ways for curses and freeloader spells to stay attached to objects. The gifting itself didn't automatically guarantee a purge. If the person receiving the gift didn't know about the spell, and the giver was devious, accepting the gift could actually make the spell stronger. The receiver's acceptance acted as a welcome for both the spell and the gift.

Of course, I did know, and we had done the purge correctly, but the thought of a spell transferring to me, especially one connected in any way to an ill wind, made my skin crawl. "What was attached to it?" I asked.

His watery, alcoholic eyes returned to me. "There's ill spells being carried on the wind. I didn't know any had gotten to my stash, but bloodstone is a likely spot for it to land, isn't it?" He nodded his own conviction. "If you need more of this stone, go to a place called 'Charms' near the plaza. I sold a batch of bloodstone there before any of the nasty wind drifted through." With a morose frown, he hefted the cloth bag in his hand. He tilted his head, then eyed me like I was a gumball prize. His arm stretched my way.

I dodged quickly to my car. "Thanks for the gift." The words had to be said because a gift had to be given freely and freely accepted in order for the purifying spell to trigger. "If I need others, I'll check out Charms." I was not taking the entire bag to help him cure the infection.

He had his work cut out for him if he was going to save that particular bag of stock.

Chapter 18

When I got home, my first instinct was to call White Feather and tell him about Martin's taint and the thugs at Matilda's shop. He was my link to the normal world and my connection to the police. Mat wasn't on the best of terms with the police considering the fact that most officials viewed her as a kook who brought problems upon herself.

Unfortunately, when I arrived, someone else waited—two of them. The white Mustang was in my yard, and Tara had scooted the silver-lined chair next to the unlined one Lynx was sitting in.

Before I was halfway to the porch it was obvious something was wrong. Lynx had never been good at concealing guilt, mainly because it had to be pretty bad before he felt guilty at all. As I climbed the steps, his eyes shifted, checking and rechecking escape routes. His shoulders tensed, and I swear the golden yellow of his cat eyes flickered.

"Hello." My feet, of their own accord, shifted into a balanced flee stance, ready to bolt for the door or the car. My fingers twitched, wanting to grab a weapon or a spell, but if I had had them on me, I would have already used them in the earlier fight.

"I came over to tell you I figured it out," Tara said.

"Figured what out?" Wary, I watched Lynx for signals.

"Water. The witching fork is set to find water," she announced triumphantly. Her gaze shifted to Lynx.

"And?" My buddy wasn't nervous because his girlfriend had guessed a spell correctly.

Neither said anything. Lynx nudged her arm in a movement so fast, I wasn't sure it happened until Tara blurted out, "We think maybe…" She trailed off and glared at Lynx uncertainly, her gaze a cross between anger and nerves.

I had a sudden, sinking thought. *No.* They hadn't been dating long enough for her to get pregnant. Well, technically, they hadn't been dating long enough to *know* she was pregnant. I shook my head. "Spit it out. Just spit it out."

"You want a ward or some protection?" Lynx asked.

My muscles clenched, and I shook my wrist to feel the silver. "A ward? You're carrying something with you?"

"I don't think it's a big deal," Tara said, whipping an oblong package out of her purse. "Lynx thinks it's bad magic because, well, he could get inside, and I couldn't."

My front door was closed. It was spelled to warn me of any breach. I stepped to the door and put my hand on the locks. There was a current. My key had silver in it that made contact with the locks when I opened the door. If someone breached it without the silver key, the current would be broken. Whatever Lynx had done, he had effectively gotten in and then relocked the door. I would never have known he was in my home unless he tripped something else once inside.

"You used silver?" My voice was high with accusation, but more than that, disbelief. Lynx was a shifter; silver would burn him as sure as fire. Lynx was also my friend, and I was stunned to find he had broken into my home.

Lynx started talking, but not fast enough. "We got here, and you weren't here. I told her we'd wait like I always do. She got thirsty. I told her I'd get her a drink."

"It wasn't his fault," Tara said. "I was thirsty, but it was all my idea. I thought it would be…cool to go inside and…wait there."

"Lynx." I fought down something akin to rage. The feeling was mixed with fear. "Tell me you know better than to go into my lab!"

"Well, sure." His defiance reasserted itself, but his muscles remained bunched as if he would spring up and escape any second.

"And you think you could have prevented her from going in there? Lynx, are you crazy?" Going off on the kid in front of his girlfriend wasn't a great strategy, but this was life and death. He may have guessed the key to picking my locks, and even learned to handle silver to do it, but getting inside my house was trivial compared to messing in my lab. There were active spells in there. Ingredients to spells. Half spells. *Real protection against intruders that could kill.*

Lynx didn't meet my eyes. "Sorry."

Tara straightened in her chair. "You don't have to apologize! It was my idea!" She stopped when I snarled at her.

The silver on my wrist warmed. The turquoise worked to cool it. "He was apologizing to you," I snapped.

It wasn't true, but it should have been. He could have gotten her killed. My threshold would not have kept him out because he was welcome in my house. Or he had been. But his ardor had pushed him into impulsive stupidity. What if he hadn't been able to prevent her from prancing right into the lab?

I shuddered at the thought of having to explain Tara's death to White Feather. He understood the need for protection spells, but if she had set something off and harmed herself or Lynx, logic wouldn't suffice.

"She couldn't even get inside your house," Lynx rushed out. "I thought maybe it was because you didn't like her or somethin' but she'd been in there before…"

"I couldn't get in until I took a running leap at the doorway and my purse fell off my arm." Tara held up a bright pink purse. "I scooped it up, but I couldn't bring it inside until a bunch of stuff fell out."

It was the same purse that had been sitting on White Feather's end table.

Lynx said, "I got her back out on the porch, and asked her what was in there."

Tara extracted a package wrapped in brown paper. "It's only a picture. But Lynx was right. When it was out of my purse, I walked right in, purse and all."

"You tried to bring evil inside my home?"

"No! I told Lynx it wasn't magic. I *know* it isn't. I just had it in my purse, because I forgot it was still in there. It's no big deal. It's *not* magic, I'd know if it was."

"And I told her ain't no witch alive gonna allow a bad spell to cross the threshold, and that thing must have voodoo on it!" Lynx said.

I sucked in air and held it. I was still so very angry. Violated and betrayed by my *friend*. The only good news was that he had recognized the threat and not let Tara talk him into anything else. I relaxed fingers that wanted to throttle his skinny little neck. "Not necessarily voodoo," I said tightly. "What is that thing?"

She started to unwrap the brown paper. It was a square of about eight by eight inches.

"Wait!" I shouted.

"It's been unwrapped before," Tara said. "It's just a picture. I had it wrapped so the sand wouldn't scrape off." The paper fell away to reveal an Indian sand painting.

None of us moved.

I finally asked, "Did you get your purse through without the picture?"

"Yeah. This and some other stuff fell out. I was picking it up from the doorway, but then Lynx got all paranoid. He shoved me out and locked the door. It's the only thing in here besides makeup. Maybe it was the charcoal in my mascara?"

That was a nice thought, but way off the mark. "My spells aren't the type to be canceled by mascara." Of course, my snootiness was obviously misplaced given that Lynx had canceled my spells and waltzed inside. I clenched my fists and wished for something to smash. "Where did you get the picture?"

"White Feather threw it out, but it's a great picture." She turned it my way, showing me the details. Colorful lines of sand represented plants and people or possibly decorated gods. The design could have been Pueblo or the more common Navajo form. Even with limited knowledge of sand painting, I already knew its nature. "Do you know what a rune is?"

"Well, sure." She didn't get the connection. Lynx crossed himself, but he did that whenever magic made him uncomfortable, whether he knew much about it or not.

Neither of them was enlightened—or protected. "Sand paintings can be-- they're essentially runes by a different culture."

Tara blinked. "But sand paintings don't have any power if they aren't done in a ceremonial tent by a shaman. This is just a picture. I know who made it, and she isn't a witch!"

"Set it down." Who knew what damage it was doing while she stood there holding it?

"See," Lynx muttered, crossing himself again. "Tol' you." He scooted his chair away when she set it on the porch.

"Put it on the dirt over there," I instructed. As long as she had already touched it, she was already contaminated. "I don't want that thing on my porch."

Rolling her eyes, she moved it. "It's harmless. It's just a painting!"

"Where did you get it?"

She remained crouched over the picture. "White Feather. Claire gave it to him--"

"The ex-girlfriend?" My rage had a new focus. I hadn't even been certain Claire was anything more than a figment of Tara's nastiness, but apparently she was real.

Tara raised placating hands. "They broke up a long time ago, but we ran into her at the plaza when White Feather took me to get some supplies. Claire was doing great, had found a new guy and was learning her own magic." Tara snorted. "She doesn't have any, never did. I think she felt guilty about what a bitch she was when they broke up so she gave White Feather the painting as a peace offering."

"How did you get it if she gave it to him?"

"He threw it in a trash bin as soon as she turned her back. It was pretty and hey, what if they got back together or something?" She leaned down and touched the edge, almost affectionately.

I did not like the way she was drawn to the painting. It was colorful, but it didn't strike me as special enough to cause a teenager to retrieve it from the trash.

"Why don't you go wait on the porch," I suggested.

Tara whirled from her crouch. "It's not dangerous! She's not even a witch! I *know* she's not! That was the whole reason my brother dumped her!"

Our eyes locked. Through my own mixed feelings of anger and fear, the insult in her comment was clear. I lashed out, automatically defending White Feather. "Your brother did *not* dump Claire because she isn't a witch."

Tara nodded emphatically. "Yes, he did. I don't care what he told you, but she wasn't good enough for him because she had no magic talent at all. He can't stand people that aren't talented!"

That made no sense, but the history was a complete mystery to me. My lack of knowledge made me almost as angry as the stupid gift lying in the yard. "Did you keep this thing in your house?" Even as I asked, my stomach hit bottom. "Was it in your purse the whole time?"

She garbled something under her breath before speaking more intelligibly. "It was in my purse, but I forget it at White Feather's house when I was there practicing spells. I meant to go back and get it because it's my favorite purse. Mom saw it yesterday in White Feather's car, and she brought it inside."

"Moonlight...Mayan crap." White Feather had been exposed to the rune for days. He probably hadn't warded his own house against Claire so when Tara brought it inside, nothing triggered. A slow acting spell, much like we'd been worried about. Only it wasn't from Sarah, as we'd assumed.

"Let me guess. You ran into Claire about two weeks ago."

She shook her head. "Nah, it was longer than that. Maybe three weeks. It was when White Feather first started giving me lessons."

It had to be spelled with something bad, quite likely on several levels and not only specific to White Feather or Tara wouldn't have had a problem getting it into my house.

Whatever the spell, it had affected Tara enough to persuade her to retrieve the picture from the trash, but then forget about it. Had it been attracted to White Feather's stronger magic? Then again, since Claire had given it to him as a gift, there were bound to be some specifics to him.

I knelt next to the picture. "When did your Mom give it back to you?"

"Yesterday."

The paw print of the bear, a symbol for the snake and at least two female characters decorated the picture. I wasn't expert enough to be anything more than puzzled. "It looks like one of the bear stories." At least one legend involved a bear competing against a monster to win a beautiful maiden.

There were both male and female characters; round heads indicated male figures, square represented females. Maybe Claire was still interested in White Feather or maybe she wanted revenge. I simply didn't know enough to judge what might be in this spell.

"I need to look something up." I turned to Lynx. "You come help me. I'm not letting it inside my house. We'll use a silk scarf to block some of the vibes at least temporarily."

Lynx beat me inside, but only after allowing me to unlock the door. As if that would soothe my feelings.

We left Tara frowning over the picture. I wasn't about to invite her in the lab. Lynx was obviously untrustworthy too, but he had a healthy respect for magic, especially of the renegade kind. Even if he had no respect for my threshold, he wouldn't do something completely stupid around magic.

As I collected supplies, I wondered if White Feather had pretended to accept the gift. Probably. Even fake acceptance could activate a spell.

But what did the sand painting have to do with the ill wind? Was Sarah the witch who spelled the sand painting for Claire? Or was the ill wind at Sarah's cabin a separate problem?

Now wasn't the time to find answers to all of the puzzles. No matter who was responsible or how, the most important task was to understand what the spell was doing to White Feather and stop it cold.

Chapter 19

After several trips to the lab, I organized the supplies next to the painting. Rune magic was a hidden magic; its aura was contained in the diagrams. I might sense something if it reacted against foreign magic, but that was dangerous, and I wasn't taking any risks.

I compared the picture to those in my reference book on Indian lore and legends. Not surprisingly, the painting didn't match any in the book exactly, but it was very similar to the bear and snake story.

I traced out the main pattern, examining each symbol against the legend. There were two pursuers, Big Snake Man and Bear Man, trying to win two maidens. In Claire's painting, the roles were switched; instead of two maidens at east and west there was a round head, indicating a male. The butterflies, which represented the maidens, took the position where the bear and snake were in the original.

Rather than bear tracks indicating pursuit, there was a worm or insect squiggle leading to the male figure being chased. There was no reference to such a symbol, but the painting tradition was generally passed down by personal teaching, so the book didn't cover everything.

As spells went it made sense for Claire to replace the original characters with herself and White Feather so that she could "win" White Feather back. But what Indian in his right mind would turn a sacred ritual into this abomination? Had Sarah gotten that desperate for business and gone rogue?

Sand paintings were an important part of the Navajo holy tradition. They were the way to the spirits, an attempt to gain intercession, a healing and a way to return to proper balance. Colors mattered, the time of creation, the types of sand used; all were of utmost importance. They weren't done for rejected girlfriends.

"How did Claire expect this to succeed?" To complete the ceremony, White Feather had to be present. The Chant had to be completed, the right words recited.

Perhaps she intended to use herself as the center rather than the Chanter. She could activate the painting by duplicating it elsewhere, paint the associated symbols on herself and hope the holy people responded to her request even though the required players weren't all present and accounted for.

Thinking of the holy people focused my attention on another peculiar aspect. I double-checked my reference, but Claire's painting wasn't a duplication of a traditional painting. It was an invented rune with an entirely different purpose.

"No, that can't be." I shifted to the other side. "Is it upside-down?" Now I'd have to figure out the orientation of the males and females all over again.

"What?" Tara's shadow fell over the picture.

"Back, back," I waved. Looking at the text I muttered, "Corn?" The corn in the original was bottom right. "This picture is wrong. The artist didn't know what he was doing!" Then again, sometimes an item was left out or changed in order to avoid setting off a spell unintentionally.

I ran my finger down the text as I read. "Tobacco...sweet tobacco to lure the maidens. It has to be there, right?" The literature didn't tell me about luring a man. "Maybe to lure the man, the artist didn't use tobacco. No, no, that's it, there at the top left in Claire's picture.

"Squash at the top right. The bean plant at the bottom right and the corn at the top left." Near as I could tell, the sacred plants had been rotated, which, if I was reading it right, left the opening to the spirits at the *west* side of the painting rather than the east. The painting was a complete reversal of the original in that aspect.

I needed another set of eyes. "Lynx, do you know anything about sand paintings?"

"Nope." He shook his head and then crossed himself.

"Hmph." He was conveniently religious when scared of a greater power. Unlike Tara, he stood well back. His hand was wrapped protectively around her arm to prevent her from getting too close.

"What is it?" Tara asked.

"I'm not sure. The four sacred plants are in the wrong place in this painting. It could be accidental, but either way, it's a problem."

Lynx finally leaned a little closer. "Why?"

I pointed. "All sand paintings are a call for help or intercession from the holy people. See these rainbows along the sides?" Without touching the picture, I pointed to the three colored bands bordering three sides. "Those are protection bars against evil. In a real painting, only the east is left open. It's patrolled by special guards, but left open for holy people to answer the call.

"Claire's picture has three sides guarded too, but the sacred crops are rotated and the people in the picture are shifted. I'm not sure which are gods and which are supposed to represent people."

Lynx came around to stand behind me. He studied the book, then the picture on the ground. He used the sun to orient the picture, tilting his head as he moved the diagram around mentally.

His ears flattened suddenly and his eyes snapped to mine for confirmation.

I nodded. "The spirit opening on this painting where spirits can enter is from the *west*, isn't it?"

Lynx frowned, but he didn't disagree.

"So?" Tara shrugged. "Maybe Claire made a mistake. She isn't a witch. She probably didn't know."

Lynx took Tara's arm and hissed, "The holy people come only from the east."

I swallowed and scooted a bit further away myself. "Whoever drew this must not have been calling for help from the holy people." That left a rather large question of just who Claire thought she was calling. The other directions were guarded for a reason; they were guards against evil. "This is bad news."

Lynx made a barely audible growl.

"Claire must have used something of White Feather's to link him to the painting." That wasn't normal for sand paintings. Links usually came during a purifying ceremony. In this case, who knew what she had tried?

More importantly, how could I reverse it? The sand had been sprayed and glued down. A real painting had to be destroyed in a specific way after a ceremony so as not to anger the holy people. "Wind," I muttered. "Sun, earth and rain." The elements could destroy this painting and in that way take back the power. "But I need him here." I wasn't about to destroy a spell unless I was absolutely certain he wouldn't be hurt by the dismantling.

Chapter 20

I wanted to find White Feather immediately, dismantle the spell and then hunt down the witch who had done this. This spell had to be the reason he had felt a need to stay home. When he had started leaving the house to solve the ghost problem, he must have unconsciously moved Tara's purse to the car, keeping the painting near his person.

"Lynx, can you convince White Feather to come here without telling him exactly what we've found?"

"Should be easy enough since I don't know what this thing is." He whipped a cell phone out of his pocket, a phone I didn't even know he owned.

"No! Not over the phone. I don't want to warn him in case this spell has some sort of trigger to prevent him from examining it too closely."

Lynx flipped the phone shut one-handed. "You're the boss. We'll find him and haul him in." He reached for Tara's hand.

"Wait!" I'd rather hire a murder convict than work with Tara, but she was my best bet at the moment. "Tara you've already handled the painting so whatever harm can be done is done. I need you to stay here and help me get started."

Tara glanced at Lynx and then back at me. Her mouth pursed into a tight line. Finally, sweetly, oh, so sweetly, she asked, "How about I be the sacrificial lamb when we get back with White Feather?"

My temper flared, but her accusation was on the money for the most part. Asking for her participation in front of White Feather wouldn't be as easy. "It would be nice to have your help now."

She rolled her eyes. "I'm not afraid of it. There's no spell on it, and White Feather will know it. He's way better than you."

Lynx frowned. His nose twitched, but spells like this didn't carry a warning smell. Gently he tugged Tara's hand, a silent plea.

I'd like to believe he took my side over hers, but his decisions were always prioritized by one factor. Survival. His.

"I'll be back," he said, drawing Tara into a kiss. He whispered something in her ear.

I ignored them in favor of contemplating how to contain the painting. It had a clay base, which would absorb many evils—and also protect it from counter-magics. The sands used in the picture were specific earth elements. If I surrounded it with more earth elements, it might accidentally strengthen rather than contain it.

When in doubt, use water. It would at least block or dilute the magic. It would also soak the clay base and start weakening the bonds.

"Boxes, bowls...no, ceramic is too close to clay. Wood would absorb and also block." After all, plants essentially "ate" soil. They were also great purifiers. If I grew a tree on top of it everything would be just fine—if only White Feather had fifty years to wait.

"Then again...Aha!" I gestured to Tara. She had long since given up on my mumblings and stood wordlessly, looking bored. "Don't disturb anything."

To the lab I went. Scooting a stool to the high window ledge, I picked up the heavy clay pot containing my largest aloe plant. The pot was clay, but the drainage dish was clay-colored plastic; my way of saving money.

I made my way along the lab shelves selecting and then discarding numerous jars. "Holy water..." It was only a small vial. I needed a pitcher-full. Maybe I should start keeping holy water in a five-gallon bucket.

"What is that?" Tara asked from the doorway.

If I didn't care so much about White Feather, I would have spelled Tara to never appear in my vicinity ever again. She couldn't follow the simplest of instructions. The idiot was more of a liability than a help. Biting back a rude reprimand, I said, "Holy water. Come on."

Thankfully, she stayed close on my heels as I raced back outside. "Put the painting in the dish while I start the garden hose."

Even though she had touched it before, I kept a wary eye on her while she did as I asked. "Okay, stand back."

She rolled her eyes and barely stepped away from the painting. I emptied the vial of holy water on top of it.

The water dribbled off the side, forming small puddles in the plant dish. Nothing on the picture moved. The sand was protected by the sprayed lacquer, but not for much longer.

I trained the hose on the picture.

The dish filled and overflowed. Unless a spell had an affinity for water, it couldn't travel through it.

Once the dish was full and the ground around it nicely soaked, I returned to the side of the house to shut off the water. Perhaps because the painting hadn't reacted to the holy water, I wasn't as guarded as I should have been.

Despite closing the tap, the hissing of water didn't stop. I doubled checked the faucet, but the tap was closed. The water was off, but the hissing escalated to a loud gurgle.

Most of the painting was hidden inside the plastic container. "Tara, get back!"

She had never really believed there was magic in that painting, not until the gurgle turned into a spray of steam that burst upwards in a mini volcanic burst.

My heart needed the blood that drained from my face. I lurched into Tara with my shoulder, knocking her away and putting myself between her and the painting.

"Mayan--" The plastic dish was *melting*.

Tara scrambled to her feet and then uttered a very unladylike word. Unthinking, I snapped my elbow back, jabbing her hard. "Shh! Never use those words around evil. Don't give evil spirits fuel, don't beckon jesters or demons. Ever."

I hurried back to the tap and turned it on full blast. It gushed across what was left of the plastic and sloshed onto the painting. "We need some wet wood. There's some sage in the garden. Do you know what it looks like?"

She nodded. For perhaps the first and only time, she rushed to help without arguing.

"Should have put some herbs in there to start with." My stomach knotted. Water should have blocked the spell, but what if my messing with the magic caused it to attack White Feather's mind or bind him tighter?

My jaw clenched. I kept the water going full blast.

Tara came running back. Her face was always pasty because of the white makeup she wore, but now her eyes were wide and scared, a lot like my own. "What do I do with it?"

That was a problem. The leaves would float away because of the water. "Keep your foot on the hose so it doesn't move away." I waited for her to position her foot. The painting continued to sit in the growing puddle of sandy mud.

"I need logs, something to get it away from Mother Earth." I was up the steps before I remembered her inclination to ignore orders. "Don't get close. Don't use curse words, spells or anything that sounds like a spell. Yell if anything changes and get yourself on the porch. If worse comes to worst, hose yourself down. Keep the water between you and the painting."

She nodded, her gaze on the painting and her foot on the hose.

I hopped up the steps.

"Adriel?"

"What?" I spun around, terrified the picture had grown horns and started to attack.

"Is White Feather going to be okay?"

My hand clenched the porch rail. "Yes!" I didn't have time for her insecurity. I yanked the front door open, determined to make my declaration right. I grabbed fresh roots, willow sticks--a bomb would be nice. I settled for a pair of clippers and my portable butane torch.

Halfway across the living room on my way out, the fireplace brought me to a halt. The logs were mostly for decoration. "Logs or fresh juniper?" I grabbed a log, set it down and extracted the cache of arrowheads from above the mantel. We definitely needed something to protect against witchcraft.

Juggling clippers, logs, and everything else, I raced outside and dumped the logs onto the ground. "Make sure the wood gets good and soaked."

Fresh juniper boughs from the trees in the yard weren't that easy to cut with small clippers, but I was motivated.

Just as I finished, Lynx drove up the dirt driveway with White Feather in tow.

White Feather jumped out of the Mustang looking perfectly normal. He strode over to the sand painting. His jaw was already tight, and the muscles in his cheek jumped. "Claire." He said it like a swear word.

Tara gulped, "I took it from the trash."

"How much did you tell him?" I mouthed at Lynx.

He gave me his cat grin, no teeth.

White Feather answered. "He told me you had a rune and were worried it had me by the balls. I assumed he was exaggerating." Each word was concise and filled with rage. His neck was flushed a deep maroon.

"Oh," I said.

"*Oh?*" The heat of his gaze went from me to his sister and back again.

Tara avoided the accusation by keeping her attention on the stream of water from the hose.

I waved my juniper branch. "We need to dismantle it."

White Feather raised a threatening hand as if he would blast it to kingdom come with a wave of wind. The problem was that he was the least useful person in destroying it. His power would probably only bind him tighter.

"Lynx." My voice trembled slightly. "Help me lift the painting on top of the wood."

"Burn it," he declared.

"It's stone. Sand doesn't burn well. We have to erase the links and diffuse it."

White Feather reached for the painting, his magic causing the hair on his arms to stand straight up. I clamped my lips shut against a warning scream. He wasn't a child; he knew magic. His home had blown apart when he attacked with the wrong timing. If he went to battle with it, there was no way to know who would win, but odds were not in our favor.

"White Feather."

He bared his teeth in a soundless snarl.

I stood perfectly still, my eyes pleading, but not daring to say anything more.

The veins along his arm bulged. There was no wind, almost no air at all.

Then, in a burst of heat, my hair lifted. Like a storm, electricity ran along my skin, racing up my face. Tara's white makeup clotted in sticky creases, forming premature wrinkles.

White Feather clenched both hands, but never took his eyes from mine.

I willed him to keep his wind, to save it, to control it. *Don't give it to the runes.*

The electricity across my skin prickled. Tears stung my eyes from forgetting to blink.

With an audible snap, as though I had rubbed my feet on a rug and then touched metal, the energy on my skin faded, sucked away as quickly as it had appeared. A breeze stirred, but it was from behind me.

I let out the breath I was holding.

His eyes still flashed dangerous green, but he stepped aside, allowing me to approach the painting.

"Wind...isn't the right weapon," I said softly.

One fist flexed, but his talent remained quiescent.

"Lynx?" I set the juniper branches across the top of the logs. My hands stung where the juniper pieces had dug into my skin.

I knelt in the dirt and picked up one of the forked willow branches.

Lynx wasn't eager to offer assistance, but he eventually positioned himself at the other side of the painting. "You already tried to burn it?"

I shook my head. "That melted mess was part of a plastic pot. The painting did the melting."

White Feather's breath hissed between his teeth.

"Shit," Lynx said.

Tara nudged him from behind. "No cursing!"

I almost grinned. That particular word wasn't likely to call anything evil, but at least she had taken my advice seriously.

"We have to erase the painting." The confidence in my voice was fake, but even illusions had their purpose. I handed Lynx one of the willow sticks. "Let's flip it up onto the wood."

"If it melted that plastic, won't it burn the wood?" His tail, had it been out, would have been jerking nervously.

"The wood is wet and the juniper boughs are fresh." I slid the branch underneath the painting, pushing it through the sandy mud. If he helped, fine. If he didn't, I would reposition it myself.

"I can move it," Tara volunteered softly.

The sleeping beast had been wakened. No way was she going to touch it again. The painting was armed and dangerous. "Keep the hose steady," I said.

Lynx gave a sub-audible growl. "Why do I always gotta be messin' with witches? Can't stick with nice, safe thieves and professionals, gotta be messin'."

We lifted it halfway up and then dropped it. I held my breath, expecting the thing to explode, but Tara quickly directed the spray from the hose onto the top of the painting.

On the second attempt, we were more coordinated.

As soon as we dropped it in place, I closed my eyes in relief, but White Feather interrupted my respite with questions. "Is now a good time for you to tell me exactly what this rune is designed to do?"

It wasn't the most coherent delivery, but I shared my suspicions about the design and how she had left the wrong side opened. "In short, Claire set this thing up to call something from the west to do her bidding, but other than binding you, I couldn't interpret all her intentions."

"Sounds like opening the east side would be a good first defense," he said.

"Honestly, I'm not sure. We need an expert shaman, but we're in short supply."

"Claire didn't have magic. She must have hired someone who didn't know what they were doing."

Our eyes met over the painting. "I think they knew what they were doing. Binding magic isn't generally considered a return to balance. Since the holy people weren't likely to answer her plea, I'm guessing whoever she hired was spelling from some other direction."

His hand reached out again, but this time he caught himself immediately. "You have a point."

"A sacred feather is the tool of choice for scattering the sand, but this thing is lacquered down, and I'm short such a feather."

"Bust it," Lynx said.

"Not a bad idea. But we should make sure we break the links in the right order." I dug in my pants pocket and came up with the arrowhead. "Let's open up the east and get some protection on our side."

Malachite was used to prevent witchery. Being a witch, I found it a nuisance, so I never stored it in my lab, but as an arrowhead it combined several magics suited for blocking evil and witchery.

I asked Tara for some of the sage leaves she had collected and palmed one and put another in my mouth. Centered through my silver and protective turquoise, I sawed at the edge of the rainbow on the east side. It didn't take long. The colored layers of sand were not deep.

For my trouble, I ended up thoroughly soaked from sitting half in a puddle and getting splashed while working. The painting didn't react to the damage I inflicted. "What next? Should we seal the other side or smash the entire thing?"

"Let me," White Feather said quietly. I hesitated, but it was his right to fight. I handed him the sage and the arrowhead.

He scraped the male figures, chipping bits and pieces of them away. When he aimed at one of the butterflies I stayed his hand. As near as I could tell, they represented Claire or at least her desires. "Not you. Not me. Too personal. There's no point in giving this thing any of our emotions. Lynx?"

He growled low. "I ain't no witch. Why you guys can't clean up your own messes—" He caught the crushed expression on Tara's face and snapped his lips into a thin line. With another sub-audible snarl, he snatched the arrowhead from White Feather. He jabbed a section of one butterfly. On the second stab, he cut the butterfly in half.

A hissing like a broken fissure in Mother earth spilled into the silence. I jumped back, but not before the stench of rotted meat permeated the air.

Before I could stop him, Lynx had his claws out. With the speed of a bobcat, he raked sharp spikes across the painting.

"Lynx! Get back!"

He ignored me. With a heavy swipe, he embedded the arrowhead in one of the lines and smashed it through the painting, snapping the sandstone in half. Smoke poured out as if it was on fire.

I grabbed Lynx to drag him away, but he was faster than I'd ever be. The smoke headed right for White Feather.

He blocked, creating a barrier of non-air like he had done before. He wasn't breathing. Neither was I.

Water poured across the pieces. The smoke could have been dissipating, so thin were the tendrils. But bits of darkness rose slowly, searching along a straight wall of nothing.

The smell of blood told me we weren't free of this thing yet.

White Feather didn't wait to be saved. His bubble slid where he commanded it, allowing him access to my butane torch. He fired it up and blasted the pieces of the picture.

Lynx rushed forward and kicked a piece of the painting my way. "Bust it!" he screamed, attacking a piece of the burned painting with a large rock.

When he didn't immediately get blown to bits, I snatched up a nearby rock and started smashing. Back to earth where it had started. Back to earth where it was nothing--not a picture, not a spell.

Tara joined us, crushing bits and pieces into the dirt.

In less than a minute the painting was reduced to nothing larger than a single piece of sand; some melted, some scorched, all of it very, very small.

Cautiously I sniffed. Burned ozone. Scorched log. Even burnt hair, but no smell of offal and blood.

I ached all over and was soaked.

Lynx, still breathing heavily, dropped his rock and replaced it with Tara's hand. "We're gonna go eat."

When no one protested, they made fast tracks to his car. I wasn't sure the painting was finished with us, but if it wasn't, I had no idea what to do next.

Neither White Feather nor I stirred. We sat there, staring at the remaining piles of dirt.

The torched glassy dirt reminded me of Sarah's cabin. "Melted sand." The grit was not completely melted and was more clumped, but my torch wasn't as hot as the explosion at Sarah's cabin. "There was melted sand around Sarah's cabin. And a sand painting inside. I wonder if it had anything to do with this one."

White Feather shook his head. "I doubt it."

"This painting wanted you to stay at home. What if Sarah's painting kept her at home until Claire acted out a sand painting ritual? Do you think Claire wanted you at home to act out this painting?"

He shook his head. "Maybe. But if Sarah had a painting that kept her at home, she wasn't being lured as a love-interest, at least not by Claire. I don't see any real connection."

"Hmm."

Quiet settled in around us. The silence was comforting; mother nature offered a hug through the twilight.

After a few moments, White Feather reached for me. He put his arm around me and we stood. "Eating would be good."

"Yeah," I agreed.

"Claire didn't have any magic."

"That's what Tara said."

He kicked at the pulverized dust, scattering bits into the wet juniper branches.

He held my hand as we headed inside, but I wasn't completely reassured. There were pieces to the puzzle missing, but Claire must have known Sarah somehow.

Chapter 21

We argued for almost an hour, minus the time I was in the shower. My focus was off. I avoided anything but the discussion about the sand painting because I didn't want to sound like a jealous shrew. On top of that, eye contact was almost impossible. I could only steal the occasional glance in White Feather's direction because he was dressed in a t-shirt and a towel.

His pants were in the dryer, and they weren't drying quickly. I usually hung my clothes out on the line because the dryer lost most of its heat to the hallway. It was imperative to my sanity that his pants get dry as soon as possible.

We were both hungry and not just for food. Most of me was exhausted. Certain other parts said to hell with food or sleep. All I needed was right in front of me, perched at the kitchen table where I almost couldn't tell he was half-naked.

His black hair was wind-blown, curling on the ends. His green eyes were tired, but bright and focused. My largest t-shirt was a guy's medium. His chest and arm muscles were going to split the seams.

He might be completely controlled by some other woman and compelled to defend her when under her spell, but I did not care. He was safe inside my house. No one was going to force him away.

I'd keep his pants if I had to.

I almost believed everything was okay, except that White Feather had decided that Sarah was likely the one who had been responsible for the sand painting fiasco rather than Claire.

"Sarah was the witch. She must have attempted a sand painting ceremony that blew up in her face," he said for perhaps the third time.

It was possible he was defending Claire, but that led to tangled, worried thoughts about whether he was under the influence of the spell she had used in the painting. Worse, what if he still cared for her, and it had nothing to do with a spell?

"If Sarah was guilty, why was she inside the sand painting? I doubt she willingly offered herself as a gift to a rogue wind spirit. Claire gave you the painting, and it was set to bind you. That was not an innocent act."

"Sarah's cabin blew up weeks after Claire gave me the painting. Claire wasn't a witch by any stretch of the imagination. She was just a marketing guru who worked at one of the wind companies I consulted with."

"So she had a natural interest in wind."

He sighed and relented a tiny bit. "There's definitely something out there. And that painting she gave me tried to bind me." He held up his hand with the ring I had given him. "But whatever she did, whatever compulsion that sand painting wrought, is gone. The ring is cold. No push to return home. Or to carry a purse in my car if I go out."

Cautiously, I touched the ring. It was cool to the touch. My shoulders relaxed at least an inch.

He turned his hand up and captured mine. We sat that way for several minutes, too tired to keep talking about it.

"I can't believe I dated such a--She didn't even know about my affinity for wind when we started dating, and I didn't tell her much."

"But she figured it out?"

He ran his hand through his hair and sat back. When he stretched his legs, one of them rubbed mine. He settled with his calf over my ankle. "I never thought twice about it, but she did ask a lot of questions. We were attacked once by a couple of thugs in the parking lot after dinner. I took care of it, obviously."

I waited impatiently.

He didn't meet my eyes when he admitted, "Looking back, she wasn't very frightened. Maybe she was even...turned on."

"You think she set you up?"

"At the time?" He shook his head. "Whether she set me up or not, she learned about my affinity for wind. She had an ample demonstration. After that," he shrugged, "her interest seemed like healthy curiosity at first, just a question here and there. But I was done with her after she started constantly begging for "a little fire" from my wind."

He put his elbows on the table. "But call a wind spirit? Could she really be that stupid?"

I bit my tongue and replaced a nasty comment with one that was more reasonable. "Some kind of ill wind was at the cabin, and it appears to be either stuck in our world or happy enough to stay."

"And homing in on me every time I use wind."

"Not just you. Martin told me his stash has been tainted. He recognized an ill wind." I told him about Martin and his stones. "The bottom line is that if Claire or someone else did a sand painting at Sarah's and left the west side open like the one on the sand painting she gave you--"

"We are seriously screwed," he finished.

There was no getting around the bad news.

I sighed, ready to suggest dinner when he asked, "What if you're only attracted to me because of my affinity to wind?

"*What?*"

"Like Claire. What if you think you're attracted to me, but it's really only the wind?"

It was a high insult to compare me to Claire in any way shape or form, but the idea was too ridiculous to take seriously. "If that's all that's worrying you, I'll just block your power, and then you don't have to worry about me being attracted to your power. I assure you it isn't your wind that...intrigues me." I raised a suggestive eyebrow and looked him up and down, at least the parts I could see. "Well, it certainly isn't *all* that intrigues me. Any woman can see that there is a lot more to you than your ability to control a breeze here and there."

He flushed slightly, making me grin. He stood abruptly, had to grab at the towel, and then stomped through the living room. "My pants must be dry by now."

I just sat and admired the view.

Right before he ducked down the hallway, he turned and caught me staring. "Block my power," he muttered.

I smiled and forgot all about dinner.

The pants probably weren't completely dry, but when he reappeared he was dressed anyway. "Can you really block me completely?"

I shrugged and stood up. "I've never tried. Your magic isn't hostile to me, but I block influences and protect against other magic all the time." I thought about a dream catcher, but that was too heavy a blocker.

He raised one eyebrow. "You make it sound easy."

"It should be doable. You wouldn't be actively fighting through any defense I mounted."

"Yes, but if it's so easy, why can't I keep my wind tamped down completely when I'm around you? Why should it be any easier for you?"

The tiniest bit of current came across the room and traveled up my arms. It felt as if he had run his hands over me. My fingers tingled. My heart tripped and then beat faster to make up for it.

"Well?" There was a challenge there. "When I'm near you, I'm barely in control. You'll have to have enough control for both of us. If you block me completely, earth would cover wind. I'd be invisible."

Given my distraction, it took me a moment to get my brain around the idea. "As in hide you from whatever might be looking?"

There was a hint of humor and heat in his voice. "And according to you it should be easy."

I knew what was coming and grounded just in time. His caress hit in a solid wave that covered my bare feet and traveled up my entire body. It was suddenly hard to breathe.

The air sparked around us, a sizzling electricity that doubled back on itself and strengthened with the bounce.

I was in my own home where I was strongest. I reached for the silver at my wrist, but made the mistake of looking his way.

He captured my eyes with his own, holding the stare while, as silent and efficient as any breeze, he glided closer, stalking me.

In two steps he had me, his hands taking the place of the wind on my arms. He was either trying to hug me or trying not to hug me. Like a shifting breeze, colors flashed across his eyes, changing from deep green to hints of brown. "Block me," he growled.

It sounded more like a demand than seduction, but when he kissed me, it was, hot, heady, and out of control in seconds.

"Cover the wind," he whispered against my lips.

I tried, I really did, but my instincts were responding to the man in addition to the magic. He moved his left hand to my lower back and pulled me close. Instead of thinking of Mother Earth, I was wishing he hadn't put his pants on.

He deepened the kiss.

When his tongue touched mine I forgot all about grounding. I gasped out, "We might have to, you know, study this problem a bit."

He choked on a laugh. "We may have crushed Claire's spell, but I don't want that thing finding me again, especially here. I have to stay hidden until whatever is hunting me either dies or stops on its own." He rested his forehead against mine, but then tipped my head back for another hungry, almost desperate kiss.

I gave as good as I got until his wind sparked uncontrollably along my skin.

He groaned. Either to convince himself or me, he said, "It's got my scent. There's no point in playing with fire and attracting its attention until I'm ready to deal with it on my terms."

Arguing was pointless, because he was right. We had to hunt down the hunter, and one way or the other, White Feather would be free to use his power again."Okay." I gave casual my best shot. "We'll just take things nice and slow until we've caught the hunter and you're safe. I'll work on a spell to hide your wind." I couldn't resist running one hand up his chest and into the curls at the back of his neck.

"Right." When the room didn't dissolve into an uncontrollable windstorm, he tightened his embrace, but kept his emotions and wind locked away.

Chapter 22

I spent the first part of the next day convincing Father Dan to bless four milk jugs filled with water. The discussion involved a lot of evasion on my part. He was left wondering if I was running a secret baptism service out of my garage.

Once home, I put pinto beans on the stove with a timer and then headed to the lab. Even with the sand painting destroyed, I was very suspicious that Sarah, the cat, or both were some kind of conduit for the ill wind.

The wind certainly had a tendency to show up where Sarah had been so it seemed wise to set a spell to block her. I really needed one that would warn me of an ill wind whether Sarah was involved or not, but other than using heliotrope, I hadn't worked out the exact technique.

By the time the beans were done, I had decided on a dream catcher as the warning mechanism. A knock at the door delayed me from starting.

Lynx and Tara were not entirely unexpected, but I was surprised at how good Tara looked. She had left off her pale base makeup. The charcoal on her face was limited to a single-stroke of black eyeliner and mascara. The stark black lipstick had been replaced by a dark plum. She still wore black, including the lace half-gloves that matched her black nail polish.

"White Feather said to stop by and set up regular lessons when it's convenient for you."

A regular schedule wasn't all that feasible considering my eclectic clientele, but I had promised White Feather I would help. "Now would be okay for a starter lesson. I was prepping spells to secure the house against ghosts. It'd be a good time for you to practice protection spells."

Her eyes slid to Lynx before she asked, "Can I use the bathroom to fix my hair and stuff?"

Her hair was already hairsprayed to within an inch of its life. Lynx didn't leave, so I nodded at Tara. She disappeared down the hall.

Lynx waited until the bathroom door clicked shut, and then talked so fast the words were hard to understand. "Thatbusinesstheotherday, where I—well, I was just showing off." His ears twitched and so did his invisible tail. "I wasn't even sure I could get in your place, but I've worked with you a long time so it wasn't that hard." Pride warred with shame. Shame won. "It won't happen again."

I didn't ask for more of an apology. "No, Lynx. It won't." Two newly planned spells would add a twist to the ones already on the door.

He nodded, understanding what I meant. The next time he tampered with my door, he had better be prepared for stronger wards. There was only one way to have a truce when dealing with a thief. You had to be on guard.

"Okay." His eyes didn't roam anywhere near the door or the lock, but a good thief wouldn't ever show obvious interest in new techniques. "You still taking the client, the one with the evil eye? He wants to move the meet up."

I sighed. "When?"

"Tomorrow morning, same place, the lodge. I didn't believe his big emergency at first, but he showed me. He's got the evil eye alright. Things growing out of him, guy looks like...I dunno. He's got green twigs sprouting right out of his arm. I pulled one out, smelled it. It's real."

That grossed me out. "That sounds like a pretty nasty spell—or a disease, maybe Morgellon's Disease?"

Lynx shrugged. "Who's Morgellon? She a witch?"

"It's the name of a disease that some people say is a spell, some say is an illness. It's basically fibers growing out of sores or causes the sensation of bugs crawling across the skin."

"He didn't mention bugs. Said the witch threw it on him. He wants it gone."

I frowned. "If she threw it directly at him, it's a spell, at least it's not the evil eye. I can probably counteract it. But if it's medical, I'm no healer. He might be better off with a witch who can do both."

"He wants the best." Lynx gave me his sly, cat smile. "Them healers, they don't like to mess with spells."

"The spell will wear off, but the witch could renew it." This problem had the potential to be a large drain on my time. "If the witch knows what soap he uses, and she put that in the spell every time he uses his soap, it'll regenerate the spell." I tapped my foot, but gave in. "Give me the details."

"Same place, just tomorrow. Meet at the lodge in the back. I tol' him early morning like you said."

"Okay, fine."

"He's got a real problem. This could be good business for a while." Lynx rubbed two fingers together.

"Yeah, sure." He wasn't the one who had to come up with counter spells for paranoid clients.

Lynx pivoted to leave, but then stilled as only he was capable. Slowly, he pointed and edged to one side so I could see around him. "That cat is just a cat."

The brown cat sat by the large juniper tree. She licked her furry chest a bit.

"I didn't think she was a shifter," I said. "But is it *only* a cat and nobody else parked inside there?" I tapped my own head.

Possessed or used as a spy or not, cats tended to know things—like when they were the subject of a conversation. The cat swiveled its head, lifting it slightly as though paying closer attention. It didn't help that Lynx hissed at me, "What you mean?"

"That's exactly what I mean," I replied. "It's been hanging around lately. I see it when I'm not expecting it, weird places. Can you tell if it is possessed?"

Lynx inhaled quickly, sniffing. "It looks like a cat." His eyes narrowed. "I followed it."

"How would that answer the question?"

Lynx shrugged. "Maybe it's an answer. Maybe not. I owe you." He scratched his ear and then it flicked on its own. "For the thing with the door."

I rolled my eyes. The thing with the door indeed. Breaking and entering. I let that go because as far as I was concerned, it was resolved. "If someone is controlling it or using it as eyes, it doesn't have to return to that place to deliver the info, Lynx."

"It's got to eat. If someone is controlling it, they'd keep it fed. Dead cat won't deliver much info."

He had a valid point. "Can you do me a favor?"

"I did already!"

"Just take it some food, would you?"

"I did that already too." He scooted away, light on his feet as always.

I was far from convinced that the cat wasn't possessed, but then again, Lynx was probably right, assuming he had followed the cat long enough. If no one was feeding it...hmm. Whether Lynx had fed it or not, I put more food on the porch.

Dallying was, no doubt, a mistake. The instigator had already been on her own in my house for far too long.

Tara waited innocently by the lab doorway. The ghost text I had been reading was open on the table, but she couldn't read it, even if she had gone in the lab. The slight smell of molten silver, a common smell in my lab, hung in the air. Nothing appeared out of place.

She trailed in behind me and took the stool where I had been reading. It didn't take long for her to ask, "You spell all your books like this?"

"Yes. I'll teach you sometime. In fact, the spell I'm working on now is a bit like it only in reverse. To keep someone from reading, the words are tuned to me. What I want to create today is a dream catcher with Sarah as the focus. It will keep everything Sarah out. Same sort of principle as letting only me in, just reversed."

"Who is Sarah?"

Talking to Tara about ghosts and training reminded me to shut the door to the hallway. Leaving it open was a bad habit. The door had special, heavy wards on both sides—no spells in and no spells out. Of course, Tara hadn't shown any real proclivity toward magic. What were the chances she'd suddenly find power and set it loose?

"Sarah's the ghost." I outlined the barest details of the explosion up on the mountain and Sarah's visit.

Tara listened, but snorted skeptically.

I ignored her opinion. "I want to make sure she can't get into the house or my dreams. The crucifixes, along with salt inside the adobe, are quite likely enough to prevent mischief. But I still want the added protection of a dream catcher."

"I have three dream catchers. I bought them though, I didn't spell them myself."

"I have a large one myself with smaller ones attached. Each piece targets different evils and spirits. We'll make one with Sarah as the target. Since she is a ghost, we'll also treat the weave with a mixture of salt and holy water."

I arranged the ingredients and dipped the cotton netting in the holy water and salt. "We'll thread sweet grass into the edges under the leather. It's not strictly necessary, but every little bit helps." I handed her the frame, the netting and the leather strip.

She was a quick study, but as she wove the sweet grass, she lacked any semblance of focus or passion.

I frowned. At this rate, I'd have to redo it. "Think about the spell while you're weaving. Some call it meditation. There's an essence that has to be embedded, almost a prayer that ghosts and spirits stay away."

"You want me to chant or something?"

"No." I stifled a sigh. "Some witches use words to help them focus, but it's not the words. Feel the magic in your fingers, tie yourself to what you need." How to teach someone to care? "Be aware of the aura of the spell. You have to see it so you can bend it."

I observed her wind a few more threads, but she was mechanical; following the technique, but completely lacking the magic. She was too self-conscious to give anything of herself.

"Let's add Sarah's essence, and I'll finish the weaving later," I said.

Sarah's spell was still in the green stoneware container. I had no intention of releasing the spell. Not only would it contaminate the lab, I needed to keep the essence to track Sarah or…for whatever else might come up. "I'll push this silver prong through the cork. The silver has notches where some of the spell will stick. When I pull it out, the cork fills in behind the prong and keeps the rest of the spell from escaping." I showed her the small pits I had made along the length of the spike.

"Then you put the silver in the dream catcher."

"Exactly. I'll cap it with a piece with wood, making it a miniature of the original awl. It's important that it look right. When you create magic you want it to be sophisticated and draw only beauty to itself, not reflect neglect or shoddiness."

I positioned the jar on the table. "Hold it carefully so it doesn't move around."

"Okay."

I pushed the spike in, turning it like a corkscrew. Usually, I attained a near trance-like state, feeling the world around me through my hands and body, but Tara's energy distracted me.

When I was certain the awl had gone far enough, I droned softly, "Hold your thumbs tight on the cork now. Envision the magic coming out through the middle of the awl, a line of light traveling along the length, like mercury in a thermometer."

Instead of turning, I gently rocked the awl back and forth, a slight reverse turn, then more rocking. "Hold tight," I warned.

The awl came free. I smiled triumphantly. The barest puff of dust hit the air and scattered like a sparkler during the Fourth of July. From outside, a yowl from the depths of a cat's soul bellowed.

Tara yanked her hands away from the stoneware jar. "Eeek!" Her screech wasn't much different than that of the cat. She stood, but one leg tangled around the bottom rail of the stool. It clattered over, trapping her foot.

I blinked, coming out of my concentration.

Tara hopped, trying to free her foot. She fell forward and caught herself against the edge of the counter top, bumping the stoneware jar.

It skittered sideways, rolling. Slowly, like a spinning top, it teetered on the edge.

I lunged for it, but it was too late.

Chapter 23

The jar was quite pretty, an almost opalescent green. It resembled water, catching the light as it turned, shimmering as it tumbled through the air.

When it hit the concrete floor, it shattered. The chemicals mixed instantly.

"OhmyGod, I'm sorry, I'm sorry!" Tara screamed.

I reached for silk to contain it, but it was past saving. Greenish blue smoke wafted up gently. It was the sky on a spring day with the forest beneath it. My head tilted, expecting the twitter of birds. The smell of juniper and pines filled the room. The smoke shifted, forming the shadows from overhead branches. No one shape was really there, just bits and pieces with light filtering down through a fragrant canopy.

The blue stayed above the green, spreading behind it, a vast horizon of possibilities. When the smoke touched my fingers, I smelled the loam and richness of Mother Earth.

The shadowy trees stretched and grew, their boughs gently swaying. Behind them, dimmer shapes implied more forest. The witch in me knew the illusion, even as I appreciated its beauty.

A huge sadness engulfed me, one that had been absent when I first realized Sarah had died. Her death had been violent. Her visit had left me frightened—for what had happened to her and what could happen to me. With the spending of the spell, I may as well have called her ghost, only instead of the frantic, pained waif, I felt the passing of a woman who had created something beautiful, meant to bring happiness and peace.

Sarah hadn't spent her life creating these types of spells and then suddenly hired herself to Claire to draw a sand painting meant to bind. Whatever part she had played, she hadn't been the one to open a gate to the west.

"I hope you're free," I whispered, watching the traces in the spell grow lighter. There were clouds, the gentle promise of a summer rain, the clean fresh smell of morning.

"Free of what?" Tara whispered back.

I didn't answer. The smoke drifted, slowly losing shape and suggestion. The smells would linger. I should open the outside door and let it drift, but I hated to do it. It was the last of Sarah.

Instead, I knelt and chose a piece of the stone jar. The chemicals were almost completely gone. Sarah probably hadn't made the jar, but there would be residual ingredients on the inside.

I set the largest piece aside and swept the other fragments into a silk pouch. They might be of use later. If not, I would bury them. Maybe up on the mountain.

I walked to the door and reluctantly set Sarah free. The wind easily captured the colored dust particles. In no time at all, the smell of the woods faded completely.

At the doorway, I bowed my head and said a prayer that she would go as freely as her smoke.

Chapter 24

It took me a few moments to compose myself enough to face my trainee. I was sad for Sarah and sad for Tara. Tara had so much potential, but there were an awful lot of obstacles.

"I skipped lunch," I said. "Let's get something to eat."

Tara mumbled, "I already ate."

"You're young. You can eat again."

Finding the forgotten beans quite cold on the stove I went to the fridge and hauled out bacon, cheese, tortillas and a jar of salsa. "Burritos it is."

When she saw the jar of salsa, she asked, "Don't you make your own?"

"You mean from tomatoes?"

"Yeah, fresh ones, with onions."

I laughed. "Who has time for that?"

She shrugged. "We always make it that way at home. If you have tomatoes, I can make some."

"I bought some for a salad. Go for it." Given my habits, tomatoes usually rotted in the drawer anyway.

She hesitated, but I left the refrigerator door open. She found the tomatoes easily. "Cilantro?"

"Only dried. Not much good in cooking."

She wrinkled her nose in agreement. "No taste after it's dried."

"Your mom probably makes fresh tortillas too." When she nodded, I sighed wistfully. "Mine too. When I make them they have arms and legs and look like a spell gone wrong."

She started to reply, and then lowered her head, juggling the tomatoes anxiously. "I—what was that awful noise? I'm so sorry. I messed it all up."

I hadn't been referring to the current lab disaster. Heck, for the first time since I'd known her we were almost speaking like normal people. "That blood-curdling scream was a cat. It's been hanging around lately. I'm not sure if it has anything to do with Sarah or not." I didn't know what to say about the jar, so returned to the food. "I warm tortillas from the store or steal them from my mom."

"You'll never take me on the scene now, will you?"

"The what?"

"The scene, the real stuff. Where you do magic for clients for real."

I sawed at the frozen slab of bacon, wondering what she was talking about. "Tara, the spells we've been working on are real."

She helped herself to a knife and the cutting board by the sink. Her words were punctuated with the chopping of onions. "This isn't the *deal*, the real deal."

"It's not?"

She shook her head. "Lynx told me you go to meets. You take the spells to the clients and work the real magic."

My eyes narrowed. "The magic in the lab is real. I do basic consultations, but only when absolutely necessary and only after Lynx has done reconnaissance. I prefer to remain anonymous."

"Yeah, Lynx says he delivers a lot of the time, but he said you do real meets where you perform the spell right there in front of them, the important stuff!"

"Tara, I do exactly the same thing whether in the lab or the field. Most of my clients don't need to know who I am or watch me work. It's better to provide the spell and let them take responsibility for implementing it."

She sniffed the tiniest bit. "Hard to get famous and make a lot of money that way."

"Easier to stay alive and avoid witch hunts." Avoiding direct contact with clients had always been my preference. "I don't hurt for business very often either."

She chopped away, her fingers flying. "You could make a lot more if you used your reputation. You'd have people coming to your door day and night and offering big money. Even Lynx said you could do more business if you wanted."

"If I *wanted*." I finished mashing the beans into the bacon grease. "But some business isn't worth having."

"Maybe you just don't want me to see your clients. I guess I don't blame you after today." Her voice was quiet, all trace of attitude gone. She focused on the onion chunk as if it required careful examination before she could proceed.

There was no denying that I didn't want her to meet my clients, but it had nothing to do with the accident in the lab. Truth be told, dressed as she did and with her mostly high and mighty attitude, she'd be very detrimental for business. Much as I wanted to help White Feather, I didn't intend to lose all my best business over it. "Tara, the accident in the lab wouldn't keep me from taking you to a client consultation. Spells don't always work as planned. In this case, I have what I need, so it isn't the worst thing that could have happened."

She reverted to food. "What about chiles?"

My hands were busy grating cheese, so I pointed with my chin. "There are some dried ones in the cupboard and frozen green chile in the freezer. My mom always gives me some."

She found the chile on the freezer door and put it in the microwave to thaw, all without any instructions from me. I started warming tortillas.

"Limes?" she asked.

"Might be some in the drawer."

She rooted around and came up with a plastic bag. There was a lime in it, but it looked more like a petrified walnut.

"Hmm," I said. "There's juice on the door. I use lemon and lime juice in the lab a lot as a preservative. Looks like I forgot to buy fresh limes."

"Yeah, since, like, last year maybe." She held the bag high with two fingers and deposited it in the trash.

I kept an eye on her while she chopped green chiles.

"Sugar?" she asked.

I pointed with my chin again. "On the table."

She found it, pinched some in with the tomatoes and began stirring. It was then that I was sure. The same stray vibes that leaked around her in the lab when she got frustrated were here now, but different. The aura was spicy like the salsa, electricity almost tamed. As she calmed down and worked, the wave hovered like a proper aura instead of spiking away from her in clouds. Unbelievable. At that moment, she reminded me of my mother.

"Impossible," I muttered. Her hair was a tangled black mass. Her makeup was still more corpse than human, but she was *right at home* in the kitchen, with a comfortable aura around her much like my mother's aura. "Healing? No way." Food was most closely related to the healing arts, although in the very talented there was a whole lot more to it.

I watched her toss the onions in the bowl. She lacked all the clumsiness and self-consciousness she exhibited in the lab. She wasn't even concentrating and the salsa came together like a spell. Granted, a lot of people could cook, but she was *improvising,* and not measuring anything.

My stare finally caught her attention. "You're burning that tortilla," she said.

I grabbed it, but it was too late. When I lifted it, smoke rose in a cloud. It was black on one side.

Tara snatched the iron skillet off the stove with a potholder. "What's wrong with you?" She waved the pan to cool it. After a minute, she set it down and flipped on another tortilla without pausing to ask permission or think about the action.

We finished preparing lunch in silence. If she had healing skills, she was out of luck. I couldn't train her on my best day. Well, unless I trained first. Given the close calls I'd been in lately, a few healing skills wouldn't hurt.

I did know someone who could help. She was an old school witch and not for hire, but if we determined Tara's true ability, we could hire a more experienced teacher later.

Chapter 25

Early morning was always the best time to meet clients. Most of them weren't too keen on "daybreak" but it worked for me because the rest of the world was mostly asleep. Rather than park at the lodge, I drove up to the second group shelter. The hike down was almost a mile through Douglas-fir trees.

The first shelter was closer to the meet, but it was also the more likely parking spot, and I avoided being predictable. At quarter to seven, there was only one other car at the high shelter, and it was from out of state. No one was around to notice me and if anyone did, I was dressed like any other day hiker.

The trail to the lodge was clear enough that a light wasn't necessary; the dim morning was a comfort, not an enemy. A squirrel scolded from a tree and at least one chipmunk scrambled across the rocks to the other side of the trail. By the time the green roof of the lodge was in sight, dawn was breaking.

I slowed and caught my breath.

From the trees, I spotted a guy leaning against the wall of the lodge. He sucked two quick drags from a cigarette. One hand clutched a square object, but rather than a weapon, it looked as though he had brought along a book to read while he was waiting.

Too bad for him it wasn't light enough out to read. The fact that he wasn't on the trail side of the split-log fence didn't surprise me because clients hardly ever followed instructions, before, during or after the spell sale.

The way he checked his surroundings did bother me. He acted as nervous as an inexperienced bank robber. Of course, some clients were afraid of witches even though they needed one.

I sighed. He was going to be a difficult client.

When I reached the fence, I left the trail and climbed over the three-rail barrier to shorten the trip.

Halfway across the packed-dirt area, my feet stopped, but for a few seconds so did my brain. Even in the low light he was recognizable as the frog-faced religious nut from Mat's shop.

"Aztec curses!" Maybe my meets should be in broad daylight. With more light, I would have identified him from behind the trees.

I backed away, but he had seen me. He ground his cigarette into the stones at his feet. "I'm David. You the witch?"

"The what?" I kept motoring backwards. It wasn't hard to act like I thought he had a screw loose.

"I've got this problem. See?" He stuck his arm straight out. The things sticking up from his arm were too thick and straight to be hair. His arm was indeed growing green things, only now I knew what they were: Petunias.

The spell from Mat's shop had seeped into his skin. Assuming he plucked at the green stems as he was doing now, the stalks probably grew close to an inch an hour.

"I'm out hiking, mister. I'm not looking for trouble." I backpedaled, fast.

The smaller storage structure should have been locked and empty at this hour, but a dark shape emerged. David's blond partner held a gun. His elation at seeing me was overdone. "Well, well!" He paced my way, jaunty and confident.

I yanked a spell off the side of my backpack and crushed the elements, setting off a heavy smokescreen before it left my fingers. Behind the billowing gray smoke, I was a gazelle; the fence might as well have been thin air. Once in the trees, I could lose the two of them easily.

Two steps into my hopeful gloating, there was more movement off to my right. I dithered. I'd have to fight if there were too many of them, and I'd likely lose. "Mayan sacrifices!" I grabbed another spell from the side of my backpack and was ready to release it when I recognized the shifting, dark-haired form.

My mouth fell open. "Lynx?" He drifted along the side of a tree, just leaving the trail that came up from the lower parking area. Hearing his name, his head swiveled my way, his eyes wide and glowing yellow.

My stomach hit my toes. He wasn't alone. "Oh no!" Tara clung to one arm, slightly behind him. "Out!" I screamed. "It's a bust, get her out!"

I turned back. If I diverted these guys back to the road...too late. David's Bible caught me in the face. He had spotted me through the smoke screen.

"Run," I screamed again.

David the Frog clamped a heavy hand on my shoulder. I kicked empty air, and didn't see the knife in his other hand in time. There was heavy panting behind me. It might have been Lynx, but I couldn't waste time finding out. Ordinarily Lynx could easily escape in his bobcat form, but he was with Tara. I clawed at David's face. He paid me back with a heavy slice from the knife across my arm.

The shock of pain penetrated my brain.

The blonde guy with the gun cleared the smoke and the fence. I heard a gasp, probably Tara.

I muttered the right words and grabbed the purple-clad spell from my pack, crushing it in my hand. This one had real fire, shooting out sparks and a long flame. It forced David back and gave me an extra half-second.

I sprinted away, hoping the explosion of noise and light would give Tara and Lynx enough time to escape. Feeling along my pack, I grabbed another spell, activated it and lobbed it behind me. Had I looked or tried for my flying spell first, I might have avoided the tackle.

He hit me hard.

Rocks tore across my knees and one elbow. My pack slid to the side.

"Gag her, gag her!"

A lot of my spells didn't need words, and if I reached my knife, it didn't need words either. I twisted, managing to get my face out of the dirt. One hand was still trapped underneath my body. The other jabbed and made contact with skin. I raked my fingernails downward.

My opponent barely grunted. I ended up with a handful of half-grown petunias.

I blocked a blow with my elbow. Frog-eyes had one leg pinned beneath his body, but I twisted, determined to knock him off.

Lynx loped rapidly through the nearby trees. He disappeared from my blocked line of vision just as gunfire popped. "Lynx!"

Setting off spells still in my backpack, which was still attached to me, was foolhardy, but reaching Lynx and Tara was imperative, especially if one or the other had already been shot.

I opened my mouth, but David the Frog slapped down, bloodying my lips. The last bang I heard was either the gun going off or the crunch as his fist crashed against my nose. Through a haze of black, I barely felt the next blow.

Chapter 26

My head ached. I wasn't seeing double, but what I did see was not good news. My stomach roiled, and pain bounced from my head to my limbs. Maybe it wasn't Patrick, the vamp, in front of me. I slid one hand across my wrist and panicked. My turquoise bracelet was gone!

I reached for my throat, but knew my silver and crucifix had also been taken. Silver was my tie to Mother Earth. Naked didn't begin to describe my vulnerability.

It wasn't possible for me to keep the shuddering breath locked quietly in my throat. I needed air, and I needed earth! My gasp caused the vamp to stop tapping on his hand-held device.

His eyes, solid black in the dim light, registered my recognition. Before I managed a second, shuddering breath, his hand was across my nose and mouth, blocking all air. Already panicked, there was nowhere to go but fight.

Biting a vampire was foolish because harming one was nearly impossible, but my silver was gone, I hadn't eaten garlic in days and my weak arms did absolutely nothing to remove his hand.

My vision went black, but I rolled away from him. The jarring impact of a bed rail loosened his grip enough to allow me another breath of air. I was *not* going to die by vampire strike. He could kill me, but he wasn't getting my blood.

"Take it easy," he hissed. "I work here. I mean you no harm."

I was already over the side and crouched. My stomach protested. On my knees, I crawled for the door.

He picked me up and deposited me back on the bed. "If I wanted to bleed you dry," he said in a passive voice, "you'd be dead already." He snapped a finger against my aching head. "Use that, would you?"

He floated away from me then, standing by a mockery of a window. There was nothing but blue curtains framing solid plaster.

Air wheezed in and out of my throat. There was only one door visible, but where did it lead? My hands twitched, searching for silver.

"I am a predator," Patrick snapped out. "Act less like prey, and I'm less likely to hunt you."

A part of my brain dissected the statement "predator." One part of me wanted to scream. The other part yelled, "Freeze." I knew the danger of running from that which hunts. Stillness was my best friend.

Patrick faced the fake window, as though peering out. "It's strange having one from the daylight hours in here."

I had no idea what he was talking about.

"I miss the sunlight. And coffee." He rubbed one arm with his hand. "The sun isn't like my memory of light and gentle heat anymore."

As he talked, my vision cleared. He was dressed in a hospital-type smock, not white, but baby-blue for God's sake. Even though it hung loose, he managed to look attractive.

That was the magic of vampires; not an ugly one in the bunch. His black hair was secured into a ponytail, exactly like the other times I had seen him. It, and a single diamond earring, were the most human things about him.

I kept my eyes locked on him, but he made no threatening moves. Specifically, no teeth.

"Sunlight." I fell back against the pillows. "I want my silver."

His mouth quirked into a smile, still no teeth or shiny fangs. "In the drawer next to the bed. I guess you miss it like I miss sunlight."

"I doubt it." I opened the drawer without taking my eyes from him. Not that watching him would do me a lot of good. I'd seen this guy in action. If he wanted to strike, I wouldn't know he was moving until it was too late.

Leaning to reach my silver almost made me pass out again. "I gotta get out of here."

"Your arm is stitched up. Your head needs watching. Doc said you probably don't have a concussion, but should have someone stay with you anyway. We kept you under to make things easier. It's not as safe for me here during the daytime."

He was back at the side of my bed.

I snarled, "Show-off."

He smiled, lips only. If he was trying to gain my trust, his lack of teeth wasn't hurting his cause, but there wasn't much he could do that would make huge inroads.

"The cat be willing to stay with you?"

"The cat?" For a second I thought he meant the little stray that had been crying outside my window, but then the fight rushed into my memory. "Is Lynx okay?"

Patrick shrugged. "He got you here."

"Lynx brought me here?" I blinked. "He knows I can't afford a hospital!" He also knew I didn't trust them.

The smile again. "He knows about the room."

"The room?"

Patrick stretched his arm to encompass the space around us. "It's a little side operation in the basement for special patients. I check on them while I'm on break from the regular hospital rounds. You don't really qualify, but Lynx figured I owed you."

I shook my head vehemently, sending waves of pain and light through my head. "No way! You don't owe me."

Patrick chuckled softly. It was a sexy, comforting sound. My fingernails nearly drew blood as I gripped my bracelet. Until that moment, I hadn't realized the pain in my arm was partly due to stitches that ran all the way up the top side. My t-shirt was intact except for one sleeve that was completely ripped away. Blood was liberally splattered across the front.

Instead of my jeans, I now wore some sort of loose shorts. They looked suspiciously similar to Patrick's hospital pants, only they had been cut off at the knees with a very sharp knife.

"I am not sure we are yet even, witch." He made the last sound like an endearment. "You helped me greatly when I was in need, and I ended up with a house out of the deal."

I scooted to the side of the bed where he was not. "That house had nothing to do with me."

"Not so much, but you did rid it of the pestilence." He waved a hand again. "Enough. The question remains, will the cat stay with you and guard you?"

"Where is he?"

"Can you reach him?" Patrick countered.

Patrick was fishing, maybe trying to ascertain how strong my powers were or how much influence I held over Lynx. Well, he was bound to be disappointed. "I can call my mother. Or sister. Or White Feather will come and get me."

He took a cell phone out of one pocket. "Call."

I didn't want to use his phone. Or anything else he had touched, but the phone was my best chance at freedom and survival. I accepted it without touching his cold fingers.

"Where are you?" exploded through the ear piece, the second White Feather heard my voice.

"The hospital—"

"I've checked nine times! Gordon has a bulletin out on you!"

"Uh, Lynx didn't tell you he brought me here?"

"Lynx?" He cursed. "Is Tara with you?"

"Uh, no." I scanned the room again to be certain. Before I had a chance to say more, Patrick leaned in and confiscated the phone.

"Come in the back way, near the dumpster. The door is marked with the number seven. She'll be waiting."

I blinked rapidly as Patrick snapped the phone shut.

"The back?"

"You aren't officially here." He extracted a folding wheelchair from behind a partition. "You're my first day creature."

"But...it's a hospital!"

He smiled, and this time there was a bit of fang. "The back room is mostly for shifters. On rare occasions a vamp requires treatment. Your friend Lynx knows about the special arrangement."

He lifted me in the chair without answering the questions running through my mind. How much of my blood had he taken before he stitched my arm?

Had he…I gulped. *Had he licked it clean? Or just sucked out a meal's worth?*

It wasn't possible to contain the shivers that took hold of me. I was suddenly freezing and near panic again. Patrick noticed, but he just threw a blanket over me. From under the bed, he extracted my backpack and set it on my lap. He recited instructions concerning care for my head and stitches.

With the roaring in my ears, I heard none of it. I suddenly missed the sunshine, but not for the same reasons he did.

The hallway and stairwell was dark; perhaps the area was for maintenance, perhaps it was long forgotten. If there was an elevator, Patrick didn't use it.

We didn't wait long at the back door. I couldn't hear a thing, not even a car door slam, but Patrick seemed to know when to open the door.

"You can hear him breathing through the door, can't you?" I babbled, unable to help myself.

Patrick gave an amused chuckle, but didn't deny the charge. He held the door with one arm and pushed the chair through with the other.

At first I thought it was still dawn out, but that made no sense. Gradually, I recognized dusk, that hovering space when everything was gray and getting darker. If there were nearby street lights, they weren't operating.

White Feather was ready for a fight, at least until he saw me. His eyes dismissed Patrick as if he were no more dangerous than a vase of flowers. "Adriel." It was half prayer, half sigh. He knelt down, his hand clutching my knee as he examined my injuries.

"She'll be fine," Patrick said. "Bump on the side of her head. Keep an eye on her. She'll get a nasty headache."

"I already have one!"

White Feather's hand moved gently up my arm, turning it to see the stitches there. "What happened?"

"Meet went bad. They were witch hunters, the ones from Mat's shop. I never found the time to tell you about them."

"Witch hunters?" Patrick echoed.

White Feather cursed. "Gordon mentioned them. He said they've been causing trouble around town, and he mentioned something about Mat having trouble with them. Some fanatic group called enlightenment or enforcement."

I groaned. "Somehow Lynx missed who they were when he set up the meet."

"You might want to leave the door open," White Feather told Patrick. "When I find Lynx, he's going to need your services."

Patrick's fangs flashed. "No credit for saving her?"

White Feather's grip on my arm was about to make me whimper. "Was Tara with you?" He kept his gaze on Patrick.

"I thought I was alone. Lynx and Tara must have followed me. Guy ambushed me from behind. But Patrick is right. I didn't get here by myself." I tugged away from White Feather's grip. "Haven't you found Tara yet?"

White Feather's hand relaxed when he noticed my pain. "No."

"How did you know I was missing?"

"Smoke up at the lodge. After what happened to Sarah, Gordon called me in from the start. There were bullet casings and expended spells. I recognized your aura. Just how many spells did you set off?"

"Not enough. I would have used my levitation spell, but Lynx and Tara showed up." I closed my eyes against the guilt. "I'm sorry, White Feather. I had no idea they were there!"

He squeezed my hand, this time gently. "Gordon found a guy inside the lodge that was mauled by," he glanced at Patrick and then remembered that the vampire knew, "a cat of some kind. The guy refused treatment and even with the bullet casings, there wasn't enough evidence of a crime to hold the guy. I looked for you first and when that failed, I tried to locate Lynx and Tara."

Patrick finally spoke. "These hunters, what are they after?"

"It's a witch hunt," I said. "Bible throwing, threats, fire."

"Interesting."

I thought I was past caring, but if something interested a vampire, and it concerned witches, it would be stupid to ignore. "Why is it interesting?"

"You're the third witch in this week. The other two were checked in on the regular floors. There's one here now who sustained more injuries than a simple Bible beating unless someone used Bibles to flog skin off."

"Flogging? Someone flogged a witch?"

Patrick tilted his elegant head. "Hikers found the witch over by Tent Rock. There appeared to be quite a bit of inebriation involved on both the part of the witch and the hikers. I ignored the witch's nonsense about snakes pinned to the ground, maidens dancing in the desert and corncobs. The witch didn't report anything about Bibles."

"Gordon didn't mention witches had been hospitalized," White Feather said. "Who are they?"

"Sorry," Patrick answered with an elegant shrug. "Neither was admitted to my special space. Privacy laws protect them unless they decide to contact Gordon."

The list of witches I knew was fairly long. Some I suspected were witches, others I knew about for sure and a few I knew by name or reputation. Because Patrick mentioned Tent Rock, it took me longer than it should have, but few witches spent time inebriated in the desert. "Martin!"

Patrick raised an eyebrow. "Clairvoyant too?"

"Who is Martin?" White Feather asked.

"He's a drunk. The guy I told you about with the heliotrope that was infected by the ill wind. He spends a lot of time alone in the desert, so those guys could have gotten to him." I called to mind everything that had been happening lately, but none of it fit together.

Patrick said, "Your friend Martin mentioned spirits, not Bibles. Perhaps I should have paid more attention."

"Spirits? Like a wind spirit?" Martin usually made sense if you knew what he was talking about. The corncobs and maidens didn't the bible-thumpers, but it reminded me of sand paintings. "Did he say he saw those things as part of a drawing? Like a sand painting?"

"He wasn't what you'd refer to as sober. Of course, we ignored most of what he said and assumed he had been flogged or beaten senseless."

"Is he going to be okay?"

"No worse than before he was admitted."

The inference that Martin was not exactly ever going to be "okay" was obvious but unarguable. "Tell him I asked about him." I struggled mightily before adding, "Let me give you my phone number. He can call me if he needs anything."

"I have it," Patrick said.

The vamp loved to make me shiver. White Feather wasn't amused. He leaned over, and though the chair was quite awkward, picked me up in one smooth motion.

Patrick held the car door opened. After I was taken care of, Patrick said, "The first witch in wasn't in bad shape. You might have Gordon do an inquiry."

"Hard to do without a name," White Feather growled.

"Try the newspapers. There was an attempted theft of several horses with the first witch. The current accident is being reported as a fall. He was drunk and wandering around at night during a full moon."

I groaned. The bible-thumpers could have found Martin at work, but under the circumstances, we couldn't rule out the wind being responsible for Martin's mauling. Whatever was riding the wind was far more dangerous than a couple of guys waving a souped-up cigarette lighter or a gun.

Then again, as Patrick floated soundlessly back to the door and disappeared, "dangerous" was all relative.

Chapter 27

White Feather used his cell to check with Gordon while he drove me home. "One found, two to go," he said after he hung up. He squeezed my hand as soon as his was free.

"If Lynx got me to the hospital and didn't take Tara there, she's probably okay," I said.

"I don't like this whole thing with my sister and Lynx," White Feather grumbled. "I wasn't sure I liked Lynx before he and Tara met."

This wasn't news to me. Lynx was my friend in some ways and in others, I felt he was my responsibility. "Because he's a shifter?"

"Because he's a *teenager*!" White Feather exploded.

I smiled and relaxed. "That's curable."

"Not necessarily in time to save my sister."

He had a point. "She's a teenager too."

"So?"

Telling him I wasn't all that enamored of her wouldn't help anything. "She's got a lot of growing up to do."

"Couldn't she find a nice--" He slapped his hand against the steering wheel.

"Yeah, she isn't going to stumble across a nice teenager. There isn't any such thing."

"But *Lynx*? He's a thief!"

"He's very protective." Listing Lynx's best qualities was challenging, especially considering I hired him for his more unsavory ones. "He's extremely intelligent. And I'm pretty sure he has turned over a bit of a new leaf since he started seeing Tara." Except for the little leaf that was Tara convincing him to break into my house and follow me to a meet.

"Where does he earn his money? Are you telling me he got money for his new car legally?"

Now there was a question. "I honestly don't know. Not everything Lynx does is illegal. He takes a lot of odd jobs, many of them magic related. That doesn't mean they are illegal."

"But he charges more for the illegal ones."

"Not necessarily. Lynx charges by difficulty. He'll even turn down some illegal stuff if it isn't worth his time." Those qualities weren't particularly admirable, so I tried again. "If he wants something and it's worth money, he'll do his own thieving, but he won't steal for someone else, not even for a large payoff. He doesn't generally do things that can get him blackmailed or that serve to enrich the guy he's working for more than himself."

"And this is good for Tara, how?"

Explaining Lynx and his ethics was impossible. He worked on projects for the money, but also for the challenge. He only worked for people he respected, but ultimately, he wanted to work for no one.

His independent streak and business ideas were usually what got him into trouble. He'd sell things to people even if those things weren't good for them. Except drugs. "He doesn't do drugs," I said brightly. "He won't touch them—not to sell them, not to use them." I was almost positive that he blamed his own abandoned condition on drugs. Then again, it could be that he knew how dangerous drugs were for a kid living on the streets.

"And that's about his best asset. I want something better for my sister. I'd like her to date someone who doesn't disappear into thin air, leaving you holding the bag! Is that asking too much?"

"No, not really. But the good news is that Lynx wants something better for her too. And for himself. He always has." I drummed my fingers on the door rest. White Feather pulled close to the house, which was good, because I was determined to walk on my own.

Someone, I assumed Lynx or Tara, had driven my car back here from the mountain. Small consolation.

As I climbed out, I said, "Maybe by the time they aren't teenagers they will have reached the point where they are better."

"If they live that long."

That was the biggest problem with being a teenager. They had to live long enough to make it to the point where they were more than just a bundle of energy and hope—and hormones.

I managed to climb the stairs and stagger inside without whimpering. There was no point in looking in the mirror. Once again, it was the shower for me, clothes and all.

White Feather interrupted that plan. "I had better check you over."

I paused in my marathon effort to make the bathroom. "Check?"

"Patrick is a vampire." His eyes were worried.

I swallowed. "I suppose so."

My t-shirt was matted on one side, bloody and stuck to me near my right arm. "I thought I'd shower this thing off." I pulled at the bottom part. Patrick must have washed me down while checking for wounds, because other than the arm and shirt, the rest of me was surprisingly clean for someone who had been rolled and mashed in the dirt.

Still, getting the shirt off with the stitches in my arm was proving tricky. "What a mess. Maybe I should cut the shirt off."

"Here, let me help." He was suddenly right behind me, almost faster than Patrick could have moved. He lifted my shirt very carefully. It stuck on my breasts, and I had to wiggle and shift my arms to allow it to move higher. His hands, with a feather-light touch, traced my back, searching for bite marks. My back was the least injured area, because it had been protected by my backpack.

Without asking, he released my bra hook.

It always felt good to take my bra off. To spring free while his hands were running across me was enough to make me moan.

His hands stilled. I tingled all over, my wounds forgotten. I didn't know if the air movement came from him or because I was half naked. His hands slid across my exposed skin again. Slowly. Like he knew he really shouldn't.

He was only checking my back, but...he kissed my shoulder. His lips traced the areas where his hands had been.

While his lips were busy, his hands inched forward, just touching the swell of my breasts. He cupped them.

I gasped out another half-groan and leaned into him.

His hands teased across me, exploring, but not for vamp bites. I couldn't feel his power because I was drowning from his touch.

When his thumbs grazed my nipples, I nearly screamed. He turned me to him in one smooth motion.

I put my bad arm up across his, giving him all the access he could possibly want.

He didn't refuse the offer. Magic rolled over me in waves with every brush of his lips.

We both breathed in, the motion a tease against his face.

One hand supported my back while he explored further with his mouth. Holding tight, I wished he would never stop, but the magic raged out of control. He wrestled with it. Against my better judgment, I helped, grounding myself to Mother Earth.

He rested his face against my chest and said, "You are so beautiful." He kissed me again, working his way up my neck until he reached my jaw and then my lips.

I held onto his shoulders, kneading my fingers into his muscles. My ground to earth was strong; I offered it to him. More than that, I pushed it over his wind, keeping him grounded too.

His wind didn't stop. It swirled around us.

"Too dangerous," he muttered. "Water blocks an ill wind," he contradicted himself. "And you need a shower."

I kissed him hungrily, my hands under his shirt, reveling in his broad chest. "You're safe here."

It was stupid. The fight had left me battered. My head pounded, my arm was slashed, and I still couldn't be happier. Well, maybe a little, but we were getting there. We had to. It was becoming a matter of survival.

"I can't repair your house and mine at the same time," he said, but his feet were taking us step by step into the bathroom. I kept my arms wrapped tightly around him, doing some exploring of my own.

He mumbled against my neck, "Where would we live if your house blew apart?"

The hospital shorts were not a tight fit. "It's not the house you're worried about, is it?" I whispered, reveling in the taste of him. He smelled of aftershave and fresh forest air.

He pulled me in tight. He could leave his hands on my bottom like that forever, and if he let go now, I'd fall over.

"My promise is for life, Adriel. I'm not taking any chances with you, especially if it's the difference between one night and a lifetime of them."

I leaned back and turned the shower on.

He growled, "Adriel!"

My head was back, arched toward the water. The cold drops did nothing to cool the currents running across my skin. I held tight to White Feather and leaned further away. The new angle pulled him off balance.

He didn't hesitate to correct the situation.

Water cascaded across my head and shoulders, slanting my grounding sideways. With his wind and the growing vapor, it was hard to tell where the magic started. There was no end to it.

He kissed my breasts, gently. His hands worked eagerly on the rest of me.

Maybe he meant to put things on hold, but when the water hit his head, the strangest thing happened. His wind mixed with my earth. Instead of two forces, they were wrapped together, circling. We were the eye in the center of a storm. There were colors everywhere, sparking across the water. I didn't have to entice him closer; he was already there.

When we finally merged, the magic was earth, wind, water and a flame that didn't go out.

Chapter 28

There were numerous things we could have done to be safer. A swimming pool would have been good. Maybe his grandfather's retreat even better. My house was warded and as safe as I could make it, but nothing was foolproof.

I hadn't cared, and was pretty sure I wouldn't care the next time either.

Drying off, I managed to ask, "So, my back looks okay, then?"

White Feather, once again in my house with only a shirt and towel, froze for a second.

"No vamp bites?" I prompted.

It took another second, but then he laughed.

The sound filled the tiny room, echoing. It was like his wind, only it was the magic of the man.

"This is crazy." He reeled me into a half hug, mindful of my arm. "Yesterday, while working on the house, I had a visit from four mini-tornadoes. The ill wind, whatever it is, came back, searching. It won't find me there. I know how to be invisible. Thank God it didn't find us here."

Goosebumps covered my bare skin. His essence was his enemy. There wasn't a worse place to be. "You're working on spells to counter it? Ones other than disappearing behind no air at all?"

"A spell to fight and one or two others to hunt it down." He glanced at the window in the bathroom, but it was opaque. The important thing was that it was intact. Whether it was luck, the water or my wards, nothing had found us here. Not yet, anyway.

"Between the water and the earth, we were well hidden," I said.

He stroked my shoulder gently. "Wind under the earth."

"That was an unexpected benefit. I've never merged magics like that."

"I didn't know it could be done."

"We should probably take more showers," I said. "Someone needs to study these things."

He laughed again. It was a very magical sound, one I wanted to hear over and over.

* * *

White Feather woke me several times during the night and not once was it for romantic reasons. After verifying I was lucid and not concussed, he tucked me to him and kissed my head. I snuggled closer and fell back into exhausted sleep.

The last time he woke me it was six a.m. I threatened him with bodily harm. Despite my grumbling, he nagged me until I got up and locked the door behind him. He was determined to find Tara. I desperately required more sleep.

If White Feather had thought about it, he'd have realized that teenagers slept in. They didn't go anywhere for any reason before ten, even if they were concerned about someone. I knew this because ten-sfifteen was when Lynx showed up to check on me.

My nose was horribly bruised and my arm throbbed, but my headache was mostly gone.

Getting angry with Lynx was a total waste of time, but that didn't cool my slow boil. Even though he had obviously returned to rescue me, there was still the blatant fact that he had set me up in the first place.

"What in all the spells gone wrong were you thinking?" I demanded upon answering the door.

He gave me slit eyes. I wasn't impressed. He could control his change. Acting angry and displaying any sign of cat was a show.

"You're okay, ain't you?"

"You turned me over to Patrick? Are you crazy?"

He relaxed. Obviously he was fine with that part of the caper. "'Trick is okay. He tol' me if I ever needed patchwork, he could help. He took care of you, right?"

"Lynx. He is a vampire."

His eyes roamed the floor. "Yeah. But you wasn't lookin' so good, and I had to take care of Tara."

I sucked in a worried breath, but he said, "She's cool. But she ain't like you. She freaked, wondered why you didn't just blow those guys away. White Feather, she said coulda done that."

"I am *not* White Feather." My voice was icy cold, unreasonably hurt by a stupid comparison.

"Why did you run right at those dumb asses?" he asked. "We'da gotten out of there!"

"I was trying to give *you* time to get *your* ass out of the fire!"

He was quiet for several seconds. "It seemed like a simple case, just a guy with the evil eye."

"Lynx—"

"I know, I know, it's a screw, but I checked!" His ears swiveled away from me. "You saw his arm! It looked legit!"

"Lynx, I do not have a problem with you mistaking the guy for a legitimate client. I have a problem with you showing up at the meet. *Any* meet of mine and with Tara, no less."

Had he run or swore I would have been vindicated. Instead, he eyed the doors and windows as if he were desperate to escape, but he held his ground. "She wanted to see you in action so she'd know how to act."

I folded my arms in front of me, insulted and betrayed.

Lynx babbled. "I forgot you get into trouble a lot. Shit, it was an easy one! Nothin' shoulda happened!"

He was not helping his case. The red line up my arm was ample evidence that something had, indeed, happened.

"I shoulda known. I know, I know." His shoulders slumped. "You think he got this infection from the evil eye like he said? And that turned him against witches?"

I almost laughed. "You did not read this guy correctly, Lynx. He did get the spell from a witch, but he was already out to cause trouble." I told him about the incident in the shop. "It's one of Matilda's spells. It mixed with another spell and super-activated."

Lynx blinked once in shock, but then he brightened. "You're saying this spell ain't gonna disappear? He's gonna have *petunias* growin' out his arm for the rest of his life?"

"I doubt that will deter him. For his purposes, this more than proves his point that witchcraft is nothing but evil."

Lynx lifted his lip into a half smile, half snarl. "If he minded his own business, he wouldn't have petunias!"

"True."

Like a cat pouncing, he abruptly switched topics. "You still gonna train Tara?"

"No. Is she with you?"

He hunched as if I had hit him with a stick. At any moment, he might wail loud enough to make the stray cat proud. "It wasn't her fault! She just wanted to watch. You can't throw her out 'cause of that!"

"Is she okay? Where is she?"

"She's at my place."

"I'm going to call White Feather and tell him."

Lynx didn't protest. I left White Feather a message on his cell. "Lynx will drive her home," I said into the phone.

As soon as I hung up, Lynx said, "Listen--"

"No deals." I held up a hand to stop the flow of his words. Sadly, I didn't have the heart to punish him too much, even though he deserved it. "I've found someone else to train her."

Lynx said quietly, "But you the best."

"Actually Lynx, I'm not the best for this." He swallowed hard like he might cry. "Lynx, this incident was not only your fault. If you're completely honest, it wasn't your idea to go traipsing around after me."

"I shouldn't have done it."

"You got that right. But she should also be smarter than that. She grew up around this stuff and knows it's not a toy."

Lynx slumped toward the door. He was not light on his feet, nor was he quick.

"Stop back with her if she gets ungrounded anytime this year. I do have a very good teacher picked out."

He stopped, but didn't face me. After a long second, the door snicked quietly behind him. His feet dragged across the porch.

The truth was, I wasn't the best teacher for Tara. My withholding training wasn't punishment. Besides, it would be a relief to have someone else help—someone who had more experience with her kind of magic—and someone who had more experience with teenagers.

I collapsed in a chair and held my now very-much aching head. There was a lot to be done. I needed to look up recent burglaries to find out more about the first witch who had been hospitalized. I should visit Martin and get more details about what happened to him. I still didn't have a wind spell, which meant I was no closer to understanding what was threatening White Feather. On top of all that, I needed to verify that Tara's new teacher was willing to take on a pupil.

It was a very bad idea to visit my mother with my face looking abused, but not only was I hungry, I wanted sympathy, maybe a thousand hugs or so and some comfort food.

Just before I left, White Feather called me back. "She can't be at Lynx's apartment. Gordon has had a car there all night!"

I waited while White Feather processed his own statement. Lynx wasn't the type to keep an apartment without several ways in and out. He also didn't need light to get around, and thieving in the night was his forte.

"You better hurry," I said. "I'm not sure she'll heed my advice and head home."

White Feather grumbled a threat alongside several more curses.

"I'm sure she returns your love and possibly the threats," I teased, glad she was his sister and not mine. I had already done my share of rescues, babysitting and worrying where sisters were concerned. I sympathized greatly, but was relieved that in this case my presence wouldn't help.

Chapter 29

Herb magic was something I understood well and used often. Healing magic was a huge step beyond herbs, a step that my talent didn't bridge. I could mix and match with the best of them, but true healing magic came not just from the herbs, but from the healer. It was a soul magic. My mother had a talent for it. She prepared recipes that relieved stress, high blood pressure and an assortment of other ills.

Healing magic was an old, magnificent magic. I lacked the patience required to understand it, not having enough for even the recipe part. While Mom's red chile posole cured most colds, mine was more likely to cause stomach upset.

Mom was thrilled to see me, even after she found out I intended an experiment to verify that the magic in the kitchen was the same as I had witnessed with Tara. Before we could possibly think about starting, she fed me a warm, gooey burrito with all the trimmings. She fussed over my stitches and my face; she scolded, worried and was my mother. She touched my forehead, checking for a fever. Under her cool hand, my headache disappeared. Sure, it might have been the burrito, but not likely.

"You need to take those stitches out after seven days. Yes, I know they are the dissolving ones, but you listen to your mother and take them out."

"Okay."

She gently rubbed a light balm on my arm. The itching and pulling eased almost immediately. I basked in her care until she probed for more details on the guys who had attacked me.

"Religious nuts," I said. "Beat me over the head with a Bible. They tried to do the same to Mat a week ago."

"Aeeeiii, these crazy people! They must be the ones sneaking about the Gomez ranch!" My mother wrung her hands around a towel, but didn't stop puttering around the kitchen, pulling out the bowls, butter and cookie sheets necessary for my experiment.

"Sneaking? Did they break-in?" I paused mid-bite and paid more attention. When it came to news items—especially illnesses, deaths, marriages or who picked up his mail and at what time, she and her friends were more accurate than any news source. The only problem was that when I asked questions, she had fifty of her own.

"Yes, yes, they scared the horses into a stampede. That's how Gomez fell and ended up in the hospital. It must have been drug addicts or," she paused and changed direction, "crazy lunatics who know nothing about religion!"

"Tony!" Gomez was as common as the anglo name "Smith," but there was only one who was a horse whisperer. Patrick had said something about horses when he mentioned one of the witches who had been hospitalized.

"Of course Tony. Your uncles and father had to take care of the horses while he was in the hospital." Mother gave me Tony's lineage, along with other people he knew and the name of his high school sweetheart, whom he had married.

"Was it two guys who attacked him?"

"At least two. They could have killed his horses. That's how Tony got hurt. The horses were trying to protect him, even though he ordered them away." She whisked my empty plate to the sink and shoved a bowl with butter and sugar under my hands. "You mix."

Dutifully, I mashed the butter and sugar. Even though Mom was distressed, there was magic in the kitchen. In fact, maybe because she was distressed, it resembled Tara's aura even more. I told her so.

"This world, it is going back to the witch hunts from your grandfather's time. It's not safe to be a witch. I don't know if I can help this friend of yours," she fretted. "Tony, he just wants to take care of his animals. Then suddenly these people come after him. They had to use magic too because Tony has the sight. How else could they get through his defenses?"

I wasn't certain how much my mother knew and how much had grown from gossip. The bible thumpers wouldn't have used magic.

Mom started her own bowl of cookies, explaining the ingredients as she added them. "Now you do the same with yours. Make sure the butter is creamed all the way before adding the eggs."

We cooked. I thoroughly enjoyed the change of pace and being home in her tiny kitchen. All the old adobes had tiny everything. The ceilings were low, the doorways rounded. The cupboard doors didn't close all the way because the wood had warped. The wallpaper that had been a bad idea had finally been replaced with fresh plaster over the adobe.

I sighed, content. We even talked a bit about White Feather, but he was too fresh a find for me to say much other than to admit he existed and was special.

Talking about him was distracting or maybe I wasn't skilled enough for the delicate touch required of healing cookie dough. My effort was taking on the properties of heavy clay.

"No, no, what are you doing?" Mom pushed me away from the dough. "You'll ruin it handling it that way."

"The magic or the cookies?"

"Fold. You have to fold. Otherwise you kill the ingredients. It's like yeast." She glared at me because the last time we baked with yeast, I had definitely killed it.

She reminded me of my grandmother, as though Gram were superimposed on top of her. Mom cooked differently, but they both did it instinctively. They both...flowed.

"You have to mix with your heart."

I peered around her shoulder. While she rolled, she hummed, but she kept an eye on me. Gram had been like that too. She'd catch me spying, as I waited for an opportune moment to steal cookie dough. She'd pretend to curse me with the evil eye, and then I'd be lost to giggles, giving her a chance to finish the cookies unimpeded.

I dusted flour across a different part of the counter top. "What do you think about?"

Mom shrugged. "You. Your father. Whomever I am baking for. Springtime. Christmas."

Just like a spell. Even more importantly, as we cooked and talked, the feeling in the entire kitchen changed from angst to...Mom. Just Mom; comfortable, happy, doing what she did best. "You add your essence. Just like my spells." I poked at the flour. "But how do I incorporate my essence? And how to recognize if Tara has any healing essence?"

Mom laughed.

"If I put my essence in, will the cookies end up tasting like Mother Earth—silver or dirt? Which ingredients have healing magic?"

Mom shrugged, sprinkling sugar on the cookies about to go in the oven. "Ingredients are nutrients, they give life. But it depends if you are healing the spirit, the mind or the body."

"Cookies...that must be spirit."

"Definitely." She slid the tray in the oven. My mouth watered. It was easier for me to be analytical rather than spiritual when devising spells. I preferred concentrating on how the baking soda helped the dough rise, rather than about how my sister Kas might react when she ate my cookies. I chuckled. She'd probably spit them out.

My tray of cookies went in after Mom's, which gave me ample opportunity to eat hers. I felt so much better than when I first arrived.

Mom packaged all my cookies to take home, but hers were the important ones. They were magic.

Chapter 30

On the way home, I dropped by the hospital to visit Martin. Not surprisingly, he had checked himself out. That is to say, he had disappeared in the middle of the night, and the nurse had no idea of his whereabouts. I considered asking Patrick if he knew when and where Martin had gone, but surely dealing with a vamp twice in one week was asking too much.

Even after arriving home, I was still pleasantly full and content. A nap would suit me fine, but it was barely noon and there were tasks awaiting my attention.

I reloaded my backpack with my normal cache of spells and then finished the dream catcher. The heliotrope from Martin had been purified, but it knew the touch of the ill wind so I included it in the design. It would be adept at recognizing such a wind and provide a warning of its presence.

Using the heliotrope was a great idea, but now I needed more and preferably samples that had never been used or touched by an ill wind. That meant shopping, and shopping meant a new place, which meant going incognito.

Before I had a chance to change, White Feather drove up. To my dismay, Tara was with him.

Even though it had probably been a few hours since he found her, she hadn't calmed down. When I opened the door, her face was red under her makeup, and her chin and mouth were set in mutiny. She stomped inside the entry and declared, "I came by to tell you that I don't need your help."

White Feather clamped a heavy hand down on her shoulder.

I ignored him for the moment. "I agree. You're better off with someone whose talents are similar to your own."

"You're just like everyone else! You don't want any real help. You never wanted me along!"

"That's certainly true." I was finished playing nice. "I spent the entire day in the hospital because of your unscheduled appearance. I'm not really keen on it happening again."

White Feather interrupted. "She came by to apologize."

My eyebrows shot up. "I missed that part."

"So did I." He eyed Tara critically. "Restoring your privileges isn't happening anytime soon at this rate."

"Don't bother," I said. "It wouldn't be sincere anyway."

White Feather turned his ire in my direction. I'd do just about anything for him, but backing down from a fight was not in my nature. His sister was the one in the wrong, and she could set her witching fork to "find happiness elsewhere" as far as I was concerned.

"You look like you're feeling better," White Feather said to break the growing silence.

"Thanks. I was on my way out to buy some heliotrope." It would be nice if he could come along, but Tara was standing there in all her glorious, misplaced fury.

"She's grounded," White Feather reported. "No running around without supervision."

It was pretty obvious that he was torn. Several suggestions burned the tip of my tongue; dropping her at home being the most polite, but if White Feather had the option of leaving her there, he wouldn't have dragged her here.

"I'd like to go with you," White Feather said, his face resigned and full of regret.

Tara was no dummy; she didn't waste the possible opening. "I'm really sorry you got hurt. I never should have followed you. It was a terrible thing to do." She aimed for earnest but fell flat into smug and manipulating. Her lips contorted as she weighed saying more.

The girl was counting on me to convince White Feather to dump her. "Well, why don't you and Tara join me?" I suggested instead.

Tara's face froze and the rage ratcheted back up. Yup. She figured White Feather would jump at an opportunity to park her somewhere. For her, that equated to a win. She would be in control of her fate and promptly disobey whatever orders she had been given.

I smiled at White Feather. "Heliotrope is a wind stone, believe it or not. Maybe you can help me learn to use it." Smashing her plans, petty as it was, made my heart sing with glee. Of course, I was older and had a sister of my own so I was much, much more practiced at keeping my smugness hidden. "Let me grab my backpack."

I hurried to the lab, conveniently forgetting that revenge was never simple, and the happier you were before taking revenge, the harder the fall.

Chapter 31

White Feather waited more patiently than Tara, but our dallying meant more trouble. Lynx knocked before I had done more than pick up my backpack.

After answering the door, I briefly considered running away, but he was blocking the exit.

Lynx blurted out, "I didn't know the rules or I would have brought her home last night. Either way, she needs to be trained by the best or it's a waste of time. Adriel's the best. But you gotta talk her into it."

The plea and half apology threw White Feather. Unlike Tara, Lynx knew a thing or two about business, and he understood focusing on the bottom line. Or in this case, focusing on the one thing he wanted. If only he'd had his priorities straight a few mistakes ago.

The tension in the air was palpable.

Instinctively I groped for Mom's cookies on the bar. They represented comfort, not stress. It was a mistake. Now I had to share. "Lynx, she will train with the best--the best for her. I'm not sure of Tara's talent, but I've sensed it, and even if the magics aren't the same, Mom will be better at recognizing her inherent strengths."

Tara didn't bother to look up from her fingernails.

"Mom is more organized than I am so she'll meet with you twice weekly, Tuesdays and Saturdays."

Lynx's ears pointed straight up. "Whoa. This is big."

I offered White Feather a cookie and gave one to Lynx. If I allowed Lynx to help himself, he'd devour the whole bag. "What is big?"

Lynx ignored me in favor of Tara. "She must have sensed something special to send you to her family. Not even *I* have met her family. You're gonna be some important witch."

I coughed cookie crumbs. Since when was meeting my family important? "Or she will be a nice ordinary witch like me, making a respectable living." I did not want Tara, or Lynx for that matter, to start building towers into a dangerous sky.

Lynx looked at me, his round eyes carrying more awe than when I did my best spells. "Yeah, ordinary." He laughed his silent laugh then, chuckling so hard he bent over, still soundless.

"Can I meet her now?" Tara asked.

Lynx straightened immediately. "I can take her."

"You're grounded," came the pronouncement from White Feather.

"I'll have her home by whatever time she's supposed to be there," Lynx said respectfully. He didn't drop his eyes either. "I didn't know about the rules before. I never had to be home at night." He paused and then added, "Or in the day."

"She knows the rules." White Feather chomped down hard on his cookie.

"We could go straight over there," Tara said. "It's training, so it isn't like a date. And I know to be home by nine. I promise, I learned my lesson, and I'll be there."

"Could we get food before we go or do we have to go straight there?" Lynx wanted to know. "Otherwise, I gotta eat here."

I shook my head. "Lynx, you never eat before visiting my mother. She'll have more food than you've ever seen in your whole life. It'll be the best food you've ever eaten too. She made these cookies."

His face lit up either because of the possible food or because he sensed an opening to take Tara there. "But she doesn't know we're coming. We'd have to call first and even then, how's she gonna have enough food ahead of time?"

I smiled and put my finger by my nose; the silly witching signal. "Mom always knows stuff like that Lynx. Trust me."

His eyes widened briefly. "Big. This is big. That's one useful skill."

I laughed. It was more useful for him than for my mother, and witch or no, she was always prepared for company. My smile faded when White Feather said, "I'll take you." His only concession was to add, "You too, Lynx. That way she'll know all the potential problems she is dealing with."

Tara snorted and put forth a last-ditch effort. "We'll go directly over there. It isn't like we won't be supervised." She made little quote marks with her fingers when she said "supervised."

White Feather was having none of it. "You'll be supervised because I'll take you."

My stomach clenched. White Feather had to meet my mother eventually. I had no particular plan, and in fact had been studiously avoiding any planning.

Well, since it was bound to happen sooner or later, it might as well be now. "Okay. Drop them off, pick them up, however you want to handle it."

He smiled. "What about you?"

I shook my head. "Nope. I have work to do. You are on your own."

He frowned. "Abandoned."

"No, not really." I was not about to introduce White Feather to my mother while Tara and Lynx were present. There were some tortures too awful to even consider. My mother knew about White Feather. I had as much as admitted what he meant to me, but I refused to stand there in front of two teenagers and endure the angst of bringing a man, the most important man of my entire life, home.

White Feather considered his options. Then he grinned.

I chewed another cookie, almost meeting his eyes. Let him charm Mom without me there to blush and be anxious. Let Mom test him without me watching in agony.

Lynx bolted. "Let's go, then."

Tara wasted no time speeding out behind him.

"You sure you don't want to join us?" White Feather lingered.

"I'm positive I don't want to be there under these circumstances. Any other time, not a problem."

He laughed. "Okay."

He didn't have to be so pleased with himself. A fluttering panic hit for a second when I imagined him asking Mom about my childhood. Or my magic. Or my...oh hell. It didn't matter. I had nothing to hide.

I followed the unlikely trio outside. Tara and Lynx whispered to each other on the side of the porch. White Feather gave me a quick kiss and whispered, "Thanks."

What was he was thanking me for? He couldn't possibly be as thrilled with the prospect of meeting my mother as Lynx seemed to be.

White Feather snorted in disgust at the two lovebirds. Well, no doubt he was glad to have help--any help--in dealing with Tara.

"Come on," he said to them.

Tara hurried off the porch, probably fearing he would change his mind.

Before Lynx followed, I grabbed his arm. Very quietly I said, "No more screw ups. This stuff is serious. You know more than she does. Quit letting her lead."

He tugged his arm away, but then did something he had never done before. He set two of his fingers against my wrist. It had to be uncomfortable because he was holding my wrist right above my silver bracelet. "Three strikes I'm out. You got my word. You and White Feather can count on me. I'll guard her better'n anything."

With a single hop, he joined Tara and White Feather in the driveway.

I closed my eyes. I had nothing to be worried about.

Yeah, right.

Chapter 32

I tarried on the porch, fidgeting. I should have gone with them. Then again...I sighed. Extra heliotrope wouldn't materialize on its own.

Time to don a disguise and get to work. Keeping my identity and reputation low-key was part of my mantra. Normally an illusion spell would be my first choice, but browsing in a magic store with any active spell was a good way to attract attention from an astute proprietor.

Wigs had created a variety of problems for me in the past, so my latest disguise substituted white locks of hair that clipped under my own black. The three streaks of platinum not only marked me as a groupie, they were striking enough to be memorable.

I also inserted plain brown contacts, because the greenish streak in my left eye was too unique a marker. If Charms turned out to be a groupie haven, that sort of flaw in my eye would get me noticed.

Jeans were the only pair of clean pants available. In fact, with all the pants I had ruined lately, it might be the only pair I still owned. My backpack could be too easily remembered, so I pocketed one illusion spell that would shift my appearance if things got out of hand. Distraction spells were standard fare, but lately it seemed everyone had real firepower except me. I selected a nettle and habanero spell in addition to the usual firecracker-type.

My flying spell needed serious improvement, as in starting over from scratch, but I packed a copy in my sneakers anyway. Even though the spell was more likely to rocket me into a tree or leave me free-floating like a helium balloon on the way to the moon, I wasn't leaving it behind, not with David the Frog and his buddy still at large. "Never enough time," I mumbled.

I doubled-checked the address before heading out.

Charms, like all shops open for tourist business, identified itself on the internet as near the plaza. Actual plaza space was prohibitively expensive, so Charms was a good half mile off the plaza and wouldn't get random tourist business unless it was from a drunk wandering through alleys.

The glass windows were covered with a dark, modern anti-glare coating, but it did little to disguise the age of the weathered building. A blue screen door was propped open permanently because the decayed wooden frame was half off its hinges.

"Charms" was painted in gold block lettering on the window of the door. Various native Indian charms, including kokopelli, a lizard, and a kachina were stenciled across the shop windows.

It looked like a tourist trap, albeit off the beaten path. I went in anyway.

Mat's shop was always well-lit. She didn't burn incense because it interfered with her personal perfume concoction. Charms was more typical of a witchery shop; the guy probably had the lowest light bill in Santa Fe, and the place smelled like cinnamon, an herb known for attracting business.

Trying not to sneeze, I wandered around the outer shelves. Several jars were marked with a cross and skull, but it was too dark to read any actual instructions.

"May I help you?" The question came from a dark lump sitting behind the jewelry case counter all the way at the back.

"Just looking." There was no point in a conversation unless the merchandise was worth asking about. The too-typical arrangement of cellophane wrapped incense blocks wasn't a great harbinger. A rack of books with unreadable titles had solar systems on the front covers. On the same rack there were two Ouija boards for sale.

I hated and feared the real thing, but these particular ones were about as magical as the cardboard packaging. Lots of glitter and shiny promises, but no aura of anything ancient, magical or lethal.

Closer to the counter now, I snuck a glance at the young guy seated on a tilted stool with one sneaker balancing against the counter. He was vaguely familiar, but maybe it was because there was nothing particularly striking about him.

He hadn't shaved in a day or so, but it was a cultivated look. He had obviously showered, combed his longish dark hair and bothered to put on clean clothes before work. The only magical thing about him was the way his black t-shirt and jeans helped him blend into the dark wall behind him.

The midnight blue wall darkened to black near the top. The solar system was a splash of colors including a cloudy, distant Milky Way and planets in bright shades; red for Mars, a pearl iridescence for Venus, and Saturn with rings in several shades of gold.

The guy kept his hands folded across his stomach in a half-asleep, bored manner. I wasn't sure if he was the hired help or the owner.

"Did you draw the solar system?" I asked.

"Yeah. You like it? I can do murals of all kinds, indoors or out."

"Ah, an art student?" There were many in Santa Fe; some in school, some here for the laid-back atmosphere. Too many of them were waiting to be discovered. At least he was working.

"Yeah. That's why the shop has funny hours."

"Oh." If he controlled the hours, he probably owned the shop, but he barely looked twenty. Maybe a parent was helping foot the bills. Inconsistent funding would explain the rather odd assortment of merchandise, half of which looked like it might have been picked up at a Dollar Tree Halloween clearance table.

"Looking for something in particular?" he asked.

"Just browsing for a gift for a friend."

The single bulb over the counter barely illuminated the cash register. The glass case held the most interesting items, including several religious objects. A beautifully crafted Star of David rested next to an exquisite Native American wedding vase. There were two sets of Buddha beads and several rosaries made from natural stone.

I didn't recognize the significance of several items, including a conch shell with carved designs and bells of various shapes and sizes. Some of the craftsmanship was quite good and likely local. Some was commercial and useless. It was difficult to build up a valid inventory of diverse magical items unless the proprietor had Matilda's contacts. This guy obviously didn't.

At the end of the counter, there were several cleaned pieces of quartz; probably local. The rocks helped me finally place the guy. He was the hiker I had studied so carefully when I was experimenting at Tent Rock a few days ago. If he collected his own stones for sale, that showed genuine interest and attention to craft.

Martin's probable contributions were next to the quartz. This was another area in which the proprietor had excelled. Many of the stones were carved into pendulums and lined up according to their appropriate astrological month.

Carefully honed pendulums retained and enhanced the properties of the stones. They were usually spelled to promote healing, hypnotism or to dispel bad spirits. Of course, there was no way to tell if these pendulums had been properly spelled.

The heliotrope was right where it belonged, lined up under March. It was polished and possibly treated to provide shine and a better color. Not helpful.

"If you need something specific, I can get just about anything."

I shook my head. "Not really. Just browsing."

"Looks like you've protected yourself well." He came over and stood on the other side of the counter from me. "That's nice turquoise on your bracelet."

Rather than verify it one way or the other, I ignored the statement.

He pressed a switch on the side of the counter. Lights brightened the display instantly. "There you go."

From his sudden motivation, it was obvious he had more at stake at this end of the counter. "You do these designs yourself?"

He nodded.

"They're impressive." A good jeweler created a balanced shape using the existing edges of the original stone. From the loosely carved hearts, rounds, and diamond shapes, he wasn't completely blind to what the natural stone had to offer.

I sniffled a bit, fighting another urge to sneeze. The sweet smell in the air reminded me of something, but other than the cinnamon, I couldn't place the scent. Truly I hated incense, a disadvantage for a witch. There were powers in smells.

Ah well, there was no point in sticking around. Even if he hadn't carved the bloodstone, he had polished it. I wanted my own stone completely unaltered.

"I'm leaning toward a chile recipe book." When he started to speak I added, "You know, something that says New Mexico. These rocks, you can buy them anywhere."

He stiffened. "I can design something specific. Maybe something in the shape of New Mexico?"

I hadn't meant to insult the guy; I was just doing my best tourist impression. "I don't need anything that special."

"Take one of my cards in case you change your mind. I'm Jack. You look like you've got great taste in jewelry."

I accepted the eagerly proffered card. Predictably, it was black. "Thanks." I read the name. "Jack." Seeing the middle initial "O" and the last name I nearly groaned aloud. "Lantern? You're kidding, right?"

He shrugged sheepishly. "Well, my real name is too long and no one can pronounce it. It's Indian. This way they remember, and it reminds them of stuff I sell."

"Uh-huh." He seemed like a nice kid, even handsome behind the locks of hair hanging in his face. The name was over-the-top, but he'd figure that out in good time. "You're right, I won't forget it." I stashed the card in my back pocket and scooted around the racks.

Half-blinded from looking down at the brightly lit display case, the sunlight outside beckoned me like a light at the end of a tunnel.

Chapter 33

Since untainted and unused bloodstone was unavailable, Mat's stone was the next best choice. Her aura would definitely be on it, but at least she was a trusted entity.

The guy at Charms was friendly and eager, but he had dabbler written all over him. No telling what he might have tried and what residue he had left behind on the stones.

Mat wasn't expecting me, but when I explained that Charms' inventory wasn't up to snuff, she was more than happy to help.

"Surprised the guy even had the shop open. I've been by a couple of times, and it was closed. You want quality stuff and service, you have to patronize the right places." She gave a theatrical sniff.

"He isn't open regular hours because he's in school. Seemed like a nice enough guy."

"He caters to drunk students willing to part with their money on Friday nights, which is why he's open until midnight on the weekends and can't be bothered to open much during the week like a quality shop." She locked the front door as she always did when she intended to access her safe. "Come on back. I actually have a couple of extra bloodstones now because Martin stopped in."

"Ah." I wasn't surprised.

"He mentioned they might be tainted so he gifted them to me. Said he couldn't sell them anymore. If I gift them to you, it would be double protection, but I know how you are about taint. I'm surprised you'll even consider using mine." She eyed me, her curiosity piqued.

Dragging her into the mess wasn't fair.

She read the hesitation on my face. With a shrug, she unlocked the safe and handed me the heliotrope.

I rubbed my thumb over it. It smelled like Matilda and would even after I left her shop. There was no humming or breeze, but the windows were closed.

"Let me give it to you," she offered. "Along with one from Martin. Between the two of them, you should be able to concoct great magic."

I grimaced. "I'm not very good at accepting gifts."

She giggled. "I know. You'll keep score and plan to pay me back because that's the way you are. And that can negate the whole gifting thing."

"I didn't have trouble taking Martin's," I lied. I had accepted the gift, but worried about it constantly since then.

"Martin isn't your friend, and the stone wasn't any good to him." She frowned and headed to the front to unlock the shop. "Do you just want mine?"

"Actually, I think I would like one of his."

She pivoted with a dancer's grace on one foot. "You're kidding, right?"

"No, I'm not. There's a chance that whatever tainted it will be more attracted to it than to your stone."

She put her hands on her hips and planted her feet. "Just what is going on? Did you call something by mistake when you tried the spell I showed you?" Her blue eyes goggled. "Ohmygosh, are you okay?"

"No, no, I didn't call a mistake. Whatever it is was already out there."

"Adriel!" She rushed over and peered at me closely.

Before she panicked further, I provided enough detail to convince her not to call the wind any time soon. "Whatever it is, it's dangerous."

"Why are you worried about *me?* You're the one about to walk out of here with the stones! You're not planning to summon this thing?"

"Not unless it shows up. Even then, I'd only be calling it away from White Feather. I haven't figured out any other kind of spell to fight it."

She chewed her lip, but released my shoulders. "Hmm. Opposite of wind. Sand paintings you say?" She turned in another graceful circle, slowly perusing the shelves of her shop. "Let me give this some thought."

"I can use ideas. I'm planning to visit Granny Ruth and see if she has any inside knowledge of sand paintings. Learning about a single sand painting takes days, and that would only cover one particular painting. You know how spells are. There are derivatives, techniques, layers and variations. Learning about sand art properly would take years."

"Isn't that the way with all expertise?"

"I definitely need more than Cliff notes. So does whoever tried to use a painting to coerce or keep White Feather home. Claire was either lazy or plain stupid."

Mat frowned. "Dealing with irresponsible idiots who believe in magic can actually be a lot worse than the ones who don't believe in magic at all."

I agreed. "Do you think Sarah would have tried performing sand paintings for clients?"

"The spells Sarah sold were all about atmosphere and aromatherapy. That type of thing ranges from quick party fun for cheaper thrills to very expensive healing potions. Sarah generally went after discerning clients who wanted something that touched their spirits. She was good at it, and I never saw her abuse power or seek power she didn't have."

"There was a sand painting at Sarah's cabin. And I know Claire gave one to White Feather." I described the melted sand around the cabin.

"You think this Claire person is using sand paintings to bind a wind witch? If so, she mistook Sarah for being more powerful than she was."

I shifted uncomfortably. "Worse than that. I don't think she bound Sarah to leech her power. I think Claire offered Sarah to the spirits from the west in exchange for some power of her own. "

Mat gasped. "Binding would definitely have been necessary to force Sarah to be a part of that kind of ceremony."

"Yeah. And if that's what Claire was doing, what came through?"

Mat shrugged her shoulders and shook her head.

That was the crux of the problem. No one had any good answers.

Chapter 34

One block outside Mat's shop my head started to overheat and itch. The locks of white hair were fine inside, but outside in the sun their straw-like construction was as irritating as a wig.

Since removing them in public would negate the disguise, I decided to duck back inside her shop, but before I could reverse my progress, David the Frog waved at me from across the street.

A scan for exits brought more bad news. Frog's buddy, Blondie, was already on my side of the street and narrowing the distance between us quickly.

"Mayan Curses." The disguise was only a prop to throw someone off who didn't know me. It wasn't likely to fool Frog and Friend. Hoping whatever spell Mat now had on her door would stall them, I turned tail and ran, dodging into the open plaza.

The footsteps behind me definitely picked up the pace, but it didn't matter too much. I crushed the illusion spell in my pocket. The spell was similar to that of heat rising in the distance. The shimmer would blur my features, letting the human eye fill in the gaps. The rose scent was spelled to encourage people's minds to drift to a pleasant memory rather than pay attention to my face.

Once around the corner, I stepped into the first shop that wasn't blocked by aimless tourists. The Frog or his buddy might follow me in, but they wouldn't recognize me.

I browsed the t-shirts and mugs without touching anything. If I had to run, holding merchandise would slow me down.

My heart slowed and my worry eased, but when the door opened again, the enemy walked in.

It hadn't taken them very long. I had been far enough ahead that they couldn't have seen me enter this place. Shouldn't one of them be searching in the next shop? Or watching the street?

Both of them blocked the doorway, scouring the shop.

Nervous, I sidled closer to another female shopper. She was plumper and shorter than either of my disguises.

The two goons conferred quietly.

There weren't enough people in the shop for my comfort. The clerk was in a middle island, surrounded by a rectangular jewelry counter. Shelves lined the outside walls. A teenager picked along the jewelry counter and a middle-aged guy, probably the teenager's father, waited close to the doorway.

The entrance was rather crowded with three men loitering by the only opening.

David the Frog caught me looking his way. He smiled. His attempt at avuncular friendliness was akin to a lizard drooling. My lip curled with distaste, but he continued to ogle me. Maybe my glare was like a love call to amphibian-people.

He checked his wristwatch and then quickly sought me out again. He couldn't identify me in my disguise, so there was no way he was indicating that he had all day to catch me, but that's the way it felt.

He whispered to Blondie and strode my way.

"Mayan and Aztec bloodbath rituals in a handbasket." I did not want to end up in the hospital again, not the front part and not the basement part where Patrick the vamp could get his...anything in me.

My hands went to my pockets. I had choices. Smoke and noise might cause enough confusion to clear the shop and give me a chance to escape.

Yeah. Maybe.

David the Frog made it halfway to my position before I wandered along the other side of the jewelry counter. I was now sandwiched between the two of them.

I palmed the nettle spell. Like a camera flash, after the membrane was broken it would take a few seconds for the charge to build up. My timing had to be perfect.

The door was two yards away. I prepared to hit the door running.

Blondie solved the problem of timing. He lunged and swallowed my upper arm with his meaty fingers. "It's been ages!" His smug smile pretended we were old friends.

"Oh!" I tripped on purpose and slapped my hand against his chest, snapping the membrane on the spell. David the Frog was closing in fast behind me. I stuffed the packet inside Blondie's front pocket. The spell crackled as chemicals reacted.

Fifteen seconds to get away.

I kicked Blondie in the shins. At the same time, I pried his thumb away and yanked my arm free.

Had the spell been a camera flash or strobe light, there would have been a nice bright light, but there was only nettle and electricity that finally snapped free right next to his skin. The magically enhanced herbs exploded, sending sparks and stinging nettle mixed with habanero pepper juice deep into his chest.

Blondie's mouth hung open, soundless for scant seconds before he screamed.

I bolted out the door, leaving him frantically batting at his shirt pocket.

David the Frog lurched at me with wide-open arms. I ducked, cursing the fact that the nettle spell wasn't lethal. Blondie was probably scared silly and from his screams, he was at least smoldering enough to worry. After the burning subsided, he'd go into an itching frenzy from the nettle.

Instead of calling an ambulance, David chased me, rudely shoving people aside as he struggled to keep me in sight. The illusion spell interfered with his ability to identify me even though running made me the obvious target.

I hugged the wall, jumped behind a group and lost myself in the crowd for two or three steps. When David plowed back into view, he had gained on me.

He stuck his arm out and checked his watch while he ran. I hoped he was seriously late for something he couldn't miss.

Before he caught sight of me again, a mass of people emerged from a shop. I zigzagged around them, but he slammed right into them.

Blondie, a block away, still screamed like a stuck pig. Frog-buddy was the only person besides me who wasn't stopped along the sidewalks to gape at the crazy man slapping his shirt.

Half-jogging, half walking, I yanked at my white locks. Illusion spell or not, another quick change of appearance wouldn't hurt.

At the end of the plaza block, I crushed another packet, threw it behind me as far as possible and sped away. Smoke billowed, covering my tracks.

Breathing hard, I ran straight into the welcoming doors of St. Francis Cathedral.

Chapter 35

Once inside, I stashed the white locks of hair in my pocket. The church was blissfully quiet, a huge contrast from the chaos outside. My panting punctuated the air as I knelt in a pew. The cool air felt as though it was channeled directly from the earth, seeping inside to breathe life into anyone who visited.

I itched to apply an illusion spell and leave a whole different person, but luckily the spell was spent. Performing a spell on sacred grounds was suicidal. I had tried it once and ended up with a bloody scalp and a headache for a week. A church was better protection than adobe. If holy ground didn't outright prevent a spell it certainly changed the outcome.

Though the cathedral emanated peace and was safe from magic, there was nothing stopping my enemies from coming in after me, beating me to a pulp and leaving me for dead. The good news was that the church had three exits on the south side of the building. If the nut cases came in the back, out the side I would go.

Lately, it seemed every time I wore a disguise, I ended up in church in some kind of trouble. Maybe a rinse-off hair dye would be safer.

I sighed. I prayed. I watched the doors.

If there was any justice in the world, anyone who entered with ill-intent would be blasted by lightning. But justice wasn't always timely, and God didn't consult my preferences all that often.

I removed my earrings and prayed through another few Hail Marys.

No enemies appeared.

"Okay." I scooted from the pew, but just before exiting, I paused, faced the altar and bowed my head. "Thanks."

The parking lot and nearby trees on the south side contained no ambush. Though it was several blocks away, I sprinted for my car.

For the first time in days, a shower was required that didn't include ruined clothing. Even better, White Feather had left a message on my answering machine. I had a date for dinner at The Owl.

Chapter 36

With Tara and Lynx busy at Mom's house, White Feather had used his free time to search for Claire. The idea of him dealing with her face-to-face was more than a little disquieting, but I'd have done the same thing in his shoes. Someone had to track her down and stop her.

He waited until we were seated in a comfortable vinyl booth at The Owl before he gave me details. "She moved. Gordon couldn't find a trace. You know, normally this would be the point where I'd start checking with my sources in the underground."

I smiled. We had met as a result of Lynx arranging a first meet for a "cop digging up information on paranormal crimes."

Of course, in this case if I'd known where Claire was, I'd have already convinced her to leave town. Permanently. She easily inspired violent thoughts. "Hire Lynx. He excels in locating desperate people, especially those dabbling in things better left alone."

"I've had about as much of Lynx as I can stand at the moment."

"Uh-oh. Did he cause trouble at Mom's?"

White Feather grinned. "Of course not. He was the model of perfection, as was Tara. And your mom wasn't buying any of it. She gave them both assignments about fifteen seconds after feeding them."

"What free labor did she manage from Lynx?" This was a magic trick I needed to learn.

"Cleaning the tops and seeds from red chile. She said something about him staying for dinner, therefore, he would want to help. She was teaching Tara how to concoct an herbal cure for acne breakouts. Tara is planning to sell it to her friends."

I wrinkled my nose. "Chamomile in amounts strong enough to kill most humans, walnut and calendula oil, right?"

"You know the spell?"

"Mom excels at it. I get requests for it, but I prefer spells that act against outside influences rather than internal body issues." I sipped my ice water, anxious to ask the more important questions about what he said and what Mom said.

Mom would call me eventually and provide the lowdown on what she thought of White Feather, but first, via her cronies, she'd run a background check on him that the FBI would envy.

Before Mom was done, she'd know the route White Feather had walked to grade school, how many days he deviated from it and whether he'd ever had so much as a traffic ticket in his life.

"I guess I should have gone with you," I finally admitted.

White Feather chuckled. "I can't believe you threw me into your family without a proper introduction."

"Aha! Mom said that, didn't she?"

"She was a bit on the flustered side."

Which had given White Feather the distinct advantage, a good place to be where my family was concerned. Had I been there, Mom would have gone into her dignified mode, inviting him into the family and then leaving him to flounder with overdone formalities—and possibly teasing me into an early grave in the meantime. "Did you compliment her on her cooking?"

"Not exactly a hardship."

"With Lynx there, though, it would be difficult to compete."

He laughed. "His reaction to the food did make my enthusiasm appear almost finicky."

"Definitely sorry I missed it." I wanted them to be friends on their own terms, not just because of me. But that sort of magic was way beyond my talents. "I'll be around when you meet Dad."

"Not taking any chances?"

"No one is good enough for Dad. You'll need someone to protect you." I smiled at his raised eyebrows. With Dad, there would be a test, and the sphinx had nothing on the challenges he invented.

Tino came over to our table, a rare thing unless he had business to discuss. "Got a guy wants a meet. You gonna be here a while or should I set it up elsewhere?"

Tino was a huge source of clients. Most of his restaurants were known to groupies as well as paranormals. The groupies thought they had access to all the cool people when in reality, Tino ran more than one place for a reason. Those of us in the approved paranormal category had special privileges in private rooms like the one we now occupied.

"Now isn't the best time for regular business," I told him.

Tino shrugged and chewed on a skewer. At well over six feet he was too large to use a mere toothpick. He usually sported at least one dangling silver earring, but tonight his ears were as naked as his shaved head. With football shoulders, he should have been intimidating, but his cool saunter and habit of "striking a pose" conveyed the illusion of just a friendly neighborhood bartender.

"Guy said to mention bloodstone. Said you'd be interested."

There was only one person right now who would use that word to gain my interest. "Martin? Martin wants to meet with me here?"

"He didn't provide his name."

"Get real." None of us used names very often, but Martin was Martin. He was like the town wino who panhandled around the bank, only in his case, he roamed the desert and made a few mad, naked dashes through town now and then. "I'll meet him. Whenever he can get here."

"Take awhile. You eat. Slow."

Tino lumbered off, dancing a little jig right before disappearing behind the bar. There was a door there to his private office and one to the kitchen. The kitchen was the dividing line between the private rooms and the more public restaurant.

Angel, the waitress, came over to take our orders. "The usual?" she asked me.

"Please."

We both looked expectantly at White Feather. He had a habit of ordering different menu items even though the green chile cheeseburger was beyond spectacular. "Green chile cheeseburger," he said.

We both exhaled, maybe a touch disappointed in his lack of creativity.

"With bacon," he added.

Angel tittered, giving him a flirtatious smile. She waved her note pad, a pad she never used. "And to drink?"

"Coke for you, water for us," he said.

Ah routine. Was there anything more comforting in life?

All two hundred very un-Angel-like pounds headed for the kitchen to drop off our orders. Her silver white hair did give off a halo effect. "You shouldn't buy her a coke. It's bad for her health."

"Who taught me the habit in the first place?"

"I can't imagine. She must have spelled you somehow." I refused to acknowledge that Angel always convinced me too.

He shook his head and changed the subject. "Tell me about this Martin guy."

I explained the basics. We rehashed whether it was more likely Martin had been hospitalized because of an ill wind or a run-in with our religious friends. "Should we hire Lynx? We need to find out more about the bible thumpers." I proceeded to tell White Feather about my close call earlier in the day.

"You don't need Lynx, you need a bodyguard."

I shrugged. "Once Lynx obtains more information for me, I have a very special spell planned just for them. Running every time they spot me isn't going to solve anything. And so long as Lynx is on the clock, we can have him ferret out Claire's hiding place too."

"I don't want Lynx involved," White Feather protested. "That automatically means Tara will be in danger."

He had a point, and it stumped me. Lynx was by far my most reliable source. Tino was great for clients, but Tino wouldn't stroll down alleyways, dig up dirt or keep tabs on religious freaks. Before I thought of an intelligent response, White Feather reached his own conclusion.

"Not involving Lynx might not keep her safe either. Will he leave her out of this if we ask?"

"He excels in secrets." I frowned. "But he's never had a girlfriend before."

"Claire's dangerous. So are those religious nuts. There's one other source I can ask first."

"Oh?"

He didn't smile. "Not my favorite informant. Lies worse than a crying crocodile, but he might know the religious freaks."

Our food came. With herculean restraint, I kept from stuffing more than one fry into my mouth at a time. Was there anything better than fresh, hot salty fries?

We were almost finished when Tino strolled in through his private door. He inclined his head and began wiping the bar.

Seconds later, Martin entered through the alley-side door, an entrance that blended so naturally with the wooden panels, it was nearly invisible. Martin, however, was not.

It wasn't possible to tell, thank God, whether he had on underwear because his very large t-shirt hung down almost to his knees. His sneakers clattered noisily on the way to our table, flopping and slapping against the tile floor. The large, colorful bag on his shoulder smacked into him with each uneven step.

When Martin finally arrived at our table, he waited awkwardly. Since he had recently been in the hospital, he didn't smell that bad, although alcohol fumes still wafted around him.

"Hello." He squinted in the dim light. "I brought you something."

Tino grabbed a free chair and plopped it down behind Martin before disappearing again without a word.

Not a speck of desert dust marred Martin's oversized shoes. The t-shirt was not new, but it too was very clean. And huge, as in Tino's size.

There was only one logical conclusion: Martin had shown up at Tino's stark naked intending to talk to me. I forced the image aside. "Heard you were in the hospital. How are you recovering?"

Martin sat down. Seated, his unconventional outfit was easier to ignore. "You heard about me? That's nice." He beamed, eyes wide and happy with a big sloppy grin. "This must be your wind fella. I'm Martin."

White Feather waited for me to signal him, but I couldn't tell him how to act. Martin was as fickle as the weather. Right now he was friendly and subdued. In five minutes he might be morose or dancing on the tables. "Yes, this is my friend. I hear you wanted to talk to me?"

Martin took his time extracting a silk-wrapped bundle from his shoulder bag. When he set it on the table, he muttered over it, but let the silk fall away.

Four lumps of stone rested on the cloth. I knew better than to touch them. "Yellow, white--" There were bits of sand in the bottom of the bundle. The fibers of the cloth were matted together in more than one spot; dangerously melted. "Red."

"The black would be charcoal, I presume?" White Feather guessed.

Martin nodded. "Found these near the rectangle patterns. It was the last pattern that sent me to the hospital. It wasn't dead yet. Hadn't finished burning when I crawled to the middle to see what was there. Bones, I think."

"What happened?"

Martin swallowed noisily. "I could sure use a beer."

"Martin, don't start."

"When you pay me, I'm getting one anyway," he said.

"Not here you won't. Too expensive. You like cheap beer, remember?"

His eyes watered. "Cheap beer." With a big sigh, he pushed a finger at the rocks. "There were smaller ones. Not all the colors were at the second rectangle. I missed the charcoal one. It was probably there, but with everything burned, I didn't notice it."

"You know what they are?" I asked.

"Took me a while to remember, but these were sitting outside the rectangle in a bark bowl just like the sand painting ceremony calls for. I collected them. There was a feather that wasn't burned. Then I noticed the wind." He squinted at White Feather. "Didn't smell right, but I can't smell much." He shifted his gaze to me. "Got myself blown all over my desert. But I went back there again after the hospital. Put these in my pack to show you."

What could I say? "Thank you, Martin."

"That wind. It knows me now. Thought I'd best carry the banner on up to Wyoming again, even though it'll be cold in the winter." His eyes watered again. "Maybe when I come back, it will be gone?"

He kept his attention riveted on the stones.

"What makes you think it will be?" I asked.

He gurgled a rough cough, but thankfully didn't spit. "You have to fix it." He reached into his bag again. This time the bundle he pulled out was soft buckskin.

"The first two rectangles didn't amount to much. There was nothing there but a few half-burned reeds, some bones. The third one," he pushed the buckskin my way with one dirty finger. "Over near Tent Rock. They're calling things best left alone; the old ones, the monsters."

If I hadn't already seen the sand paintings myself, his rambling would have been nothing more than the mad illusions of a drunk. But the sand paintings were Navajo legends done as a retelling, a plea to the spirits. The lore was about monsters, great ugly beasts and even ones not so ugly. The monsters were not friendly to the human race. According to legend, the human race would have had no place on earth had it not been for the twins—sons of father sun and changing woman. The twins traveled the world to slay the monsters and make it safe for people.

"What's in there?" I pointed a careful finger at the bundle.

"Fresh stones, the ochre from the desert. Ones not tainted. I gift them to you." He waited. I had the feeling he would wait all night and follow me home until I said the right words.

"I accept them and only them, no curse or bargain, no ill may follow."

"I wish you no ill and give it free of heart with no obligation," he said softly. "But I hope you can make use of them. The sand painters called something into the desert, but they didn't contain it. They've been practicing. They aren't done yet."

He fished out two more stones, pebbles really. "The turquoise belonged to my mother. It is protected and cannot be followed. The heliotrope is only a chip really, but you'll need gifts to attract the ones who will help." He sat quietly for a moment, fingering the turquoise stone. "The ones who could stop them are all gone now. People like your great-grandfather and my grandmother. That was when there was a council, before they came after your grandfather and his father." He peeked at me briefly. "I don't know if you can stop them. There's no council now."

My heart beat hard. "Did you know my great-grandfather?"

Martin didn't lift his head. "The right answer is no. Because no one must trace him or know where he went after he left." He handed me the turquoise stone. "She would want you to have it. For her, I gift it to you."

We repeated the gift-giving words again. When we finished, Martin said, "These stones left behind by the sand painters, it's not wise to use them. I can't give them to you."

I nodded. This was another ritual. "How much?"

"How much is the beer here?"

Surprised, I asked, "Do you really want to order a beer?"

He cackled, but softly. "It all works the same for me, good beer or cheap beer."

"It's," I slid my eyes to White Feather. "Ten dollars, I think."

Martin nodded. "That's good beer. That would buy a lot of cheap beer."

Before I could dig into my backpack, White Feather took a ten from his wallet. He added a five. "A tip."

"No obligation?" Martin blinked eagerly, but remained wary.

"No obligation."

"I don't mind obligations usually," Martin lied. "But I have to leave, you see. It's looking for me. I can't hide my smell, and the desert isn't big enough to hide me."

"No obligation."

Martin accepted the money with a gap-toothed smile. "Wheee," he sang softly. "Gonna be a good fire."

"Martin," I said hurriedly, "you might want to wait for that fire until you've hit Wyoming."

His face fell. After a short pause, he lumbered to his feet, but forgot about the shoes and nearly fell. On his way to the door, he mumbled, "Gotta feed the fire."

White Feather shook his head in disbelief. "Does he ever really go to Wyoming?"

"Usually in the summer. I don't know how he ever gets anywhere, drunk as he is all the time."

"If that thing out there really has his scent, does he have any protection?"

Watching Martin stumble out the door, I shrugged. "Only the fact that it's very hard to kill a drunk man."

We finished eating. I longed for more silk, stuff that hadn't already been half melted from exposure to whatever nastiness had nearly destroyed the rag Martin had used. He should have properly disposed of the tainted samples. There was probably some inane reason he hadn't, but I couldn't imagine what it was unless it was sheer laziness.

When I got home, the tainted samples were going straight into a glass jar filled with holy water. I'd bury that in sand until every last bit could be properly destroyed.

Chapter 37

White Feather escorted me and the bundles to the trunk of my car. He then walked me to the driver's side and gave me a kiss goodnight that made me forget my name. His wind raged underneath his skin, brushing across and right through me.

"I'm working on that," he said, pulling back. "Merging magics like we did may hide us behind earth magic for a while, but it won't keep us hidden forever."

I didn't care. His fingers caressed the back of my neck, and with the next kiss he showed how close he was to not caring either. Had we already been at his home or mine instead of a semi-dark public parking lot, caution would have been thrown to the wind; evil, good, or neutral.

He broke off the kiss, but when he whispered in my ear, it was almost as seductive. "I've developed some new techniques for hiding my wind, but I need more practice." His hands spanned my ribs, and then slid to my hips. He nuzzled my neck, while I did some nuzzling of my own.

It took me a few seconds, but I finally offered, "Do you want help? Practicing, I mean?" We were as close as we could be with clothes on, and that was enough space to make me crazy.

"Oh yeah," he laughed, nibbling the pulse at my neck and letting his lips linger there. "Definitely, and soon."

When he reluctantly peeled himself away, his eyes flashed dark forest green in the streetlight. I wanted to see the colors as his magic moved. He was so...magnificent.

"I'm going to locate Claire. I'd like to be done with this."

"No kidding."

If his house had been fully standing, I'd have followed him home. Of course, if his house had been standing, we wouldn't have these problems, and maybe we'd be holed up there and never leave.

As soon as I got home, I arranged the cactus on the porch to signal Lynx. He wasn't likely to be checking for the signal very often these days, not with Tara holding his interest. I respected that, but he was still our best bet. He had the ears of a cat, right along with the curiosity.

I called my mother to ask for Tara's cell phone number. Plus, in truth, I was dying to hear the White Feather status report. My nerves over him meeting her had settled, but like a spell, there was a ritual that needed to be completed.

Predictably, Mom ignored my request for Tara's number. "What a *nice* young man you've found!"

"Nice" was promising. That meant initial checks showed he was not a known murderer or associated with one. Of course, I knew that already, but it was a good idea for Mom to know these things also. "Yes, he's pretty cool, isn't he?"

Mom giggled. "When do you intend to introduce him to your father?"

"Sometime this century."

She laughed again. "He didn't mean to set your last boyfriend's shirt on fire. It was an accident!"

"Uh-huh, maybe." The boyfriend in question had made the mistake of talking up his supposed abilities. Dad was a rather passionate and protective sort; the hot blood of Spaniards ran through him, quite literally. Dad had either decided to shut the ex-boyfriend up or test his worthiness. Either way, it had not ended well.

"Did Tara give you her phone number?"

"White Feather is a good man to take care of his sister like this. He is more patient with Tara than you ever were with Kas."

"But I offered to teach Kas anything she wanted to know!"

"Yes, but Tara has more attitude than Kas. If Kas had acted like Tara, you might have started her on fire."

"I don't have an affinity for fire."

"I know, and Kas never wanted to learn. Tara," she sighed. "Oh, mi Dios. Tara has talent. But she will burn up inside if she doesn't learn how to give."

"She's too defensive," I agreed. "Instead of giving things an honest try, she blocks herself."

"Magic can't blossom with all that fear of failure. She has no respect for herself or the craft."

Well, at least Mom had identified the problem. Fixing it was another story. "I need to find Lynx. Did either of them leave you a number?"

"Of course." She finally rattled it off.

"Thanks. And thanks for teaching Tara."

"She needs to make peace with her own limitations first."

Hard to do when you were all raging defense and no offense.

When I finally reached Tara, she wouldn't tell me Lynx's number, but she promised to pass along a message. "Just have him stop by my place," I said. "Tell him I have a job for him."

Lynx was obviously with her because the next voice I heard was his. "Whatcha need?"

"I don't like doing business over the phone, but I suppose beggars can't be choosers."

"Beggars don't pay. You pay, you aren't a beggar. I'll be there. Fifteen."

He hung up before I had a chance to ask him not to bring Tara. White Feather didn't want her involved. Neither did I, but Lynx didn't do well with a lot of rules.

We needed to find Claire and shut down the sand painting ceremonies. Or make sure that she led us to whoever was helping her. Lynx was our best bet for either.

While I waited for him, I applied every mundane and magical block feasible to the bundle that Martin had left with me. With that task completed, there was just enough time left to enhance the lock on my door to make it extremely difficult for Lynx to pick it. He wasn't the real problem, however, so with great satisfaction, I set the final spell against Tara, not Lynx. It was a last-minute decision, but it would probably stump Lynx longer if he made the assumption that the spell was designed with elements specific to him.

Getting places was easier and faster for Lynx now that he had a car. Not only was he quick, but the best news was that he came alone.

He hopped up the steps and paused at the cat dish. "You shouldn't feed her on the porch. She doesn't like it. Too close to you and too much in the open."

"But she comes up on the porch on her own. I've seen her there several times."

Lynx shrugged, completely unimpressed with my logic. "Base of the juniper. She can go up or away. Porch, she doesn't like it."

He was the expert. "Okay. I'll try that."

He came in. Where some people might have paced or taken a seat, he stood almost perfectly still for a few seconds, exploring quickly with his eyes and ears. He scanned the counters in case any stray food was available, but he obviously wasn't hungry because he didn't go straight for the fridge. Maybe dating Tara encouraged him to eat on a regular basis.

"What's the job?" he asked.

"I need you to find Claire."

"And?"

"And that's it. Find a current address, occupation, whatever info you can dig up. She has taken an obvious interest in witchery. Find places she purchased spells, people who sold her stuff, whatever you can."

"You know what she looks like?" He didn't bother to hide his smirk.

"Is that suddenly a requirement for you?"

"Last name?"

I crossed my arms. "Since when do you need the obvious? Ask Tara. If she doesn't know, ask White Feather."

Lynx indulged in one of his silent laughs. "Just yankin' your chain. But don't worry. Tara already gave me the lowdown."

It bothered me that Tara knew more than I did, but there was no point in letting Lynx know. "This is serious, Lynx. She's dangerous."

"Claire ain't working by herself, not from what Tara says. I been doing some checking, because that painting Tara had, that was bad news."

"And?"

"I dunno where she got it from. But I did find some other stuff." Unable to resist, he wandered to the fridge, but looked at me for permission before helping himself to a soda. "I won't charge you neither because I owe you for screwing it up. On my own time I been lookin' into how petunia-man seemed legit when he was really out to get you."

"And any other witch he could beat up," I added.

Lynx nodded. "Thing is, I never picked up on the religious thing because the guy ain't religious. Ain't no one who knows him that says he's ever gone to any church."

"Not all religious nuts go to church."

Lynx gulped his soda before answering. "He's a guy for hire. I figured his curse came from some job he screwed up because he's not that bright. He's muscle."

"They carry Bibles," I pointed out.

"As a cover. People don't want to talk to Bible folks. The one guy keeps a switchblade in his and the other some kind of big-ass lighter. They go into any neighborhood they want, nobody talks to them and they get their job done if they don't screw it up."

"But why the sudden interest in witches?"

"Someone musta hired them to kick witches around. They ain't gonna do it without being paid. Didn't work out so well for petunia-man though." Lynx showed teeth. "If he wasn't cursed before, you made sure he is now."

It was Mat's spell, not mine, but the sentiment fit. "Any idea who hired them?"

Lynx rubbed two fingers together. "Now that is worth some green. I don't know that yet."

"Okay, find out. Maybe they've been hired by a religious group that has something against witches. And if you find Claire, don't approach her, just find her and anyone she might have hired."

"You gonna spell her?"

It was my turn to show a lot of teeth. "Since when have you ever had an interest in my spells?"

"Since never. Half now, half later."

I paid him and saw him out.

Chapter 38

Even with Lynx on the job, there was plenty to be done. I needed to master a technique for using the heliotrope with wind, I still had a cat haunting me and then there was about a hundred years worth of sand painting techniques to learn.

Luckily, in every generation there were record keepers. Grandma Ruth billed herself as a gardener, although the rumors about her insinuated less innocent pastimes. Some claimed she destroyed the entire witch's council in order to steal valuable grimoires; nicer people said she must have ended up with them because she was the last high priestess.

The only thing that was true for certain was that she owned grimoires—a lot of them. She also had greenhouses, but the greenhouses weren't primarily for plants. They were for the spiders. Weavers. Hunters. Spinners. Jumpers.

Some were poisonous. Many were colorful, some were ugly. All of them were the guardians of Grandma Ruth's ancient, magic tomes because their immunity to spells and their poison against the mundane made them ideal guardians.

No one in their right mind—or quite possibly even in a wrong mind—would bother Grandma Ruth or her grimoires without permission.

I hadn't done laundry yet, but jeans were an absolute necessity. My cleanest pair was on the top of the pile. I either had to do some laundry soon or buy more clothes.

Nestled into the low hills near Sunlit Hills in southeast Santa Fe, Granny's house was surrounded by a rustic wrought iron fence and greenhouses that stretched across the southeast and west sides of the house. The wrought iron was not for decoration. It was there because it provided a great foundation for spiders to spin across.

I opened the gate, breaking a fine line of webbing and probably announcing my arrival to Granny Ruth. It was not possible to detect all the webbing or draglines from one anchor to another so I waved one hand in front of me as I scooted along the greenhouse to the back of the house. Granny never used her front door and all her regulars knew it.

Several webs brushed against my legs, but I managed to avoid walking face-first into one.

As soon as I advanced around the side of the house, Granny stood up from a cushioned wicker chair. "Adriel! What a nice surprise." Blue eyes twinkled underneath her fluffy cloud of white hair. According to rumors, she'd gone prematurely white in her twenties. If I spent as much time as she did around spiders, I'd have gone gray early too.

Climbing the two concrete steps, I clasped Granny's weathered, sixty-five year old hand in mine. Dainty looking as a flower, she was five feet tall to my own five-six, but she was tougher than nails and just about that stubborn.

"How are you?" I asked.

"You never visit," she pouted.

"Uh-huh." Her hobby wasn't readily visible, but we both knew it was the reason she had few visitors. "And I suppose grimoire reading doesn't really count, does it?"

Granny laughed. I felt guilty about not visiting, but nobody stopped by just to chat. Like any good witch, Granny had her potions and they were powerful ones, so she retained many a client. But there was a natural avoidance spell in spiders. No other aversion spell was required, and it worked whether you were aware of it or not.

Granny waved me to a chair and retook her own, causing whatever tools she had in her apron to shift and rattle. Of course she had been tending her gardens. Only those who didn't know her would mistake her for a withered woman sitting on the porch watching life pass.

"One of these days you'll come as a buyer of my potions. They're usable for much more than healing."

"Or poisoning," I muttered defensively.

From the outside, Granny's main house wasn't much more impressive than mine, but hers was open in the center, an old Spanish style. An automatic watering system ran through all the greenhouses; fans controlled the air flow, humidity and temperature. I had never seen the very modern computer system she used to maintain a perfect atmosphere for her eight-legged friends, but I had met the son who installed it. Granny's spiders enjoyed the best technology in the world.

I told Granny about the rogue sand paintings. We also discussed Sarah, the cat, and even White Feather.

When all the information was on the table, she focused in on the largest problem. "I don't like the sound of that sand painting. If spirits from the west have made it through, we're in a heap of trouble." She tapped her fingers against the arm of her chair. "It's been a long time since anyone has been strong enough to fight something like that."

"Not since the council of witches," I blurted before I could stop myself.

Her eyes flicked to mine. Granny Ruth knew about the gossip, but it was rude of me to bring it up.

"Sorry," I apologized. "I just can't help but wonder if there are any of them left who can help us."

Granny Ruth shook her head. "They were hunted down and killed."

"Or disappeared." I was stubborn on that point for a reason.

She looked past me, into the yard. "Yes, your great-grandfather disappeared. Technically so did I, but that was allowed because I was too young to be considered much of a threat, but call it what you will, the council is gone. It was a necessary end to that era."

"Thankfully you ended up with the books. At least they weren't destroyed."

Her eyes suddenly darkened to an almost reflective black, as alien as those of any arachnid. The aura wasn't directed at me; she was somewhere in a different time, but for several seconds she was as foreign as the spiders she kept.

As fast as it appeared, the aura was gone. A shiver ran through my bones, the kind that makes you wonder if someone is walking across your grave before you're in it. "Granny Ruth--"

"You know, your great-grandfather wrote a book on magic. It included Indian lore."

"He did?" My great-grandfather was my namesake; the name I used for everyday. My memory of him was hazy, not much more than a wisp, a comforting hug.

"He promised it to the collection when it was barely started, but I've never seen it." She stood. "Let's get you to the books so you can do your research."

"I didn't know he wrote a book. I'll ask Mom."

Granny gave me a halfhearted smile. "She and I have talked about it. I'd like to see it if you find it. You remind me of him. Adriel disappeared under hurried circumstances."

That, I knew. Great-grandfather had possessed knowledge and magic. While he lived on and off the reservation, he wasn't one who believed in being tagged and registered, nor was he keen on revealing what he was up to, especially when it involved his talents.

Granny led the way inside. "The grimoires will tell you how to go about possessing a cat, but they'll conceal the truth about the damages. It's quite possible you could summon out and trap whatever demon or witch is possessing the cat."

That thought was more terrifying than any I'd had so far. "I only want to know if it is possessed. I'm not interested in possessing it or summoning anything. I'd rather kill the cat."

"Calling out anything inhabiting that cat would kill the cat anyway, but if the feline is possessed, it's as good as dead."

I shivered.

She opened the coat closet. "More important than possession, spend some time looking up binding. There won't be anything on sand paintings because Indians rely on years-long apprenticeships for teaching rather than the written word. But what you're describing sounds like it starts with a binding spell. If binding is Claire's mode of operation, she might foolishly believe that if one can bind a witch, one can summon and then bind a greater power from the west."

Because magic wasn't allowed near the grimoires, I eased out of my backpack, extracted a pair of gloves and then handed the pack to Granny.

She stored it inside the coat closet. "It'll be safe."

"Uh-huh. Just no stowaways, please."

She chuckled and opened a storm door that led inside the greenhouse. "Grab a stool. I wipe them down all the time so they are perfectly safe."

There were three saddle stools along the path through the plants. I picked up the first one by a leg and inspected the bottom. Her little hobby friends could invade in seconds, and we both knew it.

We strolled through fall vegetables in the first section and orchids and tropical plants in the second area. A banana tree grew out of a pool of water near the last door. "That thing should have died long ago," Granny said as we passed it. "No idea how it keeps surviving, but it does."

Before entering the last section, she adjusted the air flow. There was a three foot section with a revolving door but no plants. Another specialized door opened into the last chamber.

Wild flowers grew next to snapdragons, and desert grasses flourished next to blue bonnets. Flies and bugs were encouraged here because this was the most spider-filled area in the house.

Granny said, "When the books need a dose of sunlight to aid in their containment, the plants along this wall begin to wilt. If the evil seeps out, it's noticeable."

I concentrated on the plants while Granny relocated a spider web that was attached on one side to a potted plant. She rolled the pot away, keeping the web and the half-inch spider intact.

Of course, the arachnid scrambled around; that was what spiders do. I stayed well back, my lips firmly pressed together so that no squeak of horror leaked out.

"It's a silver argiope. Harmless to humans, but I like the colorful ones here, because they're impossible to miss."

"They're big." My resentment showed.

She nodded happily. "I try to convince the tarantulas to nest near the door even though the ones native to New Mexico aren't poisonous. The silly things prefer burrowing in the ground along the wall."

"How reassuring." Their lack of poison didn't mean I relished being tucked inside a six-foot hallway with them.

"Watch out for the black widow colony inside the room. They are the best line of defense against abuse of the books. Check each book for them before you handle it."

With the pot out of the way, Granny had easy access to a well-camouflaged code panel where she tapped out the combination. A plain wooden panel slid aside. Behind it, in case anyone got lucky or too curious, was the same adobe that formed the side of the greenhouse. There was a barely noticeable crack in the bricks, just enough to form a small door.

"Your gloves are leather and silk lined?"

I waved them. "Absolutely."

"I doubted you would forget."

My jeans were tucked firmly inside the top of my hiking boots. I wore no sleeves, although that could go either way. Sleeves might protect me from a spider, but no sleeves made my arms easier to see in case a spider dropped down on me.

I picked up the stool and firmed my resolve.

She pushed the door inward. It made a hissing sound. No, the hissing was from me. At her raised eyebrows, I said, "I know, I know. The daddy long-legs aren't poisonous. Do they have to *surge* like that, and does there have to be so *many?*"

"They like cellars and other dark places."

"Yeah, moonlight madness. There must be hundreds!"

She chuckled and hit the light switch wisely located on the greenhouse wall. No one would reach a hand inside that room to turn on a light.

The light bulbs were covered with cobwebs, preventing the bulbs from doing more than dispersing the worst of the shadows.

I bent to fit through the doorway. The shelves along the length of both walls towered over me, waiting. A desk and an old, stuffed leather chair were crammed into the far end of the hallway.

Who in their right mind would curl up in a chair in here?

As I crabbed inside, I forced slow measured breaths; too bad they sounded like a glorified wheeze. The giant daddy long-legs scrambled up and down one side of the wall at the end of the bookcase.

"'Ware the fiddlers and the brown spiders," Granny said softly. "Fifteen minutes. I've been in recently myself, and can't accompany you in any case."

No one was allowed to be exposed to the books for any length of time. They contained *power*, which influenced and attached to almost anything given enough time. Sunlight was exempt. And spiders.

I set the stool down and scanned titles. What should have been alphabetized, wasn't. In the dark, when no one was watching, books rearranged themselves, keeping score in an elaborate game of vying for the best space.

"Fifteen," Granny repeated as the door swung shut.

I shuddered, but it wasn't because of the spiders. The door closed on a tomb, and I was on the wrong side.

Chapter 39

Although I was more interested in cats than binding spells, Granny was too wise to ignore. "Bindings." There were several promising books, even a couple dedicated to the subject.

"Pentagrams...demons..." Probably close enough. Whatever Claire was calling could be considered a demon. Gifting the sand paintings ahead of time was a unique twist, but the rest of the spell wasn't exactly standard either.

According to the text, most demons required a blood sacrifice. Sarah had certainly paid dearly. Then again, if she had been devoured by a demon not even her ghost would survive.

"Callings, sacrifices for demons...transfer of power..." Hmm. Now that was interesting. If one coveted the power of a certain demon, but didn't want to bind the demon itself, the demon's power could be drawn out using a like power.

"Was Sarah your sacrifice in an attempt to capture the power of wind? And when she didn't yield enough power, you went after White Feather? Or did you go after them simultaneously, but Sarah proved easier to manipulate?"

The book couldn't answer that. I skipped over the spell cantations. Not only was such knowledge anathema to me, Claire was distorting a different form of magic.

The next paragraph was offset by a row of skulls and contained a very compelling warning on improperly bound demons and improperly bound power. "The demon may attach itself to a host, but if not properly bound, it will roam and feed on its own. Improperly bound power may require a new host." I flipped the page, but the section ended abruptly.

What did that mean? Did the demon destroy the first host? Or did the demon roam unharnessed in search of a worthy vessel? Was it out there hunting a juicy morsel such as White Feather?

I chose another book, set it on the shelf ledge and began searching for information on how to send leaked power and beings back where they belonged, but the text only verified my suspicions: "The pentagrams require exacting standards. After the spell is completed, they must be obliterated."

In that respect, pentagram rules were exactly like sand painting rituals. Both spells required proper collection and dispersal on the night or day they were drawn.

"Doesn't the cabin blowing up count?" Or had that been the result of massive amounts of uncontainable energy? Claire had summoned something, been unable to bind it to herself or anything else and had then failed to send it back. "It will feed. It will search out like powers."

I turned the page. The crinkling sound of old parchment echoed. Instead of quieting, the noise magnified and then repeated. It finally ceased, but just as I was about to continue reading, the rustling of papers sounded again.

If I wasn't turning pages, who was?

I ripped my eyes away, wondering if the book would flip pages on its own, lure me into its black depths and force a demonic spell into my memory.

I held my breath and waited, but even from my peripheral vision, the pages remained completely still. In fact...the noise wasn't emanating from the book at all.

Like a puppet on a string, my head swiveled. Books lined the shelves from floor to ceiling. Could spiders make that much noise?

"Moonlight--!" The largest scorpion I had ever seen scrabbled across the top of the desk, headed for the side. Its clawed feet scraped the surface, sounding exactly like old parchment as it scuttled.

The scorpion had no problem clinging to the side of the desk on its way to the floor. A floor I shared with it.

"Aeii!" As screams went, it was short on air.

As if the scorpion wasn't horrific enough, from under the lip of the desk a large black spider bolted across the front. White spots dotted its large black abdomen. Or maybe the white spots were dancing in front of my eyes due to lack of oxygen. My lungs were stuck somewhere between a screech and leaving, with or without me.

I stomped my feet down on the concrete, the better to kill anything coming my way. Dizziness made me feel faint. Or maybe I had fainted because from one blink to the next, the lights, the beautiful lights, shut off.

Nothing was visible, not books, not spiders, not scorpions. I couldn't even see the stool I found myself desperately waving as an inept weapon.

Instinctively, I reached for Mother Earth, but the floor was concrete and hitting the barrier reminded me that magic was against the rules here. Magic called magic and the books were dangerous. No magic in here. Ever. Bad things would happen.

Unfortunately, it seemed bad things were happening.

My body trembled with the need to feel Mother Earth.

I slammed the stool back onto the concrete and climbed on top of it. "I can handle this."

Before I lost it worse, a light near the door came on, and my head spun around in relief. Had I not climbed atop the stool, I would have run for the door and hugged Grandma Ruth until she made me stop only...the door wasn't open. There was no Granny Ruth. There was nothing but a single light, shining from around the corner of the bookcase.

I blinked. The room was only one long corridor with bookcases on either side. No side hallways, no other rooms. So what was the light doing there?

My hands went clammy. I had no silver on my arms. No way to protect myself. The dim glow near the entrance beckoned.

One foot inched near the ground, ready to run.

But....I checked the desk. The single light wasn't enough to determine if the scorpion or spider was creeping closer. I yanked my foot away from the floor and searched frantically.

Nothing but gaping darkness. I'd go to the light. It was away from the spider and the scorpion. If nothing else, underneath the light I'd be able to see better.

I slowly lowered one leg, studying the concrete under the stool. The light pulsed a gentle approval, shedding a direct beam as though it sensed my movement.

"Moonlight madness." I hauled my leg back up, just in time to see at least one spider shadow cross under the stool. The light was alive. Or magic. The only magic here was from grimoires, books that had to be kept warded against their dangerous power.

I forced my hand out until I found the book I had been reading and slammed it shut. I counted to three.

The old lights didn't suddenly illuminate and the new light didn't go away.

I was naked. No Mother Earth. Just me and the spiders.

I huddled into a tiny ball, listening to blood pound against my ears. My only defense was to do *nothing*. If I used my magic, whatever had gotten loose would latch onto me.

"I am not here. Nothing here, move along." I wrapped my arms around my legs and stilled my thoughts. With my luck, the thing probably fed off of fear, the one emotion that, right now, was attached to me like a beacon.

"The door is five or six steps away. The spiders in this room are not interested in me." The door was right there—the real one, not the one with the dim light. If I bolted for it, I could make it. Unless that light caused me problems.

I could create my own light with a spell.

No spells allowed.

My sympathy for White Feather's plight grew tenfold. He wanted to fight, but his wind meant a victory for the enemy. If I so much as tried magic, the spiders—or worse, the scorpion--would be on me like a flash. Scariest of all, whatever had been loosed in here, whatever was in that light, might notice me anyway.

More scraping claws broke the silence.

Would I feel the spiders or would they swarm over me so fast I'd never know? I rubbed my arms. My jeans would protect me. Well, unless a lot of them bit me. Right?

Before the whimper in my throat became a scream, lights blasted the backs of my eyeballs.

"Adriel?"

I didn't budge. My eyes stayed locked in the direction of the desk.

"Adriel! Time's up!"

The large black spider had been busy. It perched next to an even larger bundle of cocooned webbing. At least two legs worked away on that bundle, packaging it up tight.

"It got the scorpion," I whispered hoarsely.

"Put the book away and come out. Your time is up."

I peeled my fingers from my arms. The book could put itself away. I grabbed the stool and flew out of there, ducking through the doorway in a mad sprint.

Granny slammed the door shut and locked it. "What happened? You're as white as if you'd been bitten!"

I collapsed on the floor and came face to face with the silver web spinner attached to the pot on wheels. My harsh breathing turned into a wail until I ran out of air. Sweat drenched my face, but I was chilled as though with fever.

"The emergency generator light came on—my God, were you in there in the dark? The lights are supposed to come on immediately!"

I just kept breathing. That was enough for now.

Chapter 40

Granny hustled me outside into the fresh air where I sat on the bottom porch step and put my hand on good old Mother Earth.

She bustled in and out a few times before reappearing with fresh tea and demands. "Tell me what happened!"

It took a while, but eventually I managed a stunted, almost intelligible answer.

She dismissed the part about the scorpion and spider, narrowing in on the light. "That light is an emergency light over the door. It comes on when the generator kicks in. But all the lights should have come on, not just that one."

"It wasn't over the door. Not unless it was almost completely covered by webbing or spiders. I'm positive it was *behind* the bookcase. There was no bulb, and it wasn't over the door."

"The spiders wouldn't stay on top of a light once it came on," she said.

I thought she was merely humoring me with her questions, but then I noticed she was mindlessly dropping sugar cubes into her tea. After the fifth one, I hauled myself from the steps to the chair and grabbed her hand.

She jumped and then folded her fingers around mine for a few seconds. "Here. Your tea." She pushed a cup my way.

Since she hadn't spiked my cup with sugar yet, I added two cubes and sipped the fresh mint. It did little to soothe me. "There was another door or corridor. I saw it. I *knew* it was there. It felt like freedom and safety; anything to escape the scorpion."

"Spiders do eat scorpions. They prey on each other. Sometimes the scorpions eat the spiders and sometimes it's the other way around."

We had already discussed the scorpions I'd seen lately. "This wasn't a simple coincidence!"

"A hallucination?" Her little foot tapped the porch. "Those books are inhabited, you know. The spells, the magic, it often seeps out, forming its own message."

"It looked real."

"The room has always been full of risks. Good thing you didn't lose your head."

But according to her, I had. Because otherwise, the light would have registered as nothing more than the emergency light. Instead, I had been nearly panicked enough to recite a spell. "Maybe you should limit time in the room to ten minutes."

To my surprise, she took me seriously. "Good idea. Something caused the lights to go off. And with everything else you've told me, we can't be too careful." She shook her head, her fingers tapping nervously. "It should have been very obvious it was an emergency light above the door."

Granny abruptly stood and went inside. When she returned, she carried two books and a large bundle wrapped in cloth. "Here's my best reference for Indian legends." She set it on the table and unwrapped the cloth bundle, which contained two individually wrapped packages. "This spell is one of mine. The instructions for use are tucked inside, but you'll devise your own way of using it once you understand the properties of the poison."

My lip instinctively curled with distaste.

"Spider venom is just another chemical, Adriel. It's not all that different from drinking cow's milk."

I was being foolish. "Thank you." When I would have taken the package, she held it back. "This second package is...something of mine." Slowly she unwrapped the wool covering. "When you read the legend of Spider Woman in the reference book, you'll understand how to use this. It's much like a prayer stick, the reed ones, used in the sand painting ceremony."

My stomach lurched a warning. Every witch had special spells or objects. Some were from early training and as such, they contained a unique chaotic power combined with a power of years gone by. They were also dangerously tied to the witch in question and could be used as a terrible weapon against that person. "Granny--"

"Shh. Listen. That vision you saw or battle you witnessed--the spider overcame the scorpion. If you don't want to use my loom, then study the story and make your own. You might still need mine. You need power that was destroyed in your great-grandfather's time. Power we no longer possess."

She unfolded the last of the wool. A miniature loom, perfect in every detail rested inside. A tiny white shell dangled from one side; a bitty comb used to groom the fibers of a colorful weave that had been started. My mother and father were perhaps the only ones who had ever been so generous to me. Well, and more lately, Martin. This was not a good trend.

"In the original story, the loom was created from sunbeams, sky, lightning and crystals. It was the gift of Spider Woman to the Navajos, meant to protect them from things more dangerous than any human could handle. I have a special affinity to her." She folded the cloth back over. "I truly hope you don't need it."

"But what if I do? What if...Can any one person really stop a spirit from the west?"

"There is no council anymore," she said.

That wasn't an answer, not a real one. I thought about the fact that most witches, including Mat and my mother, knew Granny. We all did business with each other. There might not be a council, but there were witches who knew how to cooperate. "Could we form a council? Can we close a gate to the west?"

Her fingers tapped again, rather frantically. "There were those on the council who could have closed it. That was the problem."

"That sounds like the answer, not the problem!"

Granny's fingers stilled. "Adriel, the council disbanded because of a witch hunt. What nobody talks about is who was doing the killing." A dark shadow crossed her face. In the wake of it, her eyes flashed steely black again. "It was one of our own, Adriel. One of us killed all the other witches."

Chapter 41

I went straight from Granny's to visit my mother. Mom wasn't anxious to talk about the past either, but she confirmed what Granny had told me.

"There can be no council. Witches were dying left and right, usually by arcane methods, drained of magic by magic. Few dared to offer any kind of aid. No one wanted to be involved with a bunch of witches."

"So Grandfather Adriel left? Went into hiding?"

"He had pleaded to retire as head of the council many times. He was old for heaven's sake, but he still had power. And respect—until he was accused of the killings. After fingers pointed at him, they accused my father also. Then Dad was found...his remains...your great-grandfather left. He was innocent," she said fiercely. "But they were coming after all of us."

I thought about it. "But after Grandfather Adriel disappeared, the killings ceased?"

She nodded. "He wasn't the only one who left, but when the killing stopped it was proof enough for some that the killer had been killed."

"That's not proof!"

"No, but there was not enough trust to even think of rebuilding a council. Any cooperation resulted in more whispers. There were two more brutal murders a few months after Adriel left, but whoever did the killing wasn't able to drain the witches. They were nothing more than personal vendettas that someone wanted tied to the old killings. None of us were fooled." Mom's hands, busy snipping out my stitches, stopped just short of stabbing me.

She picked up a healing balm instead. "Granny Ruth and my father collected the books, storing them away from those who demanded everything be destroyed. There was more to it, of course. There were particular books that the council wanted to remove from general circulation. No witch wanted to surrender her books, and in a lot of cases the witches didn't want to admit to owning certain books.

"That was the problem. After a killing, the books belonging to each dead witch were deposited with either my father or Grandfather Adriel. It marked them as guilty. Then, someone got to my father and Grandfather Adriel left."

"Why didn't you ever tell me all this?"

"It was a long time ago. I was very young. My father's death—one doesn't forget. And after Grandfather Adriel disappeared, along with some of the others, it stopped. For the most part, the killing stopped."

She attacked the last stitch. I held my tongue until she picked up the balm again. "What about the book he supposedly had? One on magic?"

"Ah, mi hija. He never showed it to me. He said if anyone ever found it it would be because Mother Earth herself sent it."

"What does that mean?"

She shrugged. "Right before he disappeared, he came by to give you and the rest of us his blessing. Do you remember?"

I nodded, although it was impossible to separate out a single memory. I remembered his dark steady eyes, a deep laugh and walnut skin. To this day, my strongest memory was him grounding me to Mother Earth. I didn't understand magic and certainly couldn't manipulate it then, but sitting on his lap, he smelled of herbs and rich dirt, desert sand, and sunshine.

Mom said, "I didn't care about the book, not then. It was all so horrible. There were evil people after him. Some even claimed the books did the killing. Either way, he gave you his blessing and then he was gone. We never heard from him again."

I was sorely disappointed. Irrationally it seemed that if I had Grandfather Adriel's book, everything would be solved. "I want to find it."

Mom kissed the top of my head. "You aren't the first one. The priest demanded it after your grandfather disappeared. Said giving it up would purge your grandfather's sins." She made the sign of the cross. "Grandfather Adriel's magic existed with God."

"But what about the book?"

"My father talked about it, along with a lot of other books. He was one who believed that no matter who was using knowledge to kill witches, the books needed to be kept, but guarded. After he and Grandfather were gone, we searched everywhere. No book."

I sighed. "Did it have sand paintings in it?"

Mom smiled. "Who can know what Grandfather Adriel put in the book?"

I felt oddly cheated even though I hadn't known about the book a day ago.

"Now then," Mom said, pulling her earlobe, a signal that she had been conversing with her network. "My friends tell me that White Feather's house is very damaged. What is this about?"

The last thing I wanted Mom to do was worry, but this thing after White Feather was bigger than the two of us. I shared the highlights of Sarah's death and the ill wind. "Claire released something from the west. It's been plaguing us. Every time White Feather uses wind, it comes after him. That's how his house was wrecked."

Mom crossed herself again. "Ah, this is why you have all the questions about the council. Mija, a wind spirit. This is not good."

"I know."

She paced away. "We are not meant to mix in the spirit world, but this makes some sense with something Gomez said." She nodded. "Maybe you are right. Grandfather's book would do us some good right now."

"Was Gomez on the council?"

She slanted her eyes at me. "These questions will bring you trouble, mija. No one talks about who was on the council. There is no council, nothing like it. Remember that." She waited until I nodded my agreement, but her very insistence told me she was trying to protect me.

After a long pause, she sighed. "There is a reason witches stay underground. It is why I was not trained to my full potential. After my father died, my mother was not eager to see me trained only to be killed for my skills."

"Granny Ruth must have been on the council."

"Just how old do you think we are? She was too young to be on the council, and she is nearly twenty years older than I am!"

"But she has all the books!"

Mom shook her head. "She had a possible means to protect them, and she was the only one. Because she wasn't on the council and was young, Father hoped she'd be considered neutral and not someone powerful enough to use the books or be guilty of all the killing."

I snorted. "And after she perfected their protection using spiders, I bet no one was too keen on retrieving them either."

Mom smiled her agreement.

I had much to accomplish, so I exchanged a kiss good-bye for many admonitions to be careful. She also threatened to send Dad to help White Feather fix his house.

"Don't worry, Mom. When White Feather completes the protective barriers, I'll let you know. I'm sure Kas will be thrilled to have her husband do the plumbing too."

"Yes. Yes, that's a good idea."

Though she had fed me well, I stopped at the grocery on the way home because it was past time to buy cat food.

No way was I leaving Granny's spells or mine in the car, even if everyone in the store eyed my backpack suspiciously. One other shopper even winked at me when he saw it.

After the store manager accosted me to search the backpack, I regretted being overly cautious, but my remorse didn't last long. Three turns out of the grocery store, it became obvious an old green Corolla was following me.

"Shrivel and die," I muttered, recognizing the two bible thumpers. "Sit in a pew and rot." The goons had better hope they had stumbled across me at the grocery because if they caused my family trouble, I'd toss them a spell straight from their nightmares.

I set a new standard in road-rage as I raced through the winding streets of Santa Fe. A bat on steroids couldn't have caught me.

By the time they were good and lost behind me, I was dreaming of a new, lethal spell. There was no point in continuing this game. If I didn't stand and fight, eventually they'd get lucky.

Chapter 42

Once satisfied that no one with murderous intent was behind me anymore, I cruised home. After feeding the cat, I closeted myself in my lab. Granny's gifts went straight into my safe. The cat must not have liked the new food because she started wailing and screeching every few minutes.

Knowing she wouldn't starve, I ignored her.

Because of the cat, the spells for my two religious friends were suffused with an extra helping of irritation. "You think the petunias are a problem now, just wait." I mixed in enough nitrogen to keep a nearly dead flower growing well into next year. Since tear gas would hurt the flowers, I substituted the searing oils from my recent attempt to communicate with Mother Earth. As a finish, I added a healthy dose of habanero pepper oil.

I didn't dare test it, not anywhere near where I lived. "Maybe I should just carry a gun." Grumbling, I created one last spell, a last-ditch measure, but it made me nervous. What if it killed someone I didn't want dead?

The howling and whining from the cat escalated as soon as the sun went down. I offered the cat fresh water and more food to no avail. As soon as I was tucked inside, the cat hopped on the porch and scratched along the side of the house as if it were a tree.

I phoned Lynx, but he had very little advice.

"She's trying to tell you something."

"Unless she learns English, we're at a stalemate."

Darkness was deepening, limiting my ability to discern anything outside other than looming shapes. There were messages in everything, but deciphering them was magic, and I was fresh out.

Back in the lab, I opened the safe. It was impossible to ignore the loom. I arranged the books, the loom, Martin's gifts, and the heliotrope that Mat had given me on the table.

Since Mat's green stone was well-used, I dipped it in a mug of holy water to purify it.

The cat quieted for a bit, allowing me to read the story of Spider Woman. Next up was the book on sand paintings. Sand paintings were a magic that was meant for good; a combination of history and warnings. The artist created a medium for the sole purpose of calling to the good spirits.

There was no better teacher than experience.

I started with Martin's gifts. The minerals were as precious as spices, gifts of the desert. I ground a bit of each, filtering them with my fingers. The elements drew things or repelled them, much as a magnet was attracted to iron, but was repelled by another magnet.

The Indians used sand paintings to touch a deeper magic in the earth. The tiny grains were Mother Earth's building blocks, and as I painted, the sand tugged at other things. Therein lay the danger, but also the magic.

Every chant, whether it was the shooting chant, the holy man captured by thunder, or the legend of Spider Woman had specific requirements. Granny Ruth's loom watched over me as I sprinkled sand in the most common designs.

What monster had Claire called? Had she beckoned Burrowing Monster or maybe Thunder?

Thunder was known in the legends as one of the guardians of Father Sun, but also a hindrance. Thunder was used in sand paintings to heal those struck by lightning or harmed by storms. Yet Thunder was also the precursor of destructive storms.

The elements were so intertwined separating them was impossible. Calling a single one without the control of the others and thinking to harness it? Insanity.

In a real ceremony, after each painting was drawn, sand from each color would be sprinkled on the patient. In my case, I was after protection, but I needed to protect myself, White Feather and the very earth from accepting a monster through a door that should not have been opened.

We needed a real shaman. My great-grandfather, long gone, might have saved us. Perhaps my affinity to Changing Woman, a part of Mother Earth, would help me. She was the one who brought the Twin Slayers to save the world. But I wasn't a spirit or a god who could shove something powerful back into containment.

Sand paintings required real elements as an enticement to the holy ones; water, feathers or the most exquisite turquoise. I fingered the turquoise from Martin and the loom from Granny. Legend had it that Spider Woman had provided the Navajo with the secret of weaving. Granny's special prayer bundle was old and like Grandma Ruth, it was tuned to a magic foreign to my own.

Martin's gift was old as well. It had lasting magic that had seeped into it from the earth and grown over time. Both were good gifts.

I sprinkled the symbol of the hand basket for carrying wind. What color was White Feather's wind?

Green. But there wasn't a green sand, unless I counted the heliotrope. The traditional colors for wind were black and yellow.

Still, the heliotrope had been gifted to me from Mat. Just as repetition in a sand painting made things stronger, so did gifting, especially since the heliotrope was precious to me because of its natural tie to White Feather and his magic. I ground some very carefully.

From myself, I gave silver.

The finishing touch was a protective sundog; a red and blue rainbow surrounded by white on the inside. I drew a line for each of the gifts. My plea was for protection of the people who had given them.

The call to power was usually black zigzagged lines. I dug around the lab drawers and found charcoal pencil to complete the call when the time was right. The pencil would be much faster than sprinkling sand.

The painting had to be completed before sundown on the day it was made, but it was impossible to guess which day I would need it. Instead of dispersing it, I collected it inside the leather and declared the practice a prayer bundle. I whispered a chant, a Word of Power.

Words of Power were the primal shout of warning from a mother to her child in danger. My chant had to be powerful enough to call together whatever magic existed in the pitiful sand painting I had created. When the time was right, I'd say the word again.

It would then be up to whatever good spirit heard my plea to determine if the gifts were valuable enough to compel an answer.

Chapter 43

I tried to sleep, but the cat had returned to her noisy tasks. The minute my head touched the pillow, howling pierced the walls. Just as suddenly, it quieted, leaving me worrying that something had gotten the cat.

Game on.

Slumber drifted close, but meows drifted through my hovering dreams. The dream catcher did nothing to stop her, either. It sounded as if she was playing hopscotch on the porch. Maybe her food had spilled, and she was pouncing around killing each piece.

I buried my head under a pillow, determined to sleep, but when the cat finally stopped howling my dreams were of a ghost driving a car that chased me.

The cat may have given up, but the enemy had not. My first warning, my only warning, was a prickling along my leg. It was a subtle threat, but a deadly one.

My eyes flew opened. The prick of insect legs along my calf curdled a scream in the back of my throat. I searched the darkness above my head, waiting for more insects to fall and devour me. If this was the battle the grimoires foretold, I was completely unprepared.

Get it off.

Luckily, fear far surpassed logic and locked me in place. Hooks picked at my skin like tiny needles.

It had to be a scorpion, something with a delivery system that would strike with little or no provocation. Had Claire sent it? Or worse, the foul smelling wind?

The thing must be enhanced by some monstrous spell—not hard to do when the damn creatures were already evil. My household protections wouldn't keep out a scorpion or even a cockroach for that matter. "Don't let it be a cockroach," I pleaded. For just a moment, death by scorpion sting seemed preferable to being killed by a cockroach. Then again, cockroaches didn't sting so unless a witch had spelled a cockroach to eat my live flesh…I could not afford to shake. I couldn't even afford goose bumps. Anything could cause the thing to strike. Or start chewing.

Sweat doused my body, making it hard to distinguish between hallucinations and reality. Until it moved again.

"Eee!" What would Mom say if I died from a cockroach? The neighbors would never speak to her again even if it were a super-enhanced, spelled, evil cockroach. My aunt would say, "You ever met a good cockroach? No. Your daughter must have dabbled in terrible magic."

Without moving my legs, I flicked the comforter to the side, a quick inch.

Nothing. The beast rested against my leg, biding its time. Maybe it was infecting me wherever it touched.

I tugged harder, flinging the comforter off.

Could I remove the sheet without getting up?

Possibly. I could also get bit, stung or chewed.

Reaching slowly, I pressed the switch on the lamp next to the bed.

The light didn't cause a lethal reaction.

I picked up the alarm clock. It wasn't heavy enough. The bed underneath was soft.

Slowly, I sat up, lifted the sheet and...*Oh my God.* It was a centipede. I knew the legends: A spelled centipede crawled under your skin and sucked your blood, replacing it with poison. The counterspell was rumored to require burning it out with a flame. Effective, yes, but there was no way to do it without burning skin and other tissue along with it.

Maybe it was the cold sweat. Maybe I twitched my leg. Maybe the thing just decided to attack, but suddenly there was the movement of a hundred legs along mine.

"Aeeeeiiii!" I yanked my leg away and smashed down with the alarm clock. The electric cord didn't quite come free of the wall, and I missed the creature completely.

I half slid, half fell off the bed, jerking the sheet free as I went.

The six-inch centipede, blood-red in the center with straw colored legs— hundreds of moving, slimy legs--reared its ugly forefront in threat.

I screamed and smashed the alarm clock down. The grotesque body twisted and turned.

My skin jumped across my arm. Only a vampire could travel as fast as that cursed thing did. In the blink of an eye it was at the end of the bed. I tore at the sheet again. No way was it escaping to wiggle back later.

I swung the clock, knocking the centipede to the floor. "Aeeeeeiiii!!!!!" If a fireball spell had been handy I would have set my bedroom on fire in order to kill it.

Instead, I smashed the clock against the twisting nightmare until it was nothing but a smear.

The clock would never tick again.

"Ick."

I abandoned the clock and crossed myself. Centipedes were very bad luck. They were the carriers of poison.

This enemy was dead, but what if there were more? If they carried malicious spells, and of course they did, were the creatures too small to be repelled by my protections?

No, a spell was a spell. Any spell against me couldn't be activated until after the insect was lured or forced inside.

What had enticed the creature to hunt me?

I cringed and scooted away from it.

It had gotten in. Somehow. The logical response was to make certain my spells were strong enough to blow any insects, spiders, arthropods, fish…"Okay. Maybe not the fish."

I found my moccasins and stomped on the toe parts. Nothing crunched. A visual inspection showed they were empty.

I put my toes in and wiggled. "Okay. Lots of lights."

Turning everything electric on, I stared inside my closet. My cleanest pair of jeans, the ones I had worn a couple of times, sat on top of the laundry pile. If I were a centipede or a bug, wouldn't that laundry pile look attractive?

I grabbed a pair of dress pants from a hanger. Bugs couldn't get inside hanging clothes easily. Right?

I shook the pants and then put them on the floor and walked across both legs and the top.

Nothing crunched.

I still peered inside the legs before putting them on.

The lab was the most protected area of the house, but even there, I still didn't feel safe. Bugs went *everywhere*.

My safe contained at least two potions made from spider venom from Granny Ruth. Any spell against scorpions should also be effective against centipedes.

Checking the references Granny had provided against the internet, I devised a simple spell: spider venom and copper. Copper worked on scorpions like silver against werewolves.

There was only one copper scratch pad in the house, but there were two copper tubes and some copper tape for repairs in the lab. First, I'd protect weep holes, window sills and any other visible cracks. In the morning, I'd buy more copper and devise a copper barrier all the way around the house.

Cutting the copper was easy. Spelling it wasn't very difficult either because metals had an affinity for magic. If only I had known this enemy when the house was built, I would have added the spell to the chicken wire mesh inside the adobe.

By the time I was finished mixing poisons and copper, it was one in the morning. I had no intention of going outside—at least not until the cat howled.

"Okay. That's it." I marched over to the phone.

Middle of the night or not, something was out there.

White Feather answered on the first ring.

Chapter 44

After warning White Feather, I armed myself with a flashlight and prepared for battle, even if it meant facing a ghost or windstorm head-on. I pocketed my latest defense spells, my favorite silver dagger, the copper spells, and the heliotrope. My hand hovered over the ochre that Martin had provided, but there wasn't time to draw a sand painting to trap wind.

I settled on threading a chunk of raw turquoise and an arrowhead onto my silver necklace chain.

If whatever was out there was an ill wind, White Feather would be in more danger than me. That didn't mean I wasn't scared, but it did mean I was going to check before he arrived.

With all my weapons handy, I couldn't even unlock the front door without first setting down the dagger.

It was dark out. A light breeze, cooler than expected after the warmth inside, brushed my bare arms, gently reminding me that winter was on its way. Wide sweeps with the flashlight revealed that it was not the cat or a ghost that waited for me, but little lumps of debris scattered across the porch.

The lumps weren't soil and they weren't leaves. They were dead insect bodies. "Five, six," I counted frantically, swinging the flashlight. A centipede, not dead, dangled from the wooden porch railing. I hit the porch light with the hilt of my dagger.

My heart nearly stopped. "Moonlight madness!" I had never seen so many bugs, especially poisonous ones. Given the coolness of the night, maybe it hadn't even taken a spell to convince them to head inside. As for who had left them, there was no obvious calling card.

And why were they mangled and dead? Was this some kind of practical joke? Or had my defenses somehow injured them?

Once again, I heard the cat before I saw it. She pounced onto the steps, bounced and flung an object into the air before swatting it with her claws. She didn't outright eat it, but it was bound to have a few holes in it.

"*That's* why you were causing such a ruckus? Where did they come from?"

The cat didn't answer. She chewed at the bug, mangling it worse before dropping it in the dirt.

I aimed the flashlight past the porch light.

The cat had killed or maimed everything in range except for the centipede on the porch rail. With me this close, she wasn't about to stalk it.

This situation did not call for spells, it called for industrial strength bug spray. A truck full. A moat around my yard. A bazooka.

The cat licked her paw, an act so calming, it quite possibly saved me from hysteria.

"I hope you didn't get bit." With her wild nature, she'd never willingly visit a vet. "How did they get here?"

The cat didn't even blink. I debated calling White Feather to tell him not to come over, but I wasn't too keen on killing the rest of these things on my own.

I ducked inside, switched out my moccasins for my hiking boots and located some bug spray.

Fully armed, I stepped back outside. Anything that moved got blasted. Even the ones that looked dead got blasted *and* stepped on.

I used tweezers to stuff spelled copper inside the weep holes even though some evil bugs might be trapped inside. Although there had been no sign of Sarah for a long time, I kept an eye on the darkness around me. I was afraid of the cat too, but not quite as much as before.

Working my way around the house, I killed four more scorpions and a centipede that was gliding straight up the adobe. "Aaaztec curses." My beautiful brown adobe now had a chunk missing. Maybe I shouldn't have mashed the bug quite that hard, but how dare they attack me?

The very quiet purr of a car engine motivated me to gather myself. I was an idiot for calling White Feather over a few hundred nasty bugs. To avoid being mistaken for a crazed Rambo, I strapped the silver dagger above my ankle underneath my pants.

I didn't hear a car door slam. Maybe he was still inside the car testing the wind. I headed around the side of the house to explain that the situation wasn't quite as bad as feared, but...his car wasn't there.

I blinked. My Civic was the only vehicle in front of the house.

Had he parked away from the house to be on the safe side?

I stepped inside the light from the porch to prevent him from mistaking me for a ghost and sending me airborne with a wind attack.

The front yard was eerily still. "White Feather?"

The cat screamed.

I whirled around, but was too late.

A large, dark shape hit my shoulder, taking me down. "Oomph." My left side bore the brunt of the initial impact. I kicked and struggled to scramble free.

The cat screeched again and landed on my attacker. It gave me the half second I needed to wedge my fingers into my pocket. Instead of a spell, I was rewarded with the pair of tweezers I had been using to handle the copper.

The guy on top of me reared back to swipe at the cat.

I stuffed the tweezers up his nose as far as they would go.

He screamed.

The cat, either sensing impending magic, or not being one to stay around after raking her claws across a person, raced into the trees.

My spells were crammed too tightly into my pockets. The second attacker was almost on me before I even realized he was there.

Two spell packets dropped on the ground. There was no time to identify the spells; I crushed a membrane, screamed meaningless words and threw it at the second guy.

I didn't wait to see if he caught it or what triggered. I went for my knife.

Headlights cut through the darkness. This time, it was White Feather.

My knife came free. Bracing one hand on the ground, I felt a round, soft packet underneath.

It would have worked better had I crushed it against the enemy, but since the spell had already activated by being smashed, I launched it at the guy struggling to hold onto me.

The moisture inside the packet mixed instantly, and the blood on his face from the tweezers served as a conduit. Nettles and petunias bloomed across the bloody mess of his nose. The smell of turpentine and chile peppers flooded the air.

Just as his face disappeared behind wild growth, the headlights from White Feather's car lit up his blond hair and desperate eyeballs. My nemeses, David the Frog and his friend Blondie, had tracked me down after all.

"Aztec curses," I screamed. "Will you never leave me alone?"

I clawed my pocket for another spell, but came up with the heliotrope. I aimed for Blondie's screaming mouth, hoping he'd choke on it.

David joined the fray with something that in the headlight glare looked suspiciously like a garrote.

I raised my dagger and slashed.

An arm for an arm. I carved into a good chunk of flesh before the wind hit.

White Feather was skilled, and he was fast. He pushed me sideways while blasting a harder gust at the attackers. I rolled with the wind, although it would have been eminently more satisfying to sit there and chop David into tiny pieces of hamburger.

The bible thumpers weren't immune to fear, but their pumping legs did them no good. The wind smashed them against the trees.

Still angry, I threw the last of my spells, the last resort, the one I had hoped never to use. The explosion would maim at best, kill at worst.

The wind delivered it right to them. My mouth opened to say the words, but White Feather's wind, a gentle tangent, brushed along my arms and tangled my hair. The unspoken question in the breeze was, "Are you okay?"

His wind danced along my arms and legs, checking for injuries.

The mix of emotions, my hatred and anger against his worry and gentleness, made me choke. Then again, maybe it was the strong oils from the super-grow petunia spell.

White Feather loomed, his hands fisted at his sides, his attention split between the attackers and me. He controlled the wind with little effort, but he couldn't continue using it. If he did, if it wasn't already too late, he would attract something much worse than these two scumbags.

My arms shook with the need to extract revenge. I stumbled to my feet.

"Are you alright?" A sharp gust of wind from White Feather slammed David's head against the trunk of a tree. Blondie got his turn, face first.

If I had answered him, White Feather might have continued beating them until they were senseless, but I was too focused on my own intent to maim and destroy to waste time speaking. I felt the silver on my arms. I smelled the stink of plant oils. The last time I had searched through Mother Earth, the earth had literally spit up on me. Then again, I hadn't been too badly injured.

I reached for Mother Earth.

White Feather arrived at my side.

David and Blondie took advantage of his momentary distraction. Rolling with the wind, they crashed blindly through the juniper trees.

Earth, cactus. I reached for that last bit of turpentine though my feet, searching for the likeness growing out of Mother Earth. *Juniper needles, cactus needles, sap.* I grabbed for the things in the spell and shoved with everything in me.

Just like before, there was a suffocating gel. With the push, everything was momentarily displaced, but the explosion outward didn't make it any easier for me to breathe.

I pushed again, hard, but with no air, I panicked. I let go of Mother Earth and struggled to surface.

White Feather said, "That blood had better all be theirs."

My fingernails cut into my palm. Fresh nighttime air soothed me, but only slightly. Screams of pain and fury from the trees were music to my ears.

I followed White Feather's eyes to the dagger in my hand. "The blood is his," I spat out. The wailing from the juniper trees abruptly ended.

I hoped the cactus needles remained embedded in their skin forever.

My legs trembled. I put my head down, striving to completely return to myself. I wasn't dizzy, but I sat down.

White Feather crouched next to me. "Are you okay? Adriel?"

I nodded stiffly. "Okay. Yes." I started to lift my head, but there by my foot, of all things, was a watch with a giant face. It was the same one that David was wearing when I escaped in the plaza. My knife blade had slashed through the leather wrist band.

As White Feather shifted, the light from the headlight glinted off the face. There were no numbers and only one very dark, black hand.

The tip was pointing directly at my front door.

Chapter 45

I reached for the watch. If I couldn't destroy them, I would slash their property into tiny pieces.

White Feather grabbed my arm. He was close enough that my stabbing anything was dangerous. "Adriel?"

"I hate them."

"Adriel, are you okay?" He lifted my face gently.

"May the ghosts of Aztec sacrificial priests gut them."

White Feather brushed a rather large piece of dirt off the side of my face. "They're gone."

My teeth ground with frustration.

White Feather almost smiled. "We'll get them."

A sound very like a growl came from my throat.

"Careful with the knife," White Feather advised. He stepped away to give me time to get myself under control. The headlights glinted off the watch.

I half believed I could smash it, but my brain raced ahead of my intent. The watch face had only one hand and no numbers. I flicked at it with the end of the silver dagger. The watch hand swiveled, stubbornly holding its position. "What Mayan Curse is this?"

I rotated the watch again. The arrow kept its line, pointing directly at my house. "Magic. The bible thumpers were using magic." It was too late to get any angrier; I had run out of energy. "If they hate magic, why would they use it to find me? With me standing here, why does it point to the house and not me?"

White Feather crouched down again. "What is it?"

Most tracking spells required an object that belonged to a person. "Did they get a piece of me?" It was certainly possible. From the last run-in, David probably had some of my blood smeared on his person. Or his knife.

"This thing is pointing at my house." I demonstrated by turning it again, twice. "Why?"

White Feather touched my arm. "I'm going to shut off the car. Wait for me." He didn't take his hand away until I looked up. "Wait for me."

"Okay." Spells ran through my head. "If it's tied to me, it should find me as the strongest source. When did they find my house?" Had they followed me before today, and I hadn't noticed?

It was much darker after he shut off his car and headlights, but I didn't need much light to slip the flat of the blade under the watch and balance it there.

With him at my side, I carried it to the porch. I set it down and removed the influence of the silver blade.

The arrow still pointed at an angle into the house.

I positioned myself directly opposite the arrow.

The arrow didn't budge.

White Feather watched, but he had other questions. "Are you going to tell me what happened here?"

"Bugs. All over the porch, the side of the house, everywhere. I was out here killing them when I thought I heard you drive up. I came around the house, and bam, they tackled me." My voice wasn't very steady.

"I don't suppose it occurred to you to wait for me after you called me?" White Feather leaned over and picked up the watch. "If he was wearing it, it isn't likely to kill either one of us."

"I noticed the watch the other day when he was chasing me."

White Feather ignored the watch. "Are you okay?" He touched my cheek. His thumb might have been wiping away tear tracks. Or, at the very least, dirt smudges.

I gulped, but nodded. He gathered me in a fierce embrace.

I didn't resist. "I'm okay now. I wasn't so great a bit ago."

He squeezed. "Okay." He held me tight for a few seconds. "Next time maybe you should wait inside." His voice sounded strangled, like he was trying not to yell.

"I thought it might be a wind problem. And I didn't want you in any danger."

His grip tightened. "Next time." Deep breath. "You should wait inside."

His heart beat next to my own. Neither one was very settled. "Maybe, but what if that ill wind shows up? Now that you used your talent?"

He squeaked most of the air out of my lungs with his next squeeze. "You may recall I had a plan for that, and I've been practicing. When I was a kid, the first time I showed my mother some of my new tricks, she asked me if I could call back all the power I was wasting."

"What?"

"That was pretty much my reaction. With air around me all the time, who needed to conserve power?"

"Can you get it all back?"

"Not entirely, but enough that I'm not a giant beacon anymore. Instead of blasting wind and letting it dissipate, I collect it back."

"So maybe the ill wind won't find you drifting on a breeze."

"Yeah. So, next time you," he started and we both finished, "should wait inside."

He embraced me for a few more heartbeats until I ventured, "We need to find out what this thing is pointing at."

"Probably." He released me, but kept his hand protectively on my shoulder. The door wasn't locked.

A part of me cringed at bringing the watch inside, but after the scorpions and centipede episode, it was pretty obvious security had been breached. What was one more experiment?

I didn't know about White Feather, but I was waiting for disaster to drop on our heads when we crossed the threshold.

Defying all expectations, there were no explosions, and no spells noticeably triggered. The arrow swiveled slightly.

White Feather let the arrow lead.

When we reached my bedroom door, White Feather peered in ahead of me. "Do you always throw the covers across the room?"

I caught sight of the room from under his arm. It was a mess. The sheet and comforter were strewn across the floor. "The centipede I told you about. It was on the bed. Could this watch be focused on the bugs? Did they release them and then return later?"

"It's pointing at your closet."

"Maybe it ignores the dead ones?"

We eased over to the closet. The light brightened most of the corners. "Lots of laundry," I said, embarrassed at the state of my room and closet.

"It likes your laundry."

"Too bad it isn't here to wash it for me."

White Feather swiveled around, which wasn't easy because we were both crammed in the doorway.

I squeezed through, staying near the edge. My head bumped the clothes hanging down along the side. "It can't be the whole pile."

Using a hanger, I hooked the top pair of jeans off the pile and began slowly spreading the rest. If a scorpion or other nasty was here, it was probably near the bottom of the pile.

White Feather knelt down and grabbed a piece or two, testing.

"Be careful," I admonished. "There were a lot of scorpions out there. I couldn't have gotten them all."

"The jeans." He dragged them away from the rest, and then kicked them into the bedroom. "Yup. These are the target."

"I wore those yesterday. That was when they followed me." The jeans were one of my only pair that hadn't recently been mangled beyond use.

White Feather stepped forcefully on the pants. I winced, waiting for a crunch.

None came.

He checked the arrow again. "It's the pants."

"How did they taint them? Did they spray me with something?" I hadn't worn them to the meet at Hyde Park. That pair was ruined. I didn't remember which pair I had been wearing when they followed me outside Mat's shop.

Gingerly, I picked them up by the waist and shook them. Nothing fell out.

White Feather tracked my movements with the watch. "Top of the pants."

"The pockets?" I held the waist with two fingers. "I am not sticking my hands in there."

"Let me see them."

"No, no, I'll do it."

"Give me the pants."

I looked closely at the white pocket part inside the waistband. I flicked a finger at each side, but nothing moved.

"Will you give me the pants already?"

I handed them over and took the watch. While he dug through the pockets, I verified his findings. The thing pointed right at the top of the pants.

It wasn't until he checked the back pockets that we had our answer.

Tucked carefully inside, where I had forgotten completely about it, was a black business card. The word "Charms" was neatly printed across the top.

Chapter 46

Magic was a funny thing. It mingled through my life so much, it was almost mundane. Even when I knew it was around, sometimes because I knew it was around, I ignored it.

Walking through a magic shop that smelled of cinnamon, I expected magic. Not the tingle of the desert, not the heartbeat of Mother Earth, but various background prickling here and there like a musty dust mote that had been tainted by a spell just by being too close.

Still, I should have known better. "He gave me a business card with a spell attached?" I hadn't muttered a single protection or been the least bit suspicious. "I'm an idiot!"

White Feather flipped the card around. "Looks normal. Looks harmless."

"I didn't notice anything at all when he gave it to me, and I never thought about it afterward. I'm lucky he didn't attach a worse curse to it." I flapped my arms in agitation. "I never suspected a thing!"

"What kind of freak calls himself Jack O' Lantern?"

"He said his real name was too hard to pronounce. More likely it's a witch thing—he doesn't want to use his real name."

"I'm going to call Gordon. It's time we had a long conversation with this Jack person and his friends."

I trailed him into the kitchen, still venting. "He gives his card to whoever he wants. Then later, he can have David and Blondie follow them. Why not a compulsion to revisit the store?"

"You would have noticed that. So would any witch worth her salt."

"A normal probably wouldn't. Then he could make more money selling stuff."

White Feather paused with his hand on the phone. "Maybe making money wasn't his purpose."

We stared at each other for a while, wondering. He had tracked me. He had apparently tracked Matilda. And what about Gomez? Gomez had been hit by the Frog and Friend too.

But if he was after magic users to thrash them...what was his purpose? To get rid of the competition?

White Feather shook his head, the confusion on his face mirroring mine.

While he made his call, I considered why Charms might track customers. Why he would send scorpions into my home? I had suspected Claire was responsible for the scorpions, but Frog and Friend had appeared in the middle of the night, right after the scorpions appeared. They used magic.

I picked up the pants again. "Scorpions. Claire. Charms." Had Claire hired Charms to concoct her spells? Even so, how did the scorpions and the tracking fit?

I shook the pants hard, checking the pockets very carefully to be certain there weren't any more stowaways. One bottom cuff was partially rolled up from being stuffed inside my hiking boots.

I straightened it to make sure nothing lurked there, but with a sinking feeling, I realized why the cuff was rolled funny.

"Granny's house." I dropped the pants as though they had caught fire. "Oh, no!" The card had been in the pocket. The card had a spell on it. *I had taken magic inside the reading room!*

"Moonlight madness! I may have cursed myself." The scorpions must have found me because of the card—both in Granny's reading room and my home.

White Feather appeared in the doorway. He read the stricken look on my face and was at my side in two quick steps. "What?"

In a shaky voice, I told him about the reading room and what had happened. "The scorpion must have used the magic on the card as a gateway into the room. Magic is forbidden in there for a reason. It reacts with the books, sets off spells--" I shivered. "I'm lucky that scorpion didn't suck power from the grimoires and eat me alive!"

"You stopped it though."

"Not me. The spiders. That's why they are there. They protect the magic in the grimoires." I told him about the light and the other doorway. "I almost went through it!"

"Charms. Spelled business cards. Scorpions at Sarah's, here and with the grimoires. And what does Claire have to do with all this? She didn't dabble with magic, not when I knew her."

"The witch in Charms has to be in cahoots with her. The scorpion showed up in the reading room as a result of whatever spell was on that card. But why would he bother tracking me just because I visited his store one day?"

"Gordon might be able to help us with that, but I suggested we take a look first. You weren't planning on trying to sleep again tonight?"

I glanced at the bed. Even with White Feather standing in my bedroom, now was possibly the least seductive moment in my life.

He grinned at my dismay. "Between the two of us and our house problems, we might need to check into a hotel."

My skin prickled with electricity, a combination of fear, passion or...bugs. "I better change clothes." My current attire was ruined. Again.

I didn't trust my jeans, so I donned black sweat pants and a long-sleeved heavy knit sweater.

The sweat pants pockets were nice and loose, readily holding extra spells for blending in the dark. I retrieved a clean silver dagger and cotton gloves from the lab and stowed them in a fanny pack.

I was ready to go when I thought of something. "Hang on. I want to make sure David and his buddy don't sneak up on us again."

White Feather waited patiently, leaning against the doorway of the lab.

I unwrapped the dagger with David's blood on it and quickly made a witching fork. I hoped David was sweating bullets somewhere wondering how his blood could be used against him. "Okay. We'll be able to tell if they've been in Charms."

White Feather led the way out. Using his car headlights to illuminate the yard, I collected the heliotrope, my flashlight and the remains of my spells, including the most dangerous one.

We circled the house, hunting for any remaining scorpions. The witching fork spelled with David's blood pointed at the trees where White Feather had thrown the two jerks.

"Let's make sure they didn't leave anything else unpleasant behind," White Feather suggested.

"Good idea." The fork guided us to the left of the tree.

"They must have parked up the road," I said. "I heard a car, but assumed it was yours because I barely heard any engine noise. Instead I got Frog and Friend parking away from the house so they wouldn't be readily heard."

We ducked under one juniper and around another, my light illuminating broken branches and scuffed sand. Within a few yards, the fork twitched low and to the right, under another tree.

I shone the light over, but it bounced, glinting right into my eyes. White Feather leaned closer, very carefully, until we both identified a very large glass jar. There was no lid.

"How many scorpions did you kill, anyway?" White Feather asked.

"Not enough, judging from the size of this jar. It must have been a concession stand pickle jar." A quick sweep with the light found another jar. "So they delivered the scorpions and centipedes. They could have spelled the things to head for the business card. But then what? They come back later?"

"The scorpions needed time to get inside," White Feather said. "Scorpions eat centipedes. A clever witch could hide the compulsion to go to the business card underneath a normal hunting instinct. Done right, it might not be detectable as magic."

"And then what?"

"Maybe they expected you to be incapacitated from bites and be easy pickings?"

That thought was so unpleasant I nearly dropped the flashlight. "Sarah didn't die from scorpion bites. But they were at her cabin." I nodded. "Use a hidden spell to get the scorpions inside, then use them to trigger a spell that would welcome Claire or the thugs past any wards. Act out the sand painting at leisure with Sarah an unwilling part of the summoning."

"But how did Claire know Sarah? Or maybe all it took was Sarah accepting an innocent looking business card from Charms."

I agreed. "That or maybe she bought the sand painting we saw at her cabin from Charms. Claire didn't wait for you to shop at Charms. She spelled a painting specifically to you, one with a compulsion to keep you near it. Then, when it was your turn to be a part of a real sand painting ceremony, she'd send scorpions. Her thugs could waltz in, make sure you were incapacitated or defenseless, and she could perform whatever ritual she had planned."

White Feather lifted the glass jar. "And those two guys tonight were sent here to hold you captive until you could be used in a sand painting like they performed with Sarah."

The electricity of a dangerous thunderstorm raised the hair on my arms. It took me a moment to realize the energy was coming from White Feather.

He said nothing more, but his jaw clenched as he picked up the second glass jar.

"I wonder how they chose who to follow? Did they just wait for witches to come into the shop? No," I answered myself, "Frog and Friend tried to hire me through Lynx before I visited Charms. I bet they would have used the meet to either tag me for later tracking or hog-tie me right then. They also went after Gomez. He's not the type to wander into a shop like Charms. Somehow they heard about him and went after him."

My comment did nothing to improve White Feather's mood. He strode past me. The trail of snapped twigs and scuffed soil leading to the road was obvious enough that he didn't need the witching fork to provide directions.

Five or so yards away from the blacktop, we spotted several exploded pear cacti. A branch from a juniper tree was stripped as though it had exploded. The needles littered the ground nearby.

I hoped the needles had hit their target.

A few feet from the tree, we found tire tracks. David the Frog and his friend had simply parked a few yards from my driveway and snuck up to the house. Had I not been outside, I wouldn't have heard the car.

"Time to tackle them back at their headquarters." White Feather said.

I didn't like the idea, because a witch in his own territory was extremely dangerous. Unfortunately, we had no other leads.

Chapter 47

Charms, like much of Santa Fe, was quiet at three-thirty in the morning. Even this far inside the heart of the city, the desert seeped in at night. At this time of the year, she was a cold, calm presence; a dryness that spoke of peace, but also of danger. Anyone not prepared for her wrath could die of dehydration, but a spirit in need of soothing could find comfort in the cool nights as she rested, floating along with a billion stars and the moon.

I wished we were more in the desert and less in town. Charms wasn't likely to yield anything useful anyway, especially since we didn't know what we were looking for.

There was a lone light halfway up the block where another alley ran perpendicular to the main street. Typical of Santa Fe, the shops were crammed into an old building that had been one large space but was now renovated into smaller individual shops.

"It isn't wise to break into a witch's lair," I whispered.

White Feather squeezed my hand. "Gordon is watching this area tonight. The address is listed as a shop only, not a residence."

His reassurance didn't quiet my nerves. The kid could easily sleep in the building on a cot. And if he was the witch clever enough to spell scorpions through my magical wards, I wasn't too keen on meeting him in his territory. I was far less enthused about letting White Feather go it alone, however.

We crossed the street and passed Charms on the opposite side. The paving was cracked and uneven with large sections missing completely. The Charms side had part of a sidewalk, but it was only occasional slabs in front of doorways.

A beer can and some dried leaves danced just enough to make me jump.

We doubled back the way we had come on the Charms side of street and ducked into the alleyway. The dark tint on the windows prevented spying in the daytime; at night the glass was nothing but a black reflective surface.

"There's no way to know if he's there," I whispered.

"So we'll knock." White Feather did just that, tossing a few pebbles at the window.

"It's three in the morning. I wouldn't answer the door."

"Me neither." He held out his hand. "Let me borrow that heliotrope."

I felt around in my fanny pack, curious about how he might use it. He didn't need it to create wind.

My first hint was the glass shattering. The heliotrope crashed through the windowed door rather effectively. "I guess he'll know we've been here."

"If he calls it in, Gordon will respond."

"If he doesn't call it in, that doesn't mean he isn't there." Even if he wasn't a witch, a gun could cause a lot of damage, and he had the law on his side in this case.

"No, but now we can get in." White Feather, like Lynx, had a set of lock picks. "Watch my back."

I crushed a packet containing the nighttime illusion spell, shadowing White Feather closely enough to cover us both. The magic had no smell, but it clung to my presence. We melted into the dark, a hazy bit of blacker night, nothing more.

At the door, White Feather reached in, unlocked the knob through the broken window pane and then spent less than a minute on the deadbolt.

"Will your spell leave an aura?" he asked.

"It disperses with time, but the spell residue is attracted to my person."

"Good. I'd rather he not get anything of yours."

White Feather entered as though he belonged. The store was darker than a tomb. In this case, it might have been safer to enter a tomb.

He flicked on his flashlight, holding it low. At some point, he had put on gloves.

There were no shades to draw. The smell of faded cinnamon drifted in the air, but there was no incense burning as there had been on my daytime visit.

I donned my own gloves, turned my flashlight on and located the heliotrope White Feather had thrown. As soon as I dug it out of the scattered glass, I was hit with the scent of a forest, a breath of fresh air. I held it to my nose and savored the smell for an instant. White Feather must have used his wind to direct his perfect throw because the stone had absorbed some of his energy.

From the jewelry counter, White Feather announced, "He has more than one box of business cards. He can pick and choose which spells to send out."

I stashed the stone and got busy.

The witching fork didn't twitch, not even over a box of tourist scorpions trapped in amber-colored plastic. Of course, the four-inch bugs were cheap Chinese displays like half the other stuff in the store.

I joined White Feather at the counter just as he drifted from the left side of the cabinet to the far side where Jack had been sitting.

My mouth dropped open.

The mural of beautiful planets behind his head changed colors, shifting as though a shadow passed.

"Wait!"

He froze, but the planets didn't. The blue planet, Uranus, faded to a lighter shade. Understanding dawned. "Zodiac signs!"

"What?" His voice was much quieter than mine, and his whisper carried a warning. As he pivoted to see where the danger lay, the planets shifted colors again.

"Zodiac signs," I repeated, amazed at the audacity and skill that such a spell required. "It's probably how he guesses whether customers are witches or not."

White Feather grasped the concept immediately. "Without knowing a person's birth date and time he'd be missing key data, but yeah. How far out does this thing read?"

I edged closer to him. The planets reacted, some of them darkening in color, some fading. "With two of us, it confuses things."

"I don't think I've ever seen anything like this done in a--" White Feather's head whipped my way and then we both said, "painting!"

"And whoever is messing with the Indian sand painting isn't following the usual rules! Maybe he's attempting a combination, employing what he knows, but using a different medium," I guessed.

"Good way to die young."

"Or kill someone else, like Sarah."

"If I knew my signs better, it would make more sense," he said. You definitely got a darkening from Venus and Mercury, but those are also air signs. Me standing here influences it."

"The other air sign is Uranus, and that's the one that changed to a lighter blue as you were messing around on the other side of the cabinet." I slid behind the counter. The Venus, a pearl iridescent, rippled. "No telling what he has these things set to tell him." My stomach clenched. "I wonder if the changes will stay in the painting after we leave."

"I don't care to leave a calling card," White Feather said grimly.

The only option was to destroy the painting, which would be a signature in and of itself. Then again, there was a lot of magic in this store. "If we lined up various magical items from his display, maybe their magic will erase or change the signals." I picked up the box of desert rocks and dumped a few out along the bottom of the wall. "Anything?"

"With you still standing there, I can't tell." White Feather located the light for the counter display and switched it on. He grabbed the extra boxes of business cards and scattered them. The glass display was locked, but he went to work on them with his lock picks.

I searched the bottom of the cabinet for anything else that might be useful. Behind where the cards had been, there was a large box of copper bracelets. I had considered making something similar myself, dipped in spider venom and spelled against scorpions. Spotting them here made me wonder about Jack's reason for having them.

My hand hovered over the selection. Most of the bracelets were thin, the kind sold for various aches, such as arthritis. The larger ones were heavily etched with symbols.

Without touching them directly, I couldn't feel magic radiating, but there was a general taint of magical aura in the entire shop. Knowing what I knew about copper...I pulled my hand back.

The light from the glass case kept us from seeing much of the rest of the store, but it didn't stop noises. The sound of paper crinkling teased my wary ears. The last time I'd heard crumpling paper I was in with the grimoires, and it hadn't been paper rustling.

"Do you hear anything?" I whispered.

White Feather froze. "No."

"It...sounded like parchment." Had I stepped on one of the business cards? My skin crawled.

"A breeze from the broken window?" Without moving, he searched places I couldn't see.

Using his wind was a bad idea, especially here. I panned my flashlight. The place was crammed with junk across all the counters, shelves, and narrow aisles. The ceiling, much to my regret, had more zodiac signs painted around the edges. Entering a witch's domain was hopeless. Unless we burned the place down, we couldn't disguise our presence completely.

White Feather noticed the ceiling. "Tossing this stuff around is a waste of time."

The shuffling, scraping paper noise broke the silence again. This time, he heard it too. "Let's go."

My light glinted off the large copper gauntlets. Such bracelets would be very handy as a defense for someone who handled poisonous creatures. I shone the light down again, along the floor.

They were there. Scorpions the size of my fist wedged their way through the closed door panel on the far end of the display case. One by one, they dropped to the floor.

"Eee-aaack!" I bolted.

White Feather's back stopped me. I was not in the mood to be slowed down. I'd had quite enough of these evil bugs.

"They're melting," White Feather said.

"What?" My back against his, I pushed, but he wasn't budging. "Go!" I shouted. "They're coming!"

"They don't blow away."

Still pressed against him, I squealed and kicked out when the first scorpion scuttled around the side of the counter. White Feather finally moved.

He reached around, half picked me up and made a run for it. As he dragged me forward, I saw the display of fake amber scorpions. "Moonlight madness!" The plastic graves were rapidly melting, freeing the massive bugs.

White Feather blasted mugs, pencils and plastic souvenirs into the street, but his wind had no effect on the bugs. He raised his foot to smash the nearest one. There were too many of them, and they wasted no time converging on us.

I stomped first, as hard as possible, breaking the helium flying spell in my shoe. I muttered the words, hiding them, not from White Feather, but from ears that might be in some other tourist trap item. Supporting White Feather's weight on my own would have failed miserably except for the fact that he was already holding onto me in an attempt to protect me.

My flying spell, the only lousy one I had, shot us up to the ceiling fast enough to crack our heads. I led with my shoulder.

White Feather wasn't so lucky, plus he was taller. I blunted the blow as much as possible and then rolled to trap him above me against the ceiling.

The second part of the spell would blow wind at our backs, but I had gone through a window once because of that spell and wasn't too keen to set it off again.

"What the--" White Feather kept his arm around my waist but barely. "Adriel!"

"Crawl against the ceiling! We've got to get to the door!" I couldn't use my hands because I was holding onto him. "Aztec curses!" I was going to be forced to use the other spell, but we were angled wrong.

White Feather sputtered. Before I made any progress, his wind pushed us forward. We still hit the window, but in a much more controlled manner than had I spoken the words. My flashlight rolled crazily below us, throwing scorpion shadows the size of lobsters.

"We've got to get the door opened before they climb up here!" I yelled.

"Can you hold us here?" he asked.

"This spell isn't going anywhere but up for a while."

White Feather hit the broken window with a gust of air strong enough to blow out the remaining glass. I stretched to grab the edge to pull us through, but the force of my spell was too strong. I couldn't lower myself and still hold onto White Feather.

I hugged him with my knees, keeping my feet, and more importantly the magnets, pointed at the floor.

"Can you let us down?" White Feather's groping fingers barely caught the top edge of the window

"No!"

"How long will this spell last?" He grunted and yanked against the door. We nearly capsized. Tilting the wrong way was suicide.

"Are they climbing the walls?"

He growled a non-answer. It might have been yes, but it wasn't a definite no. He clasped me tight around the waist with one arm and whispered, "Hold on."

Wind shoved us again. We sailed partway through the window. White Feather's back scraped the top edge. My heavy knit sweater snagged on the side and threads yanked free. If we left blood, we were going to be trackable, spellable, and in a world of hurt.

Another blast and White Feather kicked his feet free of the door. Like a shot, we headed for the stars.

There were probably scorpions on the ground below, escaping mindlessly into the street. White Feather's wind carried us sideways along the street, but I didn't have that kind of control over my spell. We floated higher at an alarming rate.

In a complete panic, I canceled the spell.

Too late I remembered that only hard pavement waited below. We might as well have jumped off the top of the building.

I hoped the scorpions didn't eat our bodies.

Chapter 48

Of course, it would have made sense to tell White Feather that I was going to cancel the spell. He actually controlled the wind, while I used a magical concoction of helium and magnetic fields to gain altitude.

The last time I fell, at least my crash had been broken by a tree rather than concrete. I hadn't had to worry about a full-grown man crashing down on top of me either.

White Feather shifted, trying to maneuver underneath me. He managed to blunt our landing with a bare breath of wind, but we both still hit hard.

"Uhng..."

He collapsed next to me more than on top. I expected the worst and got slightly better than that.

Neither of us stirred. I wanted to ask if he was okay, but my brain was about three feet above us, floating. That and I had zero air in my lungs. If I wanted to continue using the flying spell I had better perfect it or practice my landing.

White Feather groaned. He sounded worse than a dying frog.

I tried to sit up. My arms didn't function quite right. It took several tries. "Ssssorry," I gasped. "I...haven't finished that one."

Another grunt. He felt for his head and missed.

"I'm...okay," I slurred.

He pushed himself up partway and sat still for several seconds. "What--?" He paused for more air. "In the hell...was that?"

"Needs...fine-tuning. There's nothing to prevent it from floating me too far up. Well, unless I shoot myself sideways, but I have a balancing problem with that part."

Maybe he was completely silent because he was still gasping for air. Maybe he was questioning whether the spell was the only thing around here that had a balancing problem.

I managed to climb to my knees. "I wonder if those things are tuned to us." I stood, albeit unsteadily. Both of us had lost our lights. My gloves had snagged on the door; so had my sweater. "We need to burn the door. Maybe we can take it off and incinerate it in the street."

"Hmm." White Feather swayed to his feet.

He dug his phone from a pocket. It was turned off, and now it wouldn't turn on. No surprise considering how hard we had landed. "I'll signal Gordon from the car," he decided.

If Jack arrived before Gordon's team we would have a rather large problem on our hands. But why hadn't Jack already appeared? All witches had wards and traps, and the whole point was to *know* when they were tripped. Jack had to know, but Jack had not appeared.

Maybe he was too busy calling spirits he had no business calling, or maybe he hadn't shown up because the scorpions were lethal enough.

We tripped our way back to the car, while I thought out loud. "Water would be good. Soak the place, wash off our essence. Be even better if we burned the place down."

At the car my legs were very happy to collapse. White Feather flashed a pattern with the headlights and then we waited.

It didn't take long for the first police car to pass us.

White Feather sat tight until an unmarked car glided to a stop behind us. "I'll let him know the door is a main concern, but he'll get enough people through there, we don't need to worry about our auras."

It didn't take White Feather long to reassure his brother and tell him what happened. After Gordon pulled away, White Feather came to my side of the car.

"Did you get cut?" he asked, after I opened the door.

"I don't think so. Couple of fibers from my sweater. Maybe some from one side of my pants." I was pretty sure at least one leg had scraped, but I couldn't tell how badly. It didn't hurt and the pants hadn't torn through. "You?"

"I don't think I left anything behind except the flashlight. But Gordon will have fire trucks hose the place down anyway. Did you snag anything from the shop? Anything we can use to trace Jack?"

I shivered. "No way. Besides, there's no telling what in that shop was spelled by him."

White Feather grunted. "The scorpions had active spells. Let's collect one or two and see if we can track Jack. We can store them in the glass containers."

I grabbed his arm. Returning to the shop was not only crazy, it was suicidal. "Those things were spelled to protect the shop. Even without a spell, they're poisonous. I am not trapping one of those God-forsaken creatures."

A fire truck rounded the corner with sirens blaring, effectively stopping any argument.

White Feather opened the trunk and reappeared with one of the jars and a small flashlight.

Grumbling under my breath, I climbed out of the car.

By the time we reached the alley, the first hose was already spraying full blast.

White Feather cursed. "We're too late. The scorpions have scattered."

I kept my eyes on the ground, watching for this scattering.

"We've got nothing of his. No way to track any kind of magical trail. He could be anywhere."

White Feather's flashlight caught a black pebble, reminding me of another black chunk of rock. I stared at it, filtering thoughts of sand paintings and evil creatures. "We don't need a scorpion to track him down." That was the good news.

"We don't?"

"No." I swallowed hard. "We have the charcoal. Martin collected the rocks used in the last ritual."

White Feather blinked twice. "I guess we do have that."

"If that stuff doesn't lead right to him, nothing will."

"But aren't those rocks actually tied to whatever it is he called?"

"Isn't that the thing we really have to stop?"

White Feather's head swiveled to the shop. Water cascaded through the door. "I was hoping we'd catch up with him before he had another chance at a sand painting."

"Yeah." We had many things to wish for, but I didn't think the tooth fairy was listening right now.

We returned to the car. Dawn was not far off.

Just before we settled inside, my skin prickled. I slammed the door. "Let's go." If the wind had finally picked up White Feather's scent, our troubles were about to get a lot worse. I seized his hand, coating him with silver and Mother Earth.

If White Feather detected anything amiss, he didn't acknowledge it. He peeled away from the curb and drove us to an all-night drive-through.

Since I wasn't driving, both of my breakfast burritos were gone before we got back to my place.

Unfortunately, even with daylight upon us, the nightmare wasn't over.

As we pulled up to the porch, Tara was clearly visible.

That was the best news.

A larger concern was my mother sitting in one of the chairs on the porch.

Chapter 49

My mother met me on the bottom step. "When you didn't answer your phone early this morning, I called your friend Lynx, but Tara answered."

Tara interrupted, "He's been tracking Claire! Lynx gave me his phone last night because he never takes it on jobs." She sounded nearly hysterical.

From the way Mom kept her back ramrod straight, she was obviously not pleased to have reached Tara while tracking down Lynx.

"What happened?" I demanded.

Mom said, "They ambushed Gomez again. This time they escaped with four of his horses. Your father is out helping him look."

Tara interrupted again. "Lynx has been watching Claire, but he didn't tell me where. As soon as he came back this morning, we came here looking for you, but then, when your mom showed up, he took the cat and left me here!"

"The little house cat?" I asked. "It went with him?"

"Something is wrong with that cat," my mother said.

"Lynx talked to it. The cat finally came over to him. He took the cat, and he wouldn't take me!" Tara didn't bother to disguise her bitterness. Lynx was going to have a problem when he returned to his love life.

"I doubt he cares if the cat gets hurt," White Feather said.

All he got for his pearl of wisdom was brimming tears and an angry glare.

Lynx was no dummy; he could hold his own running in the desert, but he couldn't do it with a liability attached. He had left Tara in one of the safest spots he knew, which didn't bode well for what he was up to. "What else did Lynx say?"

"Take me with you, or I won't tell." Tara's lips compressed into a stubborn line.

My mother folded her arms. Whatever small influence she might have gained with Tara was far too slim for us to force any information out of her.

I ducked my head quickly to hide the snarl on my face. "I better reload my spells." My flying spell was used up, but I had other copies. I also wanted every other spell in the house. And maybe I had better complete the sand painting I had started. As long as it was dispersed by sundown, I'd be within the rules.

Halfway up the porch, I noticed the cactus pot had been positioned to indicate a message. *Lynx.* Perhaps he had known better than to leave information with Tara. I wouldn't want her as my only hope of backup.

My mother surprised me when she said, "Take her with you."

My head shot up from my inspection of the cactus. "What?"

My mother nodded, her eyebrows frowning fiercely. "You can ruin yourself many ways. Some people don't have enough ambition. Some have too much. Some would rather die trying than live." Mom glared at Tara and then as if she was cooking with flour, brushed her hands free of it. "We can only do so much. You live with your own consequences."

Tara lifted her chin in defiance, but she wasn't brave enough to take on my mother verbally.

White Feather met my eyes, but I had no answer for him. His face was a pasty color.

"And?" There had to be more to Mom's request.

Her lips were tight, holding back whatever she really wanted to say. She touched one finger to the corner of her eye.

"Moonlight madness," I muttered. Now I had to take along a huge disadvantage. I turned back to the cactus. Lynx had stuffed a very small pouch under the needles, which meant I'd need tweezers to extract it. If it got punctured, the spell could escape and there would be no way to trace him.

Mom said, "I'm going to help your father and Gomez track the horses."

"None of this is good." I gave her a brief rundown of our visit to Charms and what we had gleaned so far. "Jack didn't show up even after his alarms went off. I think he's out there in the desert with Claire drawing a sand painting. My guess is they want Gomez or his horses, maybe as an offering."

"A gift to the spirits in the west? Dios mio."

I said, "We need more help. A *lot* more help--like maybe every witch you know."

Her eyes glinted, a kind of half smile. "Witches don't cooperate anymore. Suspicious lot." She hugged me tightly. "You will be careful. We will come to you. We will help."

"Mom, will you tell Granny Ruth what is going on? She knows some of it. I don't know what she can do, but it can't hurt."

"Of course. She's the best place for information. Everyone behaves around her because we're all afraid she'll send a tarantula up our legs if we don't."

"Tell Mat too," I added on impulse.

She took a deep breath while she thought about it. "The older witches don't much care for the younger witches."

"Mat knows her stuff," I said.

"Yes, but no witch in ten counties wants to admit they know her. They don't trust her because she mingles her trade with non-believers."

While I was more discreet than Mat, I mingled with the normals and sold to them too. So did most witches if they admitted the truth. Mom knew it, but we were still a generation apart.

Before I could say more, she planted herself in front of White Feather. "Watch over her. You bring her to me if anything goes wrong. Tara isn't trained yet. She doesn't know how to give."

She was down the steps then, focused on her own mission. The echo of her fear beat in my own heart, but I pushed it aside and went in the house to find my tweezers.

My longest pair hadn't been cleaned yet, so I settled for a shorter set.

As I extracted the packet from the thorns, I wondered who had spelled the packet for Lynx and on such short notice. He wasn't a witch. Of course he had been watching me a long time.

Hmm. Lately I'd had a lot of evidence that he was watching me closer than I thought.

Chapter 50

After retrieving the packet from the cactus, I left Tara and White Feather fighting over why she had been with Lynx when she was supposed to be home.

Obviously, I needed every spell I owned and probably a nuclear device or two. But the most important spell was the one I hadn't taken with me earlier. My sand painting was a pathetic collection of ochre, a couple of gifts from friends and heliotrope. Not much to fight off the spirits of this world let alone any other.

It was barely seven in the morning. It took time to draw a sand painting, but all the evidence suggested that Claire and Jack had been choosing sites and learning the necessary pieces. If they wanted to call the wind spirit again, it didn't matter whether it was a night painting or day. But what did they want with a horse whisperer?

They certainly weren't interested in inviting him for dinner. No, they wanted to use him as a draw for power; an enticement for some beast lurking in the west.

I set out a piece of deerskin and chose the smaller piece of heliotrope to serve as a gift. Of course, if Claire was actively summoning a wind spirit, that spirit wasn't likely to be sidetracked by a little piece of heliotrope, not with White Feather in the vicinity. The red blotches in the stone mocked me. That wind was out for blood.

My efforts would be a toothpick prick in the side of a rhino.

"How long before you're ready?" White Feather asked from the doorway.

I curled my fingers tight around the rock. The burrito that had been such a boon earlier was sour in my stomach. "Not long."

I wasn't very practiced at trickling the sand through my hand, but it would have to do. The first painting I had drawn went into a smaller bundle to be part of the offering of my new painting. Like before, I set all the lines, welcoming the spirits from the east, but left off the final lines of power. Those would be for later.

As I affixed the special gifts, I recalled how the heliotrope had smelled of White Feather after he used it.

"Touch this with your wind," I requested. "Both of these."

He raised an eyebrow, but sent a gentle breeze. Instead of wafting over and past the rock, the rock soaked it up.

Both his eyebrows jumped.

"I had no clue it would do that either until last night after you threw it with your wind."

He inspected the larger piece while I affixed the smaller piece to the deerskin. Having his aura around was reassuring. Plus, the closer he was tied to my protective sand painting, the better.

A squirt of hairspray affixed the sand temporarily so that spraying on a stronger lacquer didn't scatter the sand. "Okay, as soon as it dries it's ready."

White Feather asked, "How do you expect to find them?"

"Lynx left a message. I haven't decoded it yet." I lifted it carefully. The ingredients smelled of tea or sage, maybe both.

The tea leaf spell was similar to one I had used in the past for White Feather; a sharp odor that reminded him of the particular church where we would meet. Lynx's spell wasn't as potent as mine, but that was common with less expensive spells—or beginners. "Let me boil some water."

The burner in my lab heated water quickly. Reading tea leaves wasn't a particularly complicated spell, especially when it was only set to convey a sense of place. Had the kid actually learned it himself?

I dipped the packet in the water and released the hemp string securing it, but even before the chamisa scent hit, I was certain. There was a secondary sense of sand baking in the sun. "Tent Rock."

"Isn't that where your friend Martin ran into trouble?"

"He's not--" I started, but there was no point in arguing Martin's status. "Yes, that's the place."

Now for the other news. "We have to take Tara." I slid two extra silver bracelets on my arm, including the one with a silver ring that attached to my grandmother's turquoise bracelet. I longed for an extra copy or two of the recent spell that was my most lethal.

"My sister is staying here if I have to tie her to your kitchen table!"

"Mom isn't wrong about things like this even if her reasons sound crazy. She has something of the eye in her, a seer talent. I always thought it was limited to Kas and me, a mom thing, but apparently not."

"A seer thing." His voice grated as if his lungs were chewing concrete particles instead of air. "That's why she touched her eye."

I nodded. "She has the sight. Sometimes."

"Great." He sounded anything but. "Let's get this over with."

I grabbed the last few things I needed, called Mom and left a message telling her Lynx had indicated "Tent Rock," and hurried to catch up with White Feather.

Chapter 51

Tent Rock had a serene quality to it, but with the towering tent guardians, you were always watched. As a national monument, fires were never allowed. Nevertheless, the smell of smoke was a part of the early morning fragrance. Of course, it was against every law of nature to call otherworldly spirits and let them run amok, but that apparently didn't concern Claire or her buddy Jack either.

We parked next to the empty Mustang.

Lynx greeted us by stepping around the trunk of a tree a few feet from the Mustang. His cat eyes glowed yellow. "I tracked Claire here early last night. She met up with Petunia-man, his buddy and another guy named Jack. Jack came in a back way with some horses and a mule. He said the bait would draw in some guy named Gomez. Then he gave the orders for Petunia-man to ensure you were locked up for tomorrow night."

We'd already deduced the thugs had planned on holding me captive. "They didn't get me."

Lynx tilted his head briefly, a curious cat. "When you weren't at home this morning, I thought they might have brought you here so I came back to check."

"Have you been up there?" White Feather pointed to the top of the ridge. Thin tendrils of smoke puffed and spread from one end.

Lynx nodded. "They're drawing it. Big square thing. They had a bunch of stuff stored there."

"How long does it take to get up there?" White Feather wanted to know.

Lynx hesitated, so I answered. "Too long. An hour at a fast pace. Tough to cut it down because the last leg is very steep."

"I can make it faster," Lynx said.

Of course he could. The problem was, this wasn't a one man job. Of all Mayan Curses, it wasn't even a several man job. This was something the gods should handle.

White Feather turned to me. "Tell me how you make the flying spell."

"The spell might not go that high," I protested. "Given my method of canceling it, that height would be suicidal, and the helium might run out before I reach the top."

"Helium at your feet? That's the basic formula?"

"Magnets are the catalyst for the first boost. The helium shoots me higher. It's compressed. Very compressed." I lifted my left foot and showed him the special storage area for the spell. "I step down to break the initial membrane."

"You have it here now?"

I nodded. "It's in all my shoes."

"Both of them?"

"Well sure. Without the magnets in both shoes, I'd be off balance."

He returned his attention to the mesa, a thousand feet straight up. "I won't need much. Just the start of your spell to direct what I extract from the air. I'll need to contain it in something like your container, only in something more controllable."

Control was a big problem, I had to admit. The spell released all at once and rocketed me up until I canceled it, which was just a dispersal of the helium. Even without canceling it, the helium wouldn't last forever, which could leave us short of the mesa top.

"How about the heliotrope?" I suggested. "It gathers wind and holds it to some extent. Maybe you can use it as a conduit."

Lynx groaned. He changed it to a sub-audible growl when I glared at him. "Some of your tests don't go so well," he said. "You tell me what you want done up there. I get up there. I do it. You pay me and we're done."

"You can't do this one alone."

"I'm not flying. I'll meet you up there. That way you don't make it, I still have a way back down." Lynx didn't wait for agreement.

Tara said, "Wait!"

He disappeared without flicking even his ear in her direction.

Tara's head dropped. Whatever promise she had broken or whatever words she had said earlier, she regretted now.

I reached out and gripped her hand. Mom had seen something. Not only that, if someone didn't give Tara another chance, she'd self-destruct. If she had to die...I don't know. If I had to die, I'd rather do it fighting than waiting on a porch somewhere, waiting for people who might never return.

White Feather gave a low growl that would have done Lynx proud. He accepted the heliotrope from me and clasped Tara's other hand. There was incredible power in family. Granted, I wasn't exactly family, except by the vows said in his grandfather's hidden retreat. Close enough. A promise was a promise.

The circle closed. We were a dome that shut out all but his focused wind.

That didn't mean I wasn't scared out of my mind when I gave the Word of Power and broke the helium capsule in one shoe. Luckily, White Feather was ready. He directed the helium as if he'd been practicing his whole life.

He did a far better job of fine tuning our ascent than I ever dreamed of. Side breezes weren't an issue and since the direction was straight up, it was easy to stay on course.

My original spell drew helium from the air into the spell to keep it going. The result was like rocket fuel. White Feather's effort was a calculated, controlled process.

It worked fine until we reached the top of the cliff. Having not been able to scout it ahead of time, we didn't have a landing pad. The ledge itself was fairly narrow, and looked even narrower when I scanned it hoping for a hidden spot that would allow us an element of surprise.

Surprise might have been possible too, except for one thing.

Claire and Jack had been practicing and calling wind. Maybe they sensed the controlled wind or maybe they sensed White Feather.

Either way, one minute we were drifting, the next we were sucked into a vortex racing toward a huge bonfire even faster than if I had canceled the spell.

Chapter 52

I heard Claire before I saw her. She chanted like a demented rooster. She resembled one too with her arms whirling in a parody of taking flight. As her arms flapped so did we twirl, spinning upside down, sideways and in a circle.

I hung onto White Feather and Tara for dear life. Neither seemed inclined to let go of me either.

It took White Feather several seconds to regain control.

As suddenly as the whirlwind spun us, it was gone. For a half second, we existed with no air at all before a breath rushed back into my lungs.

White Feather's landing wasn't all that much better than mine, but at least it was his, not Claire's.

I had expected to hate Claire on sight if for no other reason than as my rival she had tried to spell White Feather. I wasn't expecting the cute elfin companion who had been hiking with Jack when I experimented with talking to Mother Earth.

Claire laughed, a deep sexy sound, one that in hindsight sounded exactly like the throaty chuckle Mother Earth had echoed, not only at Tent Rock, but also in Mat's store. I had searched for the hikers with my spell, but relied too much on sight. I hadn't recognized the laugh then nor when Mother Earth repeated it in Matilda's shop during the foretelling with heliotrope. Subtle clues were obvious when they were laughing in your face.

Because she had lured White Feather, I had built Claire up into a honed seductress prancing about in a tight-fitting, come-hither outfit. My imagination had clothed her too well. As the focus of the sand painting, she was naked from the waist up, painted with lurid symbols. Chitin ran like plated armor along her back and around her ribs. She didn't need a bra because the thick exoskeleton gave full support where her flesh was still soft.

"Aztec sacrifices!" I wasn't completely ignorant of the use of chitin in medicines, herbals and magic. It was a thickener, a stabilizer and had some healing properties. But body armor?

"I guess when you leave the west side of your sand painting open, and you have a bunch of spelled scorpions inside your painting, you end up with a few unintended consequences." Not only had wind come through and not been properly contained, Claire had somehow acquired scorpion properties better left to the insect world.

However Claire had aligned herself with the nether world, she was no longer entirely human. Bulging insect eyes challenged us, and human lips pouted. "I *own* the wind! And I'll own you!" She flung her arm wide.

White Feather never flinched. "Not in this lifetime." A tree behind us snapped. Dirt near our feet scattered, but our dome remained intact.

Her pout changed to a snarl. "You may have wind, but soon I'll have earth too! Then see how often you can tell me no! You'll beg me for a taste of wind!"

Martin had not left town soon enough. He had probably accepted a business card from Jack when he sold his stones to Charms, and he was paying for both of those mistakes now. Leather straps secured him to the center of the painting, positioning him as an offering to the gods. Claire had better hope the gods were in need of a drunken, wrinkled prune with oddball earth powers.

Four horses strained against tethers outside the circle. The dusty animals were bait for another witch, but if Dad has his way, that witch would arrive with more than Jack bargained for.

Jack held the position as the chanter. He met my glare with a smile. With the bonfire behind him and symbols drawn across his face and body, he was a plump little planet with stars all over. "So nice of you to join us. We might need another earth witch. Our friend Martin isn't so stable."

Martin wasn't stable on his best days. Strapped down and deposited in the middle of the painting, his body shook violently. The shakes could be due to alcohol withdrawal or from some other poison Jack and Claire had inflicted upon him. If the carved beads decorating the leather straps were of the earth, it might be a mistake that could help Martin, but at the moment it was doubtful he was in the right frame of mind to speak to any part of Mother Earth.

"Let him go." No one deserved to be part of this.

Jack laughed. It wasn't the high-pitched giggle of the insane. The baritone was as frighteningly normal as though he were chatting in his store selling goods. "We have wind. We're about to gain earth. We'll call the other powers too."

Claire flung her arm out again. "Mine!"

My braid lifted straight back.

"Bind them!" Jack's words were nearly lost on the wind, but she must have heard.

Suddenly, instead of being pushed, we were yanked forward. Tara's fingers slipped. She dug long nails into my fingers, but I didn't complain.

White Feather shifted slightly, letting us be dragged at least three feet. A half-smile flitted across his face before it disappeared under furrowed concentration.

We drifted sideways and then back.

"Is that all?" White Feather taunted.

He was playing with her. Instead of us continuing toward the cliff, we danced closer to the sand painting again.

Claire flung both arms wide. "Jack!" She clenched her claws and screamed, "Call! Call a power that will destroy my enemies!"

"You can't capture wind. You're deluding yourself," White Feather said.

Her next gust spun our bubble to the left and blasted dust right through the barrier. Tara coughed. I ducked my head against the debris, and finally realized White Feather's goal.

Distracted by her own tantrum, she wielded power carelessly. Sand and dirt stirred with her every attempt, blurring the charcoal lines near her feet. The very sand that denoted the edge of the painting was wearing thin.

A howl split the air from the trail head. "Bringing in the troops!" I almost didn't recognize Lynx's voice because it morphed to another wicked howl at the end. The noise was echoed by none other than the little house cat.

The caterwauling was enough distraction to allow White Feather to position us directly in front of Claire. He dropped the bubble to let Lynx inside.

Claire expected it. Like a scorpion with prey, she pounced. Her wind tore a path from the ground at her feet to ours. The black line that had blocked the east was obliterated. The east side, the side where good spirits could enter, was now open.

I spat dirt. Lynx dove, hitting the ground and rolling. His arms protected the tiny house cat.

White Feather snapped the bubble back in place.

Jack either didn't notice the missing line or didn't realize its significance. He began the chant.

Chapter 53

I ignored Jack's chant, opting to use the time to study the pile of rags he chanted over. Were they bones? Sarah?

There seemed to be too many, but they were badly charred. If the bones were Sarah, that meant Jack and Claire had two witches already in the painting. The horses were meant for another witch, and they had also come after me and White Feather.

Just how many witches did they need? Theoretically, more witches meant more practice, more power, but for a pair that hadn't even managed to harness the first wind demon properly, they were operating a few ingredients short of a spell if they believed they could summon and control other powers.

Time for defense. In the relative safety of White Feather's circle, I released Tara's hand and unrolled the leather sand painting. My hand was unsteady as I finished sketching the power lines with the charcoal pencil.

"Your mom is on the way up the trail, bringing backup," Lynx whispered. "She said your dad was ready to light the world on fire and to expect him any second."

Since we didn't know how to stop Jack, them arriving might only mean more witnesses to die. My puny painting was set to call the powers of the east, but would they answer?

I drew the final line.

"OhmyGod!" Tara yelled.

For a heartbeat, then two, the wind attacking our dome cut off. I jerked up to confront empty silence. From under my feet, thunder roiled. The turquoise on my wrist cracked across the middle.

Whatever was arriving was no friend of earth.

Jack let loose a primal scream.

"Holy--" White Feather never finished.

Jack had completed his chant. Maybe no one would answer my painting, but a putrid green fog had answered his.

It hit Jack first, perhaps because his chanting was the call or maybe because he was closest to the obliterated sand lines. The fog had no trouble leaving the painting to reach him.

The green mist wrapped soundlessly around his belly. He doubled over. "Claaaaaaire!!!"

Claire stood as if paralyzed, only her lips moving. "Tastes..." She stretched in his direction. Her mandibles chewed, her fingers clenched.

The skin on Jack's face sagged suddenly, aging him forty years in a matter of seconds. He decayed, withering like a dried out tree. His belly bloated, but the skin on his face stretched and dripped to the ground.

"Is it trying to get in? Or out?" I had to shout to be heard above the still rumbling earth.

"Both," White Feather yelled back.

A thin wisp of green smoke floated free of Jack.

Slowly at first, then swiftly, it struck at him like the tail of a scorpion.

"What the hell *is* it?" Lynx shouted.

"Age? Old age?" My voice croaked with fear and dust. Claire had demanded he call something to destroy her enemies. Her passionate request had been fueled by desperation and rage. She was inside the painting. If old age had heard her call, it would certainly destroy *any* enemy.

As the chanter, Jack should have been safe, but the lines on the sand painting had been partially destroyed. He was fodder. His skin dried and then sucked taut. There was nothing left but a full tuft of hair oddly attached to a skull.

Tara screamed, "It's coming here!"

Indeed, the snake-like wisp rose from his bones and drifted closer.

I grounded, but it did no good.

White Feather blasted at the oncoming wisp with his wind.

The undulating mass split. One piece wafted underneath White Feather's breeze.

He compensated, but I gasped, clutching my stomach as the truth hit home. "Hunger! He called hunger!" The stomach pains were not as dangerous as the wave of weakness that followed. "*Sickness.*" I knew the last one, the only one I had guessed correctly. "Old age."

"Hang on!" White Feather thrust it back again, but it had touched us. It knew our scent. Or perhaps I should say, *she* knew our scent.

Claire shrieked with laughter, slobbering as she chewed, eating up every bit of energy. As the focus of the painting, she benefited from our hunger, sickness and old age. She was feeding through the beast.

Hunger grabbed, doubling me over with pain.

Claire opened her mouth wide. "Food!"

White Feather muttered, "You didn't own me then and you don't own me now." The wind kept the hunger at bay, but only when he pushed at it. Every time he reined his wind in, hunger struck with a vengeance.

Lynx growled. When he bared his teeth, they were those of the bobcat. In hunger, he was our enemy.

Tara reached out to him either in sympathy or in pain. When she touched him his face shifted back. He was left panting, but the stress on his body and face was gone.

He straightened, staring at her unblinking.

"Healer," I gasped out. What I had sensed in her was real; she had a natural ability to heal. Such an affinity provided her some immunity.

White Feather's wind receded, and I fell to my knees. Claire was learning. He pulsed his power, but when she guessed the timing, the results were deadly.

"Tara, grab our hands!" As a healer, she had some natural protection against the ravages of hunger, disease and aging. Healing was the polar opposite of disease, and a negating force against starvation. Healing could slow some of the effects of old age.

Pain hit again before she responded, but Lynx was no dummy. He knew magic and whether he completely understood it or not, he wasn't about to waste it.

Lynx, still grasping her hand, dragged her to me before the next wave passed. Tara clutched my weak fingers. The aging didn't fade immediately, but the hunger pains abated. I wrapped my fingers around White Feather's hand.

He shut his wind inside himself, depriving Claire.

"You are miiine! I am wind!!!" She threw herself at the pile of bones, the bones that had probably once been Sarah.

How far gone did you have to be to wallow in bones?

Grabbing up pieces of the dead, she ran to Martin. There was no method to her madness. She dumped them on top of him and returned for more.

Martin whimpered. "I need..."

I felt his call to Mother Earth.

"Martin, no!" As a sacrifice, any link he provided would only strengthen Claire.

Claire snatched up Jack's bones.

"Martin, hang on! Just hang on." None of us could help him from here.

The little house cat didn't agree. It darted from behind Lynx and scampered to Martin. It was too small to do more than scatter the bones and grab one of the smallest.

Claire gave a howl that was worthy of the cat, but she didn't slow in her intent. She didn't care that one was missing. She just added more.

Sarah's bones had already opened the west once before. When Claire dumped her next armload on top of Martin, Mother Earth cracked.

My heart stopped.

I fell flat on my face, not knowing whether to ground or stop grounding. The silver at my wrist flickered. All sound ceased for me as a jagged line ripped across the ground.

"Adriel!" White Feather grabbed my arms and shook me. "Adriel, breathe!"

It was nearly impossible to force a breath, and I wasn't sure it mattered. Behind White Feather, a deadly tunnel of screaming wind and smoking sulfur snaked up from the crack in the ground.

Before I could warn him, a blast scattered us like leaves. There was no holding on to anyone.

Wind lifted me straight up and then smashed me back down with equal force. I hit the dirt, slapped flat, but still moving. "Aaaagh!" I scraped painfully across the dirt and sand, right across my insignificant attempt at a sand painting. Lacquered into place or not, it was now destroyed.

Well, the thing had to be scattered by dusk, and my flying butt had done a good job of it. I was all about following magical rules. I should have put a sacred feather in my back pocket to do the job right.

If the protective gods from the east weren't already insulted, I had likely sealed the deal.

Claire screamed, "Bring them!" She flung her arm, believing she was in control, but instead of attacking White Feather, the faceless wind focused on her. She may have loosed a snippet of this beast at Sarah's, but that had been a mere imp compared to the hell she had freed now.

The sand painting was meant to contain the forces that she summoned, but Claire had ignored the rules all along. The tail of the funnel swirled. The strange cloud at the top split into two eye-like funnels spinning in opposite directions. There was no mouth, but the thing devoured Claire in a single crush. If the chitin was supposed to protect her, it was so much debris; there one second and splintered the next.

She did not satiate the beast, not even close.

"White Feather!" I screamed. He was the logical place for it to head next.

An arm of the beast, a small dirt devil, started on the west side of the painting, probing along the crack in Mother Earth. It danced for a few moments, but there was nothing of interest there. Instead of exploring the perimeter, the dirt devil died.

The larger force, fed from the crack, paused. The eyes separated further, rolling up, down and sideways as it studied this new environment.

The next dirt devil appeared near the ground at White Feather's feet.

It swirled, sniffing him out.

His barrier held. There was an obvious lack of air between White Feather and the little storm, a window where the force hit, but bounced.

Whether it was his need for air, or the greater power of the attacking tornado, his hair and clothes suddenly tangled. A tunnel of wind the diameter of a large tree trunk slapped his barrier hard enough to fracture the surface into a maze of webbing. Slivers of wind as sharp as blades squeezed through the cracks. His raised arms were suddenly bloodied by hundreds of tiny cuts.

"White Feather!" I sprinted against the storm while fumbling to find the last piece of heliotrope in my pack.

He fell sideways, fighting. The air behind him was sucked into the maelstrom through him. The beast was calling back its own and would not stop until every bit of air was drained from this world.

"Your wind," I yelled. "Push it into the heliotrope!" I wasn't sure what I'd do with it, but it didn't matter. He couldn't hear me. Even if he had, such a tiny stone was no match for the power before us.

The tail of a breeze lashed onto me so quickly, I never saw it coming. Like a snake, it wrapped around me, grinding me face-first into the dirt.

My hands clutched Mother Earth, but scraped only sand and a soft mass of sticky tangled fibers as I was dragged to the gaping crack that split the ground.

My feet were already over the edge when White Feather intervened. "Hold on!"

The pulse of his wind, a giant hand, squeezed into the turbulence. I held on with my silver, grounding like I had never grounded before. I was a heartbeat through Mother Earth, just another piece of her.

White Feather, flat on the ground himself, fed the swirl above our heads. He lunged for me.

I stretched.

The wind sucked me back.

His essence touched my fingertips.

The tornado stole everything White Feather directed at me.

A unexpected screech of incredible power distracted the beast for a scant moment. It was a mother's call, one that tore through time and space. "Adriel!" There was a flash of flame, but it was too far away to feel the heat.

"Mom!" She and Dad had made it to the top of the ridge, but they were too late.

With no further warning, the edge of the gaping wound in Mother Earth swallowed me whole. A tint of blue sky winked for only a second before it was blotted out by White Feather as he jumped in after me.

Chapter 54

There was no sense of air inside the tornado. I tried grounding, hoping to find Mother Earth, preferably before I landed, if I landed. I lifted my hiking boot to smash the helium packet. Maybe if I smashed the packet at just the right moment, I wouldn't be crushed against whatever I landed on.

Sand rushed by my senses, a falling through earth that was liquid. In the Navajo legend, the world came from the belly of the earth. So did the monsters.

My silver heated against my skin. As if being low on oxygen wasn't enough, silver heating up was never a good sign.

I looked up. White Feather was still above me, caught in a swirl that kept him in place, dancing with the wind. There was the tiniest sense of him every time I took a breath.

Ah. He was the reason breathing was possible inside the maelstrom. Each shallow breath was a small bubble of air that I had to grab quickly or it was gone.

I crushed the helium packet in my shoe and aimed for White Feather.

The first burst of helium was always the strongest. That being the case, I was in real trouble.

In the belly of this beast, the helium was whisked away. I wasn't going up. For a few seconds all the helium did was keep me in place.

It was almost enough. I clawed toward White Feather. He did his best to meet me halfway.

I wished I hadn't dropped the heliotrope because it might have helped. I had no link to anything here. My silver was still hot, still warning me—*silver!*

The thought was action. He wore my ring, made from the same silver as my bracelet. I searched for it with my very heartbeat.

Like to like, even in a storm. I pulled myself to him with every ounce of my being.

White Feather wrapped his fingers around mine and reeled me close. "Got you!"

Breathing was not any easier. White Feather held tight, but his eyes were barely slits. His skin was taut as though it was being blown back--or sucked dry.

I wondered how far we had fallen. The sky was still visible. I tucked my head against White Feather's heart. Instead of a pounding heartbeat, his faltered each time he created the tiny air bubbles that allowed us to breathe.

The tornado was draining him dry.

I panicked. I couldn't surround him with Mother Earth. My silver was linked to his, but with no way to regenerate from Mother Earth, the link was weak and getting weaker.

With the debris and the moving air, it took several seconds before I realized we were not being drawn underground. At first I thought White Feather was pulsing us out, but as much as I wanted it to be true, nothing on earth had that kind of strength.

The tornado had dragged me over the edge, but instead of depositing me deep in the belly where the spirits resided, we stayed nearly level with the sand painting as the tornado renewed itself with power from the belly of Mother Earth. We swirled around and around in the circulating air.

A tattered and tiny group held court outside what had once been the edge of the painting. They were insignificant, unable to surround it, unable to keep the beast locked inside. In the first swirl, I recognized my parents.

Mom huddled on the ground. Granny Ruth stood next to a large net that was anchored by thick lines into the sand.

The wind stole my vision again, spinning us away, but my mind filled in the blanks. Granny was weaving. Mom was drawing. Dad and Gomez surrounded the entire group with a herd of horses, protecting them with a magical barrier. I couldn't hear the chants.

It was nearly impossible to concentrate because with each breath, a bit of White Feather was lost. His heartbeat and therefore the air we breathed was random. The silver on my arm turned cold, icy across my wrist.

The tornado gathered itself and washed easily through the breach in Claire's painting. It bore down on the group.

The horses ran, but not away. They headed in a line around the tornado.

Fear owned every part of me. My hand tingled as though stabbed with needles. We were trapped inside and the group on the ground could not contain this thing. Even if they somehow succeeded, we had no way out.

A flash, not unlike lightning, burned the backs of my eyelids. I looked to the heavens because the ground was rapidly receding.

Chapter 55

The wind had upended us. Up was down, down was up.

"Can't...control...nothing...left."

It took four breaths for White Feather to relay the message. He needn't have bothered because I knew. We were in a place humans were not meant to go, never mind survive.

Across the sky, horses thundered straight at us. Green sparks shot from their hooves, trailing out behind them, a giant cascade of northern lights too far south.

At first I thought they were Gomez's horses picked up by the winds, but then we tipped. Gomez's horses remained below, but a green tint surrounded them also. The horses in the sky were a mirror of what was on earth.

"Look," I tried to shout. One of the clouds was the shape of an old woman, weaving, just like Granny Ruth was weaving on her loom. A long, thin line of clouds spun out from the old woman's loom, flowing across the sky.

I had no air to tell White Feather that maybe the spirits from the east were answering.

We dipped low again, but weren't thrown free. The little cat was there briefly, but then its features blurred until it became the shadow of a coyote, the trickster. It ran through the opening on the east side of the painting, grabbed a bone and dragged it to the outside. Once there, it picked up a flaming branch and deposited it along the west side.

Dad mimicked the coyote. He threw a log into the heart of the beast, igniting it as it hit. The fire was the beginning of a line along the west side of the crack.

Right before we rotated away again, the coyote started chewing through the bindings that held Martin in place. The trickster was dismantling the painting, piece by piece.

Faster, my heart pleaded. Even though they couldn't save us, they might save themselves.

I scanned the sky, fearful of what Martin might have as a mirror image in any other realm. He, like me, was of the earth. Only with him, we might get naked angels or drunken sprites.

Granny Ruth came into view again. A white thread spun out from her, just as it did from the cloud. My hand tingled from the lack of oxygen...but the jabbing was only in my left hand.

I peeled my fingers away from White Feather.

The sticky mass from the dirt was Granny's miniature loom. From one end, a tiny string spooled outward.

The weavers in the sky and on the ground were linking their design. The miniature in my hand unwound and floated toward the threads.

It didn't matter. Breathing was painful and not often enough. Some of the debris scraped through White Feather's protection. His heartbeat had slowed to an erratic, hopeless rhythm.

"I--" There was too much I had never said to him.

His eyelids flickered.

One more bubble. I gasped it in. He did not.

I waited, but there was no more air. No more heartbeat. He had given me his last breath.

The strand in my hand dragged my arm away from White Feather. "No!!" I wasted my last breath, but I would not leave him. Not for death, not for life.

The weavers pulled. I resisted, clutching White Feather for all I was worth. We were too high up to save and White Feather...I expelled the very last bit of air in my lungs and prepared to join him.

Chapter 56

The earth was full of living things: bugs, worms, soil, decomposing bits. There was water, trees and minerals, a tie that for me was an energy stream. Being without any of those things made them much more noticeable when they reappeared.

I couldn't see them, but I sensed them rushing closer. The world was without color, a black pit. I only knew we were free of the storm because there was air for my lungs again.

It was a waste, really. As high up as we were, any landing would be too hard to survive. I sighed, wanting to give my own breath to White Feather.

The thread on my hand went suddenly limp. My silver sparked electricity as it felt Mother Earth arrive, but instead of smashing to bits, we bounced. A net closed in around us, confining and constricting us. It floated down slowly, gathering speed as gravity asserted itself.

By the time we hit the loom, the impact was not all that gentle, but considering the circumstances, it beat being crushed to bits.

The sky was dark except for lightning from the east, an eerie green. The horses still ran across the sky and on the earth. The pounding of their hooves beat around us.

My mother went straight to White Feather, but issued orders my way. "Don't get up, mija."

Moving was an impossibility. I held his hand as she began working to save him.

The silver at my wrists and fingers pulsed like lifeblood for me, but the beat wasn't steady. The rocks beneath my back shuddered as the horses pounded along the ridge.

Dad yelled, "Keep them going! The wall is finished."

Gomez answered, "They won't stop."

Tara flashed by and then Lynx.

Granny Ruth squeezed my hand. "Link to earth, dear. We're going to circle it. We're sending it back."

White Feather was on the other side of me. Dead or alive, I linked to the ring. To my surprise, there was barely any silver left circling his finger.

I traced the loop slowly. The arrowhead in his ring had been blown out or used completely, and what was left of the ring was no more than a thin wire. My own bracelet was smooth as silk. The design had worn completely off.

I touched his chest. It rose and fell, slowly. Tears of gratitude filled my eyes.

Mom smiled down at me. "He's a fighter." She stayed on his other side, giving him strength and forming her part of the circle.

"The circle...?" I struggled to sit.

The light from the east grew brighter as if it were sunrise. The horses were now end-to-end, seemingly galloping in place. They completed the circle that we humans couldn't finish alone.

Dad focused on the painting, his eyes a reflection of a fire. He controlled flames that created a turbulence meant to contain the tornado.

Surrounding the flames was water, a solid ring of it. Moments passed before my frantic search finally located Mat. She channeled water from a crystal bowl to the outside of the fire.

We humans were the outer circle. Then water, then fire.

I probed the heavens. No Spider Woman in the clouds. No horses. But they were there. I had seen them.

"Fire, water, earth," my mother chanted. Granny echoed it from the other side.

I repeated with them, "Fire, Water, Earth."

The circles snapped into place. With a roar, the tail of the tornado sucked back into the crack of earth.

"Hold the circle!" my father yelled.

We continued the chant.

Instead of fighting, the wind turned in on itself. It ducked into Mother Earth, and I thought it was gone.

The sand at my feet moved, slowly morphing into the shape of a box. One side remained missing. Mother Earth had drawn this symbol before, warning me of sand paintings with the west side opened.

"'Ware," I shouted. "It's not contained! The west is still open!"

When nothing stirred, I thought maybe I was reading Mother Earth wrong. But the silence didn't last.

As suddenly as it had disappeared, the raging wind screamed back into existence. It had gathered strength from its base. Four eyes instead of two now threatened us. The mouth stretched wide with hunger.

The wail of the wind was met by a flash of green from the heavens. Thundering hooves sparked lightning.

I burrowed deeper into Mother Earth, sending her strength along the circle. A whisper of magic the color of gold spread from Gomez to his charges. "Stand. Steady. Courage."

The wind howled. My feet dug in deeper.

Granny Ruth hissed, "Spin!" Threads of silk from the net that had broken our fall unraveled. Strand by strand, the pieces snaked out around the horses, another giant woven circle. Tiny spiders secured the links.

The wind shuddered, but didn't back down. Debris hung inside the anger of a confused spirit. The lowest pieces sank beneath the crack. For a long protracted moment the world was silent, but then, the earth shuddered and split again.

Granny Ruth screamed, "Spin!"

A jagged crater opened next to the horses' hooves on the west side, scattering them back.

My hand in Granny's slipped.

"Hold on!" I fought to maintain my grip on her weathered fingers. Two of hers snapped free of their sockets, but I refused to let go.

I flinched when a spider dropped from her hair and scurried across her fingertip to mine. It may have bitten her, but she did not protest. The spider wove first around her fingers and then around our hands. I wasn't about to complain.

The burned logs that formed the west wall tumbled into the crevice. Dad was bullied back by an invisible hand that ate at the fire he had created. Sparks flew from his fingers as he tried to burn the air to keep the wall alive.

Three horses slipped.

Gomez fell to one knee as two paints and a palomino screamed. They were too close to the new crack in Mother Earth. Gomez gasped in pain as they were sucked over the edge into the maelstrom.

"*Stand.*" The circle of horses wavered, but Granny's spider silk held just long enough for the remaining horses to find their footing. Their tails and necks stretched to keep the circle intact. There was a snort and then a whinny. It echoed along the line.

The magic of the circles snapped back into place.

Still, the wind rose up as though our efforts were nothing.

My mind barely grasped the impossibility of trying to mend Mother Earth, but Martin shouted, "Connect!" He paused but a second to allow Gomez to take Mat's hand from him.

Then, Martin jumped on the back of the first horse, a short pony. He hopped to the next, a mule or burro. Martin, as naked and bloody as the day he was born, skipped from mount to mount, his very own circus act. When he finally reached the opposite side, he slid down.

I screamed a warning. "Martin, you're inside the circle!" He couldn't possibly be drunk after all we'd been through!

Martin lay down on the west side almost directly underneath the hooves of a short bay stallion. He completed the missing edge of the painting.

Then, he sang. His voice was the whisper of sand against the tent rocks. It was the deep rumble of Mother Earth, a molten burping. It was the same rumbling I had heard in Tent Rock when Mother Earth spoke. Martin was not just talking to Mother Earth. As I had tried to merge with her to mimic White Feather's wind spell, Martin was surely melding with her now, but more completely than I had ever intended.

"Oh, Martin." He couldn't have heard my whisper, but I lent him my strength. It occurred to me that maybe Martin drank because he was too close to Mother Earth, because he heard her voice too clearly. Chanting sounds not meant for human ears vibrated underneath us.

The wind sucked back so violently, we jerked forward.

"Hold," my father yelled.

We chanted, "Earth, Wind, Fire, Water."

Earth slipped into the crack, but we held true.

Martin stayed in place.

Sand from an errant breeze or a direct gift from Mother Earth dusted him with fine particles. His wrinkles filled with ripples of sand. His leathery skin was full of shadows, a mix of earth weathered by sun, wind and rain.

He turned his head our way for only an instant before again gazing straight to the heavens. The crack in Mother Earth rumbled. In concert with a clap of thunder from the sky, the earth screamed. Rocks and boulders scattered and flowed.

The shaking tossed me sideways across White Feather. My father caught Mom before she fell, but Granny Ruth and Mat both crashed to the ground. Gomez held onto one of his horses.

I blinked. There was a flash of green, and the fires went out. For a long, silent moment, there was no light. When I blinked again, my vision cleared. Everything remained in place except for Martin. He was gone.

Well, not entirely. The shape of a man encased in rock, wrinkled sand and all, formed the wall where he had closed the painting and the rift in Mother Earth.

Final rest, indeed.

Chapter 57

Time seemed to stop while Mother Earth shifted restlessly, sand filling in gaps. My body felt her wounds as a long ache in my heart, but it was still beating, both hers and mine.

The heavens echoed her complaints, rolling with thunder and threats as the spirits retreated. Rain, almost a gushing river, slashed across the mountainside. The smell of sulfur and smoke gave way to wet sand and water on the desert wind.

For several minutes, we huddled, letting the rain beat down on us. The sun was setting somewhere behind the dark clouds. This was one sand painting that would not see nightfall.

Mat panted, "Water is a cleanser."

Mom said, "Although we'll catch our death of cold."

Dad laughed, a booming relief. He leaned over to touch my shoulder. His eyes were lit from behind, flames that still flickered, ready to burn the enemy. "Good thing he went in after you," Dad said. "I'm not dumb enough to have jumped in there."

It was a lie and we both knew it. I grabbed hold of his forearm and squeezed. "Yeah, good thing." Maybe now Dad wouldn't have to test White Feather. Seemed to me he should have an automatic passing grade. "Good thing you guys showed up and that Granny Ruth was able to spin so quickly." I flexed my hand, but there were no fibers there now.

The sand from the painting was fast becoming a mixture of mud and rocks. Shattered pieces of chitin floated in a pool of water. Claire was nothing more than leftover garbage.

Gomez said, "Time to get the horses down the mountain. They can't make it through the canyon." At his whistle, the stallion raised its front hooves. With a scream of triumph, it headed in the opposite direction of the trail, leading the herd into Indian land.

Lynx said, "He's right. Canyon could fill with water. Maybe I'll go with him." He held the cat in his arms, the tiny insignificant house cat. His body didn't do much to shelter it from the rain.

There was a darker flicker around the cat just before I recognized Sarah.

The cat emitted an impressively feral hiss. Lynx scooted away from the dark pattern, offering a hiss of his own.

Just before the wisp faded into the rain, Sarah nodded in my direction. Whether it was appreciation or something else, I would never know.

Lynx said, "When she died, her ghost hid in the cat. She hid so they couldn't eat her spirit, or take her to the nether world where you just about went."

"The cat told you this?"

Lynx gave me his usual smile, the one with no teeth and knowing, yellow eyes.

Chapter 58

Mom was only slightly suspicious when I insisted on White Feather's shattered home for his recuperation. Since she wasn't keen on doctors or hospitals and she had already given him her strength, she agreed to leave us there.

I paid Lynx to bring food and told him where to leave it without telling him where we'd be.

Mom was instructing him to come to her house and pick up said food as they left us in what remained of White Feather's home. As soon as the door closed behind them, I heaved a barely responding White Feather into the safety of his grandfather's shelter. I probably should have worried that it wouldn't open, but the dresser answered my touch without a squeak of protest.

"Come on," I whispered softly. The sides were rounded and comfortably hollowed. White Feather already had a sleeping bag snuggled into one side.

I fixed the other side with blankets and rugs.

The walls were a comfort and a healing.

Over the next day and night I read the stories on the wall often. I was on my third reading of the lower panel, sometime during the second day, when it occurred to me that my great-grandfather had probably hidden his "book" in plain sight. All along people had been hunting for a traditional book, but there were many ways to tell a story.

I chuckled softly.

"What?"

I sat up instantly. White Feather was already sitting, having propped himself against the opposite wall without my noticing.

"How do you feel?" I asked.

"About like you'd expect after being eaten and then vomited by wind."

I adjusted the small battery light so that it illuminated more of the room and reached for his hand.

"I take it we lived. Although this wouldn't be a bad substitute for heaven if there was food."

I smiled. "I've got some." I rummaged around in a small cooler and extracted cold herbal tea and burritos. "The burritos aren't warm any longer. I can heat them if you want."

"Don't bother." He accepted the tea and then tugged me over to his hollow. "If I recall correctly, didn't you feed me some soup?"

"Twice."

He swallowed some tea and then rested his head against the wall. He ate a few bites of burrito, but his heart wasn't really in it.

I stashed it back in the cooler.

He worked his fingers along one of the carvings above his head. When he found the spot he wanted, he pressed gently. He was still weak, but his essence radiated around him. He was healing.

The space behind the knot in the wood contained a miniature railroad car. After a brief rest, he handed it to me. "I found this train piece while I was cleaning up. Two of the cars made it through mostly intact. I'll put the other one in the new model railroad I'm building, but this one is for you."

"Oh!" A silly grin lit my face. The rail car had a small dent on one side, but otherwise was in perfect condition. The lingering scent of coffee had me breathing deep in appreciation.

When I lifted the top, light reflected off the contents.

He said, "I set the diamond in my grandmother's ring. I used some of the silver from the ring you gave me and kept some of the gold for my ring. There are probably things you can do to improve the design. No one works earth like you do, but I did the best I could."

The glint of light and promise froze me in place.

White Feather plucked the boxcar from my nerveless fingers and extracted the ring. The gold filigree band was a delicate, intricate laced pattern. Instead of a simple round design, the top part was woven into a raised latticework where the diamond winked in the light.

"I worked the gold myself because there wasn't originally a place for the stone. See," he pointed to the top. "I opened it here and put in two drops of silver from the ring you made for me. The weaving in the band allows earth magic to travel and be multiplied, and if the ring takes a hit, it spreads it out."

He gifted me with a crooked grin. "I'm hoping it will protect you better than your own magic can by itself."

My voice was nothing but a squeak, so I had to try again. "But White Feather! You know what can happen to a diamond. And your grandmother's ring!" Emotions rushed over the jumble of words, nearly drowning me.

White Feather chuckled softly. "I know what you do with stones, Adriel. You use them."

"If I use it--" My voice was muffled behind his hand.

When my protests stopped, he slipped the ring on my finger. "I know. After you left The Owl the other night, Martin was still in the parking lot. I offered him a ride, and he told me that if you're ever in need of a lot of Mother Earth, you will likely sheer one of the planes right off the diamond." He smiled. "But he also said there's no tougher stone out there or one with more power. Given the messes you find yourself in, I thought we'd better make sure you had at least one diamond. I'm saving up for a pair of earrings as backup."

My eyes goggled. Not at the expense, which was bad enough, but because White Feather *understood*. A diamond was clear, able to reflect colors. It had facets. It was created by Mother Earth using incredible pressure. It was *old*. A gifted diamond on top of all those other properties, and...well.

I had thought about buying a diamond more than once. But the possibility of destroying it and the expense was simply too much. I never had the money or the nerve.

I made a fist, wrapping my fingers around the ring. It sparkled, teasing. If I added a tiny piece of turquoise from Grandma's bracelet, some silver...I flexed my fingers. I had no right to own such a thing. "White Feather. It's your grandmother's ring." It was detailed, old and lovingly made.

The colors in his eyes flickered from green to brown. "And you'll wear it every day, no matter where you go, no matter what spells you are working on. If I'm not around to protect you, and the diamond wears completely away, that gold has the love of the ages in it. Including mine." He squeezed my fingers, testing the ring to make certain it wouldn't slip off.

I threaded my fingers through his. "I'll wear it." I would never take it off.

"With this ring, I can find you anywhere—in this world or any other," he said, leaning in to seal the promise with a kiss.

There was nothing between us now, not even wind.

Other Works

This series continues with Under Witch Curse and Ghost Shadow.

Most of my other works are cozy mysteries. Some contain magic and romance, such as *Dragons of Wendal* and *DragonKin*.

The Sedona O'Hala series (*Executive Lunch, Executive Retention, Executive Sick Days, Executive Affairs, Executive Dirt*) is a series of contemporary cozy mysteries: Sedona must solve a few crimes while fighting her way up the corporate ladder. Mostly she dangles from her fingertips just trying to survive.

Soul of the Desert is an historical mystery. Bo must escape to the desert of New Mexico to avoid the mob in New York.

Catch an Honest Thief is a stand alone mystery, combining a stealthy caper in the New Mexico desert with high-tech gadgets. Alexia must try to save her career—and her life.

You might also enjoy *Year of the Mountain Lion, Tracking Magic (Max Killian Investigations)* and *Sage (Tales from a Magical Kingdom)*.

Visit me at: www.BearMountainBooks.com.

CPSIA information can be obtained at www.ICGtesting.com
Printed in the USA
LVOW06s2159150915

454364LV00004B/315/P

9 780615 533926